Death By Duck

Death By Duck

John Wilson

Matador
9 Priory Business Park,
Wistow Road, Kibworth Beauchamp,
Leicestershire. LE8 0RX
Tel: (+44) 116 279 2299
Fax: (+44) 116 279 2277
Email: books@troubador.co.uk
Web: www.troubador.co.uk/matador

ISBN 978 1780885 759

British Library Cataloguing in Publication Data.
A catalogue record for this book is available from the British Library.

Printed and bound in the UK by TJ International, Padstow, Cornwall
Typeset in Minion Pro by Troubador Publishing Ltd, Leicester, UK

Matador is an imprint of Troubador Publishing Ltd

To my dear wife, Tedi.

Contents

Introduction

"It was a dark and dreary night, and the rain was beating on the windowpane."

"No, no. Dreadful. That's no way to start a book."

"How about – the sun was smiling cheerfully, and small clouds grazed like errant sheep in the azure sky."

"Please! This is sickening. Try again."

"You want something in a modern vein? Something earthy? World-weary? Cynical? That sort of thing?"

"Yes."

Attempt number three: "His feet did not exactly stink. But the faint, stale aroma in the room had to have a source. And the dean's stocking feet seemed the most likely culprit."

"Is this another story about Dean Massoud Ansari?"

"Yes."

"And all the people at Crabshaw School of the Law?"

"Well, perhaps not all, but we'll certainly meet many of them again."

"I thought the dean got Alhaji Baba Shoppa's money and lived happily ever after."

"In that place? You must be joking. The faculty stopped their shenanigans for a while, but the quiet didn't last. How could it? Not with them. And anyway, God got bored, and He – or is it She? – decided to stir things up again."

"So what happened?"

"Well, there was a murder. Or so it seemed. And for the longest time no one could figure out who did it, although it seemed rather obvious, and… wait a minute. I'm telling you the book. There's no point relating the story when you can read it – in the same words."

"All right. Let's start back at the beginning."

"That's what I was trying to do."

Chapter One

Our Story Opens With a Bang

It was a dreary day, the kind that occurs in mid-March. The vigil for spring had become interminable. Only scattered clumps of snow remained with patches of ice beneath the firs and pines, but a cold, driving rain belied any promise of warmth to come.

The dean had just returned from the president's office. He had stood for endless minutes at a trolley platform. Save for a few ugly moments when gusts of wind slanted the rain nearly sideways, his umbrella had protected his upper body. The whipping skirt of his raincoat, however, had been scant protection for his pants, and beneath his knees he had been drenched.

Entering his office, Dean Massoud Ansari peeled off his dripping raincoat and hung it on a hook by the door; he then removed his shoes because the leather was soaked through. Carefully, he placed them under a radiator in the corner to dry. His socks also were wet and emitting a faint odor, but he opted to keep them on and maintain some semblance of decorum. There was nothing he could do for his pants, although he tried vainly with his fingers to press a crease back into the damp cloth.

The office was large, in appearance like a comfortable reading room in a Victorian mansion. It had oak wainscoting and a plump leather sofa at one end near the door. An oak coffee table, flanked by wooden chairs, stood in front of the sofa, and at the opposite end of the room there was a large desk, also of oak, graced by a banker's reading lamp and stacks of journals and memoranda. The occupant was in his late middle age, tall and stooped with a prominent, aquiline nose, sad eyes often hidden behind thick reading glasses and receding, brownish-gray hair. His expressions varied from harried to a toothy grin that wrapped around his lower face. Invariably, he was dressed in a brown herringbone tweed jacket with patches at the elbows.

Abandoning the effort to return a crease to his pants, the dean turned on a standing lamp at one side of the couch; crossing the room, he also turned on the lamp on his desk. On such a day, there was insufficient natural illumination, even though it was early afternoon. He glanced at a couple of messages on his desk. One, from a former student, caught his eye. Penciled on the message slip was a notation that the graduate wanted to see the dean for five minutes and would only be in town for a couple of days.

Inwardly, he sighed. 'Five minutes' meant fifteen at a minimum and more likely half an hour. But chatting with graduates was part of the job. One never knew who might, sooner or later, make a sizeable donation to the school.

He walked to the door. "Mrs. Ackerman, don't I know this man? The name sounds familiar."

Mrs. Ackerman, the dean's elderly, care-worn secretary and sometimes confidante, looked up from her typing. "Of course you know him. Sometimes I think you're more forgetful than the professors. Don't you remember? He's John Vandervoort."

"John?… oh yes, of course." He laughed. "How could I forget? Well, I'm glad I asked. It will be a pleasure to see him again."

Dean Ansari had never discussed with anyone his conversation two years before with Junker, a member of the faculty. The latter's transvestite dance routine at the Lace and Leather Lounge had been largely forgotten, at least by the dean, although a certain tense awkwardness was never absent when the two men met or conversed. Because the subject was never raised, John's role in 'outing' Junker had faded from his active memory.

"I'll give him a call," he said, turning to reenter his office.

"After you do," Mrs. Ackerman interjected, "I'd like you to sign these letters. We need to get them out."

"Sure. Give me five minutes."

The dean walked around his desk to his telephone and dialed the number on the message slip. After two rings, John's familiar voice sounded in greeting.

"Hi. Dean Ansari?"

"How did you know it was me?"

"You're the only person I called," John responded. "Actually, that's not true. You're the only person I left a message for to call me back."

"So how are you?"

"I can answer that when I see you, but the short answer is that everything's great. Really great." The voice was genial, self-assured. "When can I come by and pay a social call? I'm only down the street at the Harvest Inn."

The dean cleared his throat, trying quickly to remember his schedule. "How about in, say, half an hour," he said, "unless you'd rather not walk through the rain."

"Half an hour would be perfect. I'm supposed to see a faculty member at the same time, but I'm sure a ten or fifteen minute delay won't matter."

The visit arranged, they chatted briefly about current events at the school and then terminated the conversation. Seeing a light go out on her telephone console, Mrs. Ackerman picked up a sheaf of correspondence and entered the dean's office.

"Will he be coming by?" she asked.

"Yes, he should be here in a few minutes."

Dean Ansari held out his hand, and Mrs. Ackerman handed him the letters. Then she sat down in a chair before his desk. The dean, who had been standing, leaned backward and sat, legs outstretched, on the edge of the desk.

He signed two letters. Part-way through the third, he frowned. "No, no. I couldn't have said it this way. The word is 'meritorious' service, not 'meretricious' service. And look here. I said 'your cooperation' is needed, not 'your cooption.'"

He handed her the offending communication; Mrs. Ackerman peered at it. "That's the way you dictated it," she said quietly and reproachfully.

The dean looked at her. Why did he feel it was always his fault, when he could not have made such a mistake? Muttering, "No matter, no matter," he carefully inspected the remaining items. There were only a couple of minor errors in them. It was worth appearing slightly illiterate in his correspondence rather than risk Mrs. Ackerman's further tart reproval.

"With that one exception, these are fine." He returned the stack of letters to her. Mrs. Ackerman beamed, having survived another inspection.

"Everything seems so quiet," she ventured. "Not like the old days." Mrs. Ackerman enjoyed talking with the dean when there were no meetings or telephone calls to hurry her from the office.

"Maybe a little too quiet," he answered reflectively. "You know, after we got all that money a couple of years ago, I thought my troubles with the faculty would die down. Not forever, of course. That would be out of character. But certainly for a few months."

Mrs. Ackerman nodded in affirmation.

"I'm surprised, though," the dean continued, "that there's not been a complaint out of them for – what is it now, two years? Maybe I'm doing something right for a change, although I'll be damned if I know what it is."

To himself, he wondered whether his good fortune stemmed from his bargain with Junker: good behavior in return for secrecy. It was difficult to credit their agreement as the sole cause, however, and in any event a Faustian arrangement of that sort was bound to unravel over time.

"I think they realize what a good job you do," Mrs. Ackerman volunteered loyally. "Now that we have more money, and they get paid more, it's no wonder they're quiet."

"You give them too much credit. More is never enough. For the life of me I almost think it's in their interest, or the interest of some of them, to keep the place quiet. That *would* be in character, but I can't figure the reason."

Mrs. Ackerman looked at him quizzically. "You know," she said, "speaking about old times, I heard that Ruth Dinsmore and Prigley had a baby. She never changed her name. Young people seem to do that these days." There was a hint of disapproval in her voice.

"A baby!" the dean exclaimed. "Why didn't you tell me? Is it a boy or a girl? What are they calling it?"

"See, that's the problem when you don't take the same name. Now they have to figure out both the first and last names."

The dean laughed. "I thought you weren't happy about them having a baby. We should probably send something, unless it's far too late. I mean, when did this happen? How nice for them. Perhaps we could… "

There was a respectful cough at the door.

Dean Ansari, who was talking to the rug, looked up and to his left. John Vandervoort was standing in the doorway.

"Well, I'll be damned. Come in. Come in." The good news about Ruth and Prigley had buoyed his spirits. "How good to see you again."

John stepped into the office, and Mrs. Ackerman rose to her feet. "Why," she said, "you haven't changed a bit." She studied him. "No, I think you do look a little older, and it's becoming."

John, still a young man, had graduated only two years before. He was square-set with sandy hair and open, genial features. He smiled. "Getting older seems to be a fact of life."

"Getting a bad back is another fact," the dean added. And he stooped over with a mock case of lumbago and took a couple of halting steps forward.

Mrs. Ackerman surveyed his weak acting skills with embarrassment. "You must have plenty to talk about," she said, "and I know you don't have much time." Turning to the dean, she added, "I'm alone in the outer office today, and I'd like to go down the hall to xerox these letters, unless you need me at the telephone."

"No," he replied, "I can take calls, or I'll just let it ring."

Mrs. Ackerman departed, and the dean, who was now standing, repeated his opening remark: "Come in, come in – and take a seat." The two men shook hands.

John sat in the chair that Mrs. Ackerman had just vacated, and the dean sat in a chair opposite him facing the doorway.

"You look prosperous. Life must be treating you well."

"I can't complain. Not at all. In fact I never imagined things would go so well in such a short period of time."

"You mean since graduation?"

"Yeah."

"So, I guess I asked when you called – or, rather, when I called you back – what have you been up to?"

"I passed the bar. Honestly, when I walked out of the exam, I was sure I hadn't. It was pretty depressing. But then, the following December, there was my name on the list of the people who made it."

"Maybe they made a mistake," the dean interjected wryly.

"Maybe they did. I'll take whatever gifts I can get. And then I joined up with an older lawyer – sort of an office-sharing arrangement, to learn the ropes – and I got into some business deals on the side."

"Is that what brings you here?"

"Sort of. I need to see a member of the faculty."

John had dropped his voice, and the smile faded from his features.

"Is there something wrong?"

"No. Well, actually, yes… yes there is."

"Anything I can do to help?"

The rain had eased, but there was a faint drip at the window casing. The radiator hissed, disguising a footfall in the outer office.

"I don't think so. But it's one reason why I came by. Something's going on you should know about."

His voice had dropped to a murmur. "Do you remember when I last saw you in this office? The time I told you about that incident at the Triple L Ranch? Well, that wasn't all. There was more, but I thought it would go away, so I didn't say anything. Now – well, now I'm scared and think I should."

The dean was listening attentively. He frowned.

"I'm in real trouble," John said, his hands clasping and unclasping in his lap, "and I'm going to the police and see if I can cut a deal."

The footfall sounded again, this time at the door.

The dean started to his feet. Seeing him rise, John, who had his back to the door, shifted to look behind him.

The apparition was wearing a floppy Donald Duck mask. A cheerful grin forced up one side of the bill, and the little round holes for eyes were topped with arching eyebrows. Beneath the mask, the figure had on a misshapen poncho and wading boots. In its gloved hand was a black, gleaming, semi-automatic pistol.

"What is this? Some... some kind of joke?" the dean questioned haltingly.

John, staring at the strange figure, was immobile in his chair.

Donald Duck in wading boots glanced cheerfully, if blandly, from one to the other. He – or she – walked to the center of the room and waved the gun at the dean, who cowered back. Then, steadying one hand with the other, in a smooth upward motion, Donald Duck turned quickly and pointed the pistol directly at John. It uttered three popping noises.

John clutched his neck. His hand slid to his chest, where a red blotch formed on his shirt, and he uttered a low, strangulated, gurgling cough. Slumping forward, he fell from the chair like a spent sack of potatoes, landing unceremoniously in a crumpled heap on the floor.

The dean had not moved. He was rooted, motionless. For a long moment – a warp in time, like a movie halted in mid-frame – there was silence. And an acrid smell of smoke.

The apparition spoke in a husky voice. "Here, honky." Or had it said "turkey"? It tossed the weapon to the dean, who caught it, uncomprehending, still standing in mute stupefaction. Slowly the dean looked at the object in his hand, then at the sprawled body on the floor. His mind clearing, he dropped to one knee.

"Are you all right? Are you all right?" He rolled the recumbent form over. Blood had bubbled into the rug. John was not breathing, and his eyes had rolled upward. Staring in disbelief, the dean had his answer.

Exhaling in fear and in a convulsive reaction to the sight, he looked around the room and then back at the doorway.

No one was there.

Dean Ansari ran to the door. The outer office was empty.

Halting, he stumbled back. "Honky! My God, that thing called me a honky! I can't believe it. A honky!"

His mind had centered on that inconsequential detail, as if nothing else mattered. He was standing in the middle of the room, a bewildered expression on his face, the pistol still in his hand.

"What's that smell? What are you two doing, setting off firecrackers?"

It was Mrs. Ackerman. She appeared at the door. Her cheerful smile vanished.

"What… what happened?"

The dean stared at her dumbly.

"My God! He's been hurt. Don't just stand there. We've got to get help."

Still staring, first at her, then at the corpse on the floor, the dean roused himself. In a flat monotone, he asked, "Did you see it? It called me a honky."

"No. When? What on earth are you talking about? Hurry! I'll dial 911. We've got to get an ambulance."

Then Mrs. Ackerman seemed to take in the entire scene for the first time. Instead of moving forward to the telephone on the desk, she recoiled a step backward.

"Dean Ansari! What have you got in your hand? I can't believe this. You killed him!" Her face grimaced in horrified disbelief.

The dean snapped awake.

"Killed him? Killed him? Don't be ridiculous. It killed him."

They were standing about five feet apart. Quickly, the dean scanned the room, grasping his predicament. "You're quite right. We must get a doctor immediately." He took a step forward. "I don't need this."

Placing the pistol on the edge of his desk, he walked around Mrs. Ackerman. At the door, he turned. "Call an ambulance. I'll be right back."

Mrs. Ackerman moved quickly to the telephone, stepping over the prone, inert form of John Vandervoort. She reached the hospital emergency room without difficulty, then thought to call the police.

The sergeant's voice was gruff and matter-of-fact. It acquired a tone of urgency, however, when she described the reason for her call. Murders in this small, midwestern city were not the fare commonly found in large, urban centers.

Aside from events two years ago, they were unknown within the university and its law school.

"Don't touch anything," the sergeant admonished.

"I won't. How soon will you be here?"

"It'll take a few minutes. I'm radioing a squad car right now."

Mrs. Ackerman put down the telephone. Where was the dean? She had thought he was going to summon help. Poor man. Mrs. Ackerman was confused and agitated. The comfortable prism through which she refracted the events of her life had ceased to exist. The crystal lay shattered with the figure on the floor – and her vision of the dean standing over it, a pistol in his hand.

She walked out of the room, pulling the door nearly shut behind her to discourage intrusion before the arrival of the police. In the outer office, she noticed the wet imprint of the dean's stocking feet leading down the hall. Anxious to find him and, despite her horrified impression that he was the killer, to report to him what she had done, she followed their path. The tracks led to the men's room but did not emerge.

Delicacy forbade her entry. A lifetime of training inhibited a knock. Desperately, she looked around. A male student had just entered the corridor.

Mrs. Ackerman fluttered to him. "Excuse me," she importuned, "would you go into the bathroom and get the dean. It's important."

"Certainly."

The student entered the sanctuary. After a moment, she heard him call the dean's name. Doors banged, and a few moments later he emerged, a puzzled expression on his features.

"He's not there."

"Are you sure? He has to be there."

"I'm sorry. I looked. There's no one in there."

Chapter Two

Mrs. Ackerman

"Let me get this straight. Tell me again, and don't leave out details because you think they're unimportant. I'll be the one to decide that."

Lieutenant Walsh was speaking. He had arrived shortly after the patrol car that had been dispatched by the desk sergeant. He and Mrs. Ackerman were seated in the dean's office, she in her accustomed secretarial chair and he facing her, straddling a straight-backed chair in reverse. His hands rested on the top of the back. Two minutes before, with the permission of the assistant dean, he had asked the officers to look through the building for anyone who seemed suspicious.

And he was suspicious himself, although he concealed the fact behind a practiced, professional demeanor. Moreover, he was not an unkind man, and he was obviously dealing with a highly distraught, and confused, elderly woman. For all that a casual observer could tell, he had infinite resources of sympathy and time as he waited patiently for her halting answers.

This was not his first visit to the dean's office. Two years before, he had been called, along with his colleague, Antwan McCallister, to investigate the homicide of two law students. The law school – Crabshaw School of the Law – was a component of Heidelschmidt University, known fondly by legions of graduates as Old Heidelschmidt. The university occupied a campus on what was formerly the outskirts of a midwestern city; its head was an energetic – and some thought crafty – sparrow of a man named Druzolovic Zo. The law school, on the other hand, occupied a dilapidated building near the city center, and its occasionally embattled dean was Massoud Ansari. On the prior occasion, Lieutenant McCallister had dealt with the dean and had come to like and respect him. After a frustrating lack of definite leads, a confidential letter to the dean from a stupendously rich African, who had a son in the law school, revealed that the culprit was the university provost, a large, forbidding woman named Allison Fetherheft, formerly known to students as Dean Dreadnaught. This letter revealed also that Fetherheft had flown beyond the reach of the law and justice to be with her African lover, and it implied a future, huge gift, in addition to a large, current donation, in return for the dean's silence. Since then the school had been quiet.

Lieutenant Walsh had been in his office in the station house when Mrs. Ackerman called. Being a detective, he was not dressed in uniform. His brown suit was rumpled and, to the discerning eye, had obviously been purchased off a rack in a discount store. In places it was shiny. A light blue shirt with flaring collar capped his inelegance. He might as well have purchased his tie with his eyes closed, although in fact it had been a birthday present from his favorite sister. The form within this sartorial disaster was middle-aged and stocky. He had changed from the time he had first visited the school – a time for him of personal turmoil due to his wife's terminal illness. Then he had been paunchy and disheveled with a full beard. Now he was clean-shaven with an open, friendly expression, florid cheeks, penetrating blue eyes and incipient jowls. The paunch was gone. His eyes missed very little.

"So, after the student told you the dean was not in the men's room, what did you do? And by the way," he added casually, "do you know that student's name? Or could you identify him? I'd like to speak with him."

"It was Larry Stolwitz. He's the head of our Environmental Law Society."

"Good." Lieutenant Walsh asked for the spelling and wrote the name on a small pad. "I'd like his telephone number, too, if you could get it later. Let's go back now to my question. What did you do after… " Lieutenant Walsh glanced at his pad, "after Stolwitz told you that there was no one there."

"I looked around in a couple of offices where he might have gone. But, but… there wasn't any sign of him. What's happened to him?"

I wish I knew, thought Lieutenant Walsh. *Yes, indeed, I wish I knew*. But he merely pursed his lips and shook his head.

Mrs. Ackerman appeared close to tears. Lieutenant Walsh paused for a moment, impassively. Then he resumed his questioning.

"You say you followed his footsteps down the hall. Please explain that. How did he leave footprints, and how do you know they were his?" The marks had quickly evaporated, and the detective had ascertained that they were gone. He had seen nothing.

"Sometimes," Mrs. Ackerman answered, "he would remove his shoes and walk around in his stocking feet. It sounds odd, I know, but he used to do it. And today his shoes and socks were wet… oh dear, I think his shoes are still under the radiator… I noticed that he left footprints from just outside his office door, and I followed them. And I'm sure he wasn't looking behind himself as he went down the hall. He wouldn't have thought that someone would follow him. They had to be his."

"We've already ascertained that there's only one door to the men's room and no window. Could he have removed his socks in there, dried his feet, and walked out barefoot?"

Mrs. Ackerman looked at him blankly. "Well, yes," she said finally, "I suppose he could have. But why would he do that? It's cold out, and raining, and he didn't have his raincoat." She glanced at the hook by the door and blinked. "My goodness, it's not there. I'm sure he was wearing it when he returned from the president's office." Hurriedly, she scanned the dean's office. No raincoat was visible.

"Umm." Lieutenant Walsh also surveyed the room, poking the end of his pencil against his cheek as he did so. He had already ordered a search of the men's room, and no socks – or anything else except a bottle of germicidal solution – had been found. The detective furrowed his brow. Mrs. Ackerman had a Kleenex in her hands that she was knotting and twisting. Throwing it in the wastebasket, she retrieved another from a dispenser on top of a low file cabinet and blew her nose.

"Did he say anything… anything at all about what had happened, or where he was going?"

"No. He said he was coming right back." She hesitated. "You know, he did say something odd. He said *it* killed him."

"*It?*"

"Yes. I don't think I got it wrong. *It*. Oh dear, lieutenant, I just can't believe Dean Ansari would do such a thing. He couldn't have. It's not like him. You must believe me. There's been some terrible mistake."

"All right now. All right. For the moment, we're not sure what he's done."

Mrs. Ackerman sniffled.

"Now tell me again," Lieutenant Walsh continued. "You came back to the office from xeroxing letters, and Dean Ansari was in his office, and there was a body on the floor."

"Yes," Mrs. Ackerman whimpered. "I came back, and the young man who had come to see the dean was on the floor. I've never seen a dead person before except in a funeral home, but he looked dead to me. Just lying there, sprawled out and horrible. And… and… and, oh dear, Dean Ansari was standing next to him, over him, and… and he had a gun in his hand."

She burst into tears.

Lieutenant Walsh waited. Mrs. Ackerman regained her composure with difficulty and the aid of two more tissues.

"The gun on his desk?" he inquired.

"Yes, he put it there."

"Make sure you don't touch it. Now tell me again. After you looked for Dean Ansari and couldn't find him, you returned to this office. Is that right?"

"Yes, I came back to see if somehow he had returned, because I couldn't find him."

"And what did you see when you entered the office?"

Mrs. Ackerman surveyed him bleakly. "I know you must think I'm crazy. Except for the blood, it was gone."

"What was gone?"

"The body. It wasn't here. And neither was the dean."

Chapter Three

The Party

Duxbury was standing in the small front hall of his home, an elegant townhouse located several blocks from the law school. He had acquired his nickname from his frequent use of the town of his birth – Duxbury, Massachusetts – in his hypothetical questions in class discussions. The students had conferred nicknames on most faculty members, and if they were apt, they stuck over time. In Duxbury's case, the name had superceded Baked Bean, awarded because of his flatulence, and long usage had made it permanent.

His professor's salary could not have been sufficient to afford either his dwelling or the expensive furnishings in it. Each room contained antiques of exquisite good taste, and large, hand-woven oriental rugs accentuated the gleam from polished teakwood floors. Those who knew him assumed he had inherited money, and there was much about Duxbury that confirmed this suspicion. He had graduated from excellent schools. His demeanor was civil, his tone soft-spoken. And he possessed a casual indifference to his surroundings and attire that suggested an early and long association with great wealth.

At this moment, dressed in an old cardigan sweater whose rumpled fullness only poorly disguised his lanky frame, he was talking to the first guest to arrive. That person was Boomer, a faculty member who occupied the office adjacent to Duxbury in the faculty office suite of Crabshaw School of the Law. It was not difficult for anyone to discern how Boomer had acquired his particular nickname. His whisper had an intimate quality at fifty feet, and his raucous laugh could be heard clearly at treble that distance. Indeed, only the loudness of his attire – white shoes, a red shirt with a flaring collar, a tie advertising a recent family visit to the Grand Tetons, and a checkered jacket – eclipsed his vocal cords.

"It's sure nice to be here," Boomer said conversationally, removing his topcoat and stuffing his slouch hat and plaid scarf into the sleeves. Despite long association, Duxbury stepped back a half pace at the sound.

"It's good of you to come. Here, let me take that coat and hang it up."

"Why don't you ask the maid to do it?" Boomer laughed. The wind whistled about Duxbury's ears; faltering, he maintained his position.

"She has the day off." Duxbury was unsure whether to be pleased at the recognition that he could afford domestic help or displeased at the impertinence of the question. Also, he knew, it was best in the company of his colleagues to assume an egalitarian pose. He had, in fact, deliberately invited them to come on the evening when his maid would not be on the premises.

He took the proffered coat and opened the hall closet door. As he did so, the trailing edge of the garment caught the pearl handle of his umbrella that was nestled in an umbrella stand beside the door. The entire stand teetered, about to fall. In consternation, Duxbury clutched at it, dropping the coat. Boomer lunged forward and grabbed the umbrella.

"Don't worry about the coat. A little dust won't hurt it," Boomer brayed again.

"Dust?" The floor was immaculate. Observing that Boomer was holding his umbrella, Duxbury snatched it from his hand. "I'll take that. Thank you. Thank you for catching it." He seemed a trifle discombobulated as he replaced the umbrella in the stand, retrieved the coat from the floor, searched in the closet for a hangar and finally hung the coat inside.

"Crisis number one averted," Duxbury murmured with a deprecating smile.

Boomer seemed amused. "Who else is coming?"

Again, an impertinent inquiry, but Duxbury let it pass. Teaching Boomer manners would be the effort of a lifetime, and one, he reflected, destined for failure.

"Two or three of our group: Jane and Rick." He was referring to The Duchess and Junker, two other members of the faculty. The latter's first name was actually Heinrich. In a burst of pro-Nazi fervor, his mother had bestowed it on him at the time he was born shortly after the Anschluss in Austria. Those glorious days, when she had attended frequent meetings of the Bund, were gone forever. But little – or kleine – Heinrich had developed into everything she had wanted. The only pity was that he had anglicized his given name, but the students caught his essence when they nicknamed him Junker.

"I've also asked Aaron," Duxbury said.

"Why him, for God's sake?" Boomer frowned.

"Because it's better to include him than have him gossiping on the outside." Aaron was also known as BN due to his ingratiating manner and eagerness to please. If the wind blew west, he traveled west; if south, he journeyed south. Duxbury had a reason for this gathering – he usually had a calculated reason for everything – and he wanted to enlist Arron before anyone else did.

Boomer, who knew Duxbury well, had assumed a mere social occasion was not in the offing. Duxbury's last remark confirmed his guess.

"So our get-together this evening is not just to have fun and relive old times."

"Of course not. You know me too well."

Boomer laughed appreciatively, and this time Duxbury stood his ground.

"Come. Let us go into the living room," Duxbury said. "What can I get you to drink?"

"I'll have a bourbon on the rocks… Do you still have that Jack Daniels?" he added hesitatingly. "I had it the last time I was here, and it was awfully good."

"Of course."

Duxbury turned to enter the kitchen, but the doorbell interrupted him.

When he answered the door, the three remaining guests, huddled against a chill wind, were standing on the doorstep. The Duchess and Junker had come together. They had met Aaron on the sidewalk before the house. All were talking animatedly about the recent events at the law school.

Cheerfully, Duxbury asked them to come in. This time, with greater care, he took their coats and hung them in his closet. He then ushered the new arrivals into the living room where Boomer was already standing before a low, crackling fire. The room exuded Christmas cheer, although that season had passed over three months before. The décor was masculine, as befitted Duxbury's bachelor status. With its paneling, leather sofa, brass lamps and old, framed maps crowded upon the walls, the room would not have been out of place in a men's club.

As requested in the invitation, the guests were dressed casually, with the exception of Junker, who was wearing his invariable dark suit and tie. A closely shaved skull and flaring mustaches made him seem the perfect Ruhr industrialist or Prussian aristocrat. His cuffed trousers were neatly creased, and his jacket, with a European cut, fit snugly on his trim frame.

The Duchess, on the other hand, was wearing beige slacks and a nearly matching, heavy-knit turtle-neck sweater. Once beautiful, with a slender figure and wavy blond hair, she was still in mid-life an attractive, if rounded, woman – except for the lines of worry across her brow and etched at the corners of her mouth. Her blond hair had given way to gray, and, unless knotted in a bun, she could still toss it seductively when she laughed. Increasingly, however, she did not laugh but rather fretted fitfully about the encroachments and absurdities of life.

The third of the late-arriving trio, Aaron, was as distinctively attired as the others. Only his manner of dress was designed to make him blend without notice into an upper-crust, old- money background. To his regret, he had grown up in a lower middle-class family in New York City, a closely guarded secret that oozed out occasionally to his considerable mortification. A graduate of Queens College, he nevertheless looked as if he had just emerged from an alumni gathering of the Ivy Club at Princeton. Aaron was wearing loafers, Oxford gray flannel slacks, a blue button-down shirt and a dark green, Shetland wool sweater slightly worn at one elbow. He had close-cropped, dark hair and balanced heavy, tortoiseshell glasses on a beaky nose. He was earnest, insecure and likeable. Duxbury found him barely tolerable.

"You interrupted me getting a drink," Boomer bellowed as the three greeted him and moved near to where he was standing by the fire.

"Alcohol makes you even less clear than usual," rejoined Junker. "We've saved you a modicum of additional embarrassment." The remark was uttered with a smile, and the others laughed nervously. Boomer, impervious to all but the grossest insult, joined them heartily.

"What will you have?" asked Duxbury genially, moving among them. Each made a request, and Duxbury departed to pour drinks in the kitchen.

In the awkward silence that followed, The Duchess stooped and placed slices of cheese on some crackers on a plate at the end of the coffee table. She then passed the plate, and each took one. Looking uncomfortable, a cracker stuffed in his mouth, Aaron said finally: "Well, isn't it nice we're all here. But I was puzzled when my wife wasn't invited. It looks almost as if we've been invited to a secret meeting."

"Of course we've been invited to a meeting," Boomer replied with a snort. "You know Duxbury. You don't think he'd go to the trouble to invite us here to be friendly."

Boomer had uttered Duxbury's nickname. As it was relatively innocuous and one of the least insulting, even his colleagues used it on occasion. But never to his face.

"Did I hear someone call my name?" said Duxbury, smiling, as he entered with the drinks on a small tray.

There was laughter again, this time genuine. Only Boomer looked discomfited, but as before, he joined in. Junker moved to a nearby chair and sat down, taking another cheese and cracker before doing so. Aaron folded his frame onto the couch.

Junker knew Duxbury well. He had guessed the invitation to a pasta dinner was in fact the occasion for a meeting. Boomer had confirmed his suspicion. As he did not enjoy idle cocktail conversation, Junker decided to broach the subject directly and immediately.

"Apparently we are here for a meeting,," he said, looking directly at Duxbury.

"Well, not exactly a meeting," Duxbury replied. "I thought, though, that we could discuss events at the school while we were having dinner. The pasta's cooking right now. And I have some excellent red wine. We should be able to sit down in a few minutes."

"Why don't we talk now?" The Duchess spoke. "It's on everybody's mind." A worried frown tugged at her mouth.

"No reason not to."

"There's something fishy going on. I think Mrs. Ackerman is covering up something. She knows why the dean left."

"Maybe. Maybe not," Aaron broke in. "But why should she make up such a fantastic story? She isn't that creative."

"Massoud gave her the story," said Duxbury. "She'd do anything he asked."

"He isn't that creative either," added Junker sourly. "I don't think he could figure out how to put his pants on in the morning without a manual." Junker had not criticized the dean since their private conversation two years before. Now it seemed safe, and his feelings had emerged.

"I thought you'd grown to like him," said Boomer. "Or maybe he just bought you off with all that money. This sounds like old times."

Junker's smile was frosty. He said nothing.

"Frankly," The Duchess spoke again, "there were lots of excuses the dean could have used to get away. He could have invented a death in the family. Or he could have said he was sick. Or he could have just quit."

Boomer glanced at her. "Yeah. Why invent a murder? If that's what happened. It makes no sense."

"None at all," growled Junker. "And then that idiot secretary of his had to keep chattering about it being one of our former students. A lot of them ought to vanish. We'd be better off."

The last comment drew a wry smile from The Duchess. "Except for the blood, the blood on the carpet. I heard that the police lab said it was human. No one could bleed that much in the dean's office without someone knowing about it."

"Maybe it was the dean's," said Aaron.

"No, he was okay when he went to the men's room, according to Mrs. Ackerman. But she seems very unreliable, and she has to be a prime suspect in a missing persons case. I even heard she tried to clean up the blood with some paper towels."

"Probably," said Duxbury. "She was fanatical about always neatening Massoud's office, even if the cops had told her not to. And she's no bolt of intellectual lightning."

The discussion ambled on, without focus but with gleams of acerbic wit. It circled back to the rape and murders two years before and the rekindled fear of violence against a member of the faculty. Could one of them be next? Mrs. Ackerman took more than her share of caustic comments, but with her personal idiosyncrasies, she seemed an unlikely candidate for perpetrator, or for anything more than accomplice liability. A well-grounded reputation for bemused integrity was her stout shield in adversity.

Finally, Duxbury spoke. He was standing by the couch, balancing an old-fashioned glass of scotch whiskey in his hand. "Well, this is all very well and good, but what are we going to do? The man is gone, and for all we know he may never return. We can't let the associate dean go on running the school. He's good, but he's not that good. The faculty needs to agree on an interim dean."

So, thought Boomer, *this was the reason for the meeting. Why didn't I guess it?*

Junker's voice interrupted his musing. "You're quite right. We need a new leader. This time let's get one to our liking. We almost got rid of Massoud two years ago, but he outmaneuvered us."

This same group, over two years before, had attempted a palace coup, the object of which had been to convince President Zo to appoint a new dean. They had failed when the dean unexpectedly became central to a gift of twenty million dollars from an African multibillionaire whose son was attending the school. No one had forgotten.

"What kind of qualities do we want?" said Boomer. "We ought to think about the needs of the school right now and then figure out who seems best for the job. And would want it." He laughed.

Duxbury peered at him. "That's a good point. We've had one style of leadership – what I call the bland, friendly type – and it seems to me that we need more vigor getting things done."

"The money helped," broke in The Duchess. "Do you remember what bad shape we were in? Let's give credit where it's due. Massoud has done a lot more than we'd like to admit. The place, I think, has turned around."

"Yeah," contributed Boomer. "And we really need to push the momentum. Things are moving. We need a person who can go out into the community and sell the school. And meet lawyers who might hire our graduates. Beat the alumni drum."

Duxbury added, frowning into his glass: "And not least, my friend, we need someone who will push the faculty around. That's my main concern. The associate dean can't do it. Not enough clout. We've got to have a man, or woman, with a much thicker skin than Massoud had to make us – yes, us – work harder."

"I agree," Boomer replied emphatically. "We can get better students and line up more jobs, but the critical thing is what we do with the students while they're here."

The group fell silent. Each was thinking. The fire crackled on the grate. Junker munched noisily on a cracker.

Aaron broke the unusual quiet. "This may sound a little forward," he said hesitantly, "but I would be willing to take on the job, if I were asked… and my colleagues wanted me, that is."

Junker's jaw froze, and the munching ceased. He swiveled his neck to stare intently at Aaron. The Duchess pursed her lips, and Boomer gaped openly in astonishment.

Only Duxbury retained his aplomb. "An excellent suggestion. Yes, excellent. You are definitely deanship material." The others stared at him incredulously. "But consider whether your talents would find proper scope in this school. Looked at that way, I have my doubts. Your name should be put before search committees at bigger and more established institutions. Anyway, whether that's true or not, and I believe it is, I don't think this faculty could afford to give you up as a teacher. You're too valuable where you are, and we need our best in the classroom."

"He's quite right," The Duchess joined in, grasping the thrust of Duxbury's remarks. "I don't know how we could replace you. There's no question that we need to concentrate on the quality of our teaching."

Only later, reflecting on the evening and slavishly grateful for the compliments and the acceptance they implied, would Aaron realize that no one had responded affirmatively to his suggestion.

Again, there was a lapse of silence. Each reflected on the new idea, with the exception of Duxbury. He had already reached a conclusion, and his efforts were directed toward casually, but persuasively, nudging the group toward his point of view. He had little interest in the position for himself. Its burdens were too manifest, its extra compensation too paltry to offset them. Neither, he knew, did Junker aspire to the job. It might lead to unnecessary exposure of his personal life of which Duxbury had an inkling. The Duchess was a suitable candidate, but adversity – and there was always adversity – would probably overwhelm her worrisome nature. Aaron's recent bid had been rejected, and no other member of the faculty, in Duxbury's opinion, was qualified.

Except, perhaps, Boomer. No one would consider him at first blush. Indeed, it never occurred to Boomer to consider himself. His idiosyncrasies were too manifestly antithetical to calm, reasoned management of an institution. Boomer often criticized Massoud for being inconsistent. Had he the job, he would double the quantum of inconsistency in a fortnight. Bellowing insensitivity would become a hallmark of his administration.

But, in Duxbury's eyes, he had two cardinal attributes, perhaps three. Duxbury had given the matter substantial thought, and he had concluded, albeit reluctantly, that these attributes made Boomer the most acceptable nominee. His very insensitivity, for one thing, would be an aid in bullying the faculty into greater productivity. Compliant and without notable curiosity, he would also be responsive to the wishes of his friends. One of those friends, and a person who had long since acquired ascendancy in their relationship, was himself. Boomer would be a useful, willing tool. Not least, he would leave Duxbury alone to pursue his own interests.

For some time, he allowed the silence to continue, well aware that the others would likely follow his thought processes in rejecting other members of the faculty.

Finally, Duxbury spoke.

"Your silence," he said, "reflects perplexity. And no wonder. The choice is difficult. The school is at a critical juncture. We need a dean who can guide us through this transitional period, yet on reflection I cannot think of any of our colleagues who would be suitable.

"The problem, though, may be that our thinking naturally tends toward considering who will be dean for the next few years. Or until we get rid of him... or her."

Boomer chortled, and Junker smiled frostily.

Duxbury continued: "At this point in the school's history, it might be advisable to seek a woman as dean. Jane, for example, might be interested in placing her name before a search committee. She would be a superb choice."

At this comment, The Duchess blushed and looked modestly at the floor. Junker shifted uneasily in his chair. The proposition struck him as only faintly less ludicrous than if Eva Braun had been asked to be the Führer.

"All this, however, is in the future," Duxbury said. "We don't know whether Massoud is gone for good or only temporarily. But even if he comes back, he should relinquish office until there's been an investigation. After all, we can't have a dean who is accused of murder, and he knows that. So we're going to need someone for an interim period, maybe a few months or a year, and as I understand the way it's usually done, that person can't apply after being acting dean to be the regular dean if Massoud steps down or disappears.

"In short, we need someone to administer the school for the next few months. Now, let's be sensible. It's in our interest to have one of us occupy the position, because the person who is acting dean will have a lot to say about our compensation and the composition of the search committee. He'll probably sit in on the committee meetings, and naturally he'll have the ear of Zo and, through Zo, the board of trustees.

"I don't want the job, as you all know. I'm nearly certain Rick doesn't want it either." At this, Junker nodded his head. "Aaron is too valuable as a teacher, and Jane should hold back and wait to be considered for the regular appointment."

At which time, he thought to himself, *we'll find a reason to reject her*. Duxbury had concluded that she would be too nervous for the job and insufficiently compliant, although she had been compliant enough in the past. Deferring her candidacy, however, bought time for a more convenient rationale for rejection and ensured her continuing loyalty. It would also buy time to rearrange his affairs and, perhaps, reluctantly propose himself for the job.

"That leaves only one solution," Duxbury concluded. He clapped Boomer on the shoulder. "Last but hardly least, I recommend that we urge the appointment of our friend here."

Boomer was caught unawares, as was everyone else. He gaped at Duxbury, trying to sort out the import of such an unexpected accolade. Aaron blinked; The Duchess stared in astonishment; and Junker winced noticeably and, had he been wearing a monocle, it would have fallen as his eyes widened with surprise.

"I... I'm not sure I'm the person we need," Boomer faltered. His voice, uncharacteristically, had fallen to a murmur. "I mean... I've never thought of myself for the job. I don't have any experience."

"You don't need any," Duxbury said reassuringly. "If administrative ability were required, do you think Massoud would have been dean?" He snorted a response to his question. "Anyway, you'll learn quickly, and we'll be around to help you. Believe me, you're the right person at the right time. There's none better."

He beamed at the group, confident of both his persuasive ability and the lack of a viable alternative to his suggestion. Once again, he clapped Boomer on the shoulder.

And once again, Junker winced. His lips had tightened, giving his face a stern, frozen quality. With narrowed eyes his glance shifted from Duxbury to Boomer, then back again. What could he say? He knew Duxbury too well to believe his remarks were spontaneous. He appreciated the logic of his position. Nevertheless, it was painfully hard to second, much less be enthusiastic about, the recommendation of a man he regarded as a bumbling incompetent. He longed for Frederick the Great, Bismarck, von Moltke, von Runstedt, Rommel or, yes, even the Führer himself – but Boomer? The thought produced an involuntary shudder. Yet he was speechless to object.

The fire continued to crackle cheerfully. Ice tinkled in Aaron's glass as he set it on the coffee table. Boomer, absorbed in his own thoughts, was oblivious to the mute stupefaction around him. Only Duxbury retained his aplomb. The purpose of the meeting had been accomplished. A seed had been planted; with occasional watering, he knew it would grow. There was no alternative.

"Well, Jane," Duxbury said, "let me get you another drink."

As if waking from a bad dream, she nodded affirmatively.

"Go a little lighter this time," she said.

"Why?" Duxbury replied. "Afraid you might lose control in the company of such attractive men?"

"Don't get your hopes up," The Duchess said, also smiling. "I hate to see grown men cry."

The banter served its purpose. The return to relaxed amiability was palpable.

Duxbury had one more arrow to shoot. It sped swiftly. "Why don't you all sleep on my suggestion," he said. "We can talk about it in a few days. I think we'll all agree it makes the most sense." So saying, he grasped Boomer at the elbow and began propelling him toward the dining room.

"I'll get your drink," he said over his shoulder to The Duchess, "after we're all seated. The pasta must be nearly done. It's time for dinner."

Chapter Four

The Dean Escapes

Now what do I do? Think!
To avoid the pouring rain, the dean was standing in a doorway on a back street not two blocks from the school. He had walked there briskly, but the rapidity of his pace was not sufficient to avoid a thorough drenching. Without a raincoat or topcoat, a hat or umbrella, he had been defenseless. Worst of all, he was still in stocking feet, and his toes were beginning to ache from contact with the chilly pavement.

His only advantage was that few people were out walking on such an inclement afternoon. Those who were, heads bowed, had not observed either him or his condition. A police siren sounded in the distance. Was it for him? Dean Ansari shivered, as much from his predicament as from the cold, and tried to collect his thoughts.

Should I go back? They'll think I did it. Mrs. Ackerman saw me with the gun. But they can't arrest the dean of a law school, can they? Why not? What makes you think you're any better than anyone else? I'll deny it. In the face of a smoking gun? The circumstantial evidence is overwhelming. Then I've got to run away – run until the murderer is found. Maybe I can find him. Running makes it look even more like I did it. How is anyone ever going to find someone in a Donald Duck mask who isn't there?

Panic gripped him. Without intervening steps, his mind leaped to prison for life, a grim cell amidst vicious fellow prisoners, and sadistic guards dragging him to the electric chair. Closer this time, the police siren sounded again.

In a desperate effort, the dean shut his eyes, trying to impose dispassionate reflection on his fragmented thoughts. The effort was partially successful. Unable to dispel his dread or the urge to flee, he was nevertheless able to devise the first, halting movements necessary to effectuate his escape. Unaware that the body had vanished, that the corpus delicti of the crime had ceased to exist, he applied barely rational thinking to what, had he known, was an irrational conclusion.

Dean Ansari's apartment was only a few blocks from the school. It became his first objective, and in a matter of minutes he made his way there, traversing the distance through back streets. An elderly woman, carrying groceries from a car, glanced in astonishment at his shoeless, disheveled appearance and lack of a coat in the rainy weather at this time of year. Annoyed that the mendicant homeless had apparently invaded her neighborhood from the downtown area and that the authorities still had not gotten these screwballs off the streets, she brandished her umbrella at him before disappearing behind a door to a rear garden.

Furtively, glancing quickly up and down the alley behind his apartment building, the dean opened the rear door. He closed it softly, then listened. It was a small building, with only four tenants, one to each floor and the basement. There was no sound – no growl of men's voices, no rushing feet on the stairs. Quickly, quietly, he walked past the small laundry closet in the basement hallway, then mounted the steps to the first floor. Still there was no sound. His apartment was on the second floor. Restraining an urge to bound up the next flight, he again listened intently, fearing a trap. The silence continued. At last, convinced of his safety, he walked upstairs deliberately and, after fumbling with his key in the lock, entered his sanctuary.

It was as he had left it in the morning: dishes neatly stacked in the kitchen, a careful pile of mail on his dining room table, the ouch and adjoining tables in predictable order in the living room. All conveyed the image of an unruffled life, and in this scene he was the only point of incongruity. He stared wildly about for a moment, then nearly ran through the kitchen to a back storeroom and retrieved a suitcase. Unceremoniously, banging it against a door jamb in his haste, he lurched to the bedroom and threw the bag on his neatly arranged bed.

What to take with him? Disposing of his dripping clothes, he threw them in a corner and donned clean, warm apparel and a dry pair of shoes. *The next season is summer,* he thought. *Take some summer clothes! There'll be time enough to purchase sweaters and wool socks when the time arrives!* Hastily, he ransacked his bureau and closet, retrieving shirts, slacks, underclothing, sneakers and an old tennis hat. All of them he jammed helter-skelter into the suitcase, throwing in a penknife and address book at the end.

After only a few minutes, the task was done. Dean Ansari laced a tie around his neck, put on a summer blue blazer and placed his checkbook in a trouser pocket. Advancing to a front closet with his suitcase, he secured a waterproof jacket, an old crumpled hat and a black umbrella. His hurried preparations were complete. In near panic, hefting the heavy bag, he opened the door, carelessly leaving it ajar behind him. The suitcase bumped down the stairs. He retreated whence he came, through the rear door of the building to his automobile parked nearby in the alley.

His next destination was the bank. A branch office was located around the corner, but he needed to withdraw all his funds, preferably in cash. He drove, therefore, to the bank's larger main office downtown, parking in an adjacent garage. With an assumed air of nonchalance, but with his brown, slouch hat shadowing his features while it simultaneously protected him from the rain, the dean entered the building and took a seat to wait for the next available vice-president to assist him. In consternation, but with external composure intact, he observed a police car turn a corner near the bank. It maintained speed, however, and soon disappeared amidst traffic down the street.

When his turn came, he took the proffered chair next to the desk of a prim young woman wearing large, gold-rimmed eyeglasses. Her brown hair was drawn back severely into a bun, and she surveyed him with a pinched smile.

"I'd like to withdraw all my money in cash from my savings and checking accounts," Dean Ansari said. His voice was even and composed, but under the desk his fingers twitched in his palms.

"You are aware, I assume," she answered, "that there is a penalty for early withdrawal of your savings."

"Yes," he replied, although he was not.

"May I have your name and the account numbers."

She looked at him, wondering why her customer seemed somehow ill at ease and nervous. *Odd,* she thought, *that he doesn't remove his jacket and hat. They're still dripping on the floor.*

"Would you care to hang up your jacket and hat?" she volunteered. "We have hooks on that pillar." She pointed in the direction of a gleaming marble pillar several feet away.

"No… no," the dean said, "I'm… quite comfortable, thank you."

He continued to sit before her, his hat pulled low over his eyes. The young vice-president recalled the story of the million-dollar account that had been transferred to a rival bank because an employee, misjudging the appearance of a customer, had been rude. *I'd better be nice to this fruitcake,* she thought, *even if he's acting weird.*

Her fingers danced over the keys of a computer on her desk, calling up the relevant information about his accounts in green numbers on the screen.

"You have approximately sixteen thousand dollars."

"Yes," the dean said slowly, making a rapid calculation in his mind, "that should be about right."

"I'm sorry, I can only give you ten thousand in cash. That's a rule of the bank. We can give you the rest tomorrow, if you'll come back."

"No, I think I'd rather take it all today," the dean said as if he were considering the offer. "Is there some other way I can take out the rest of my money?"

"If you're going on a trip," the young vice-president responded tartly, "I suppose we could provide the remainder in travelers' checks."

"That would be fine," he said, not conceiving an alternative. A certified check in such a large amount might elicit questions.

"Do you have a preference for denominations?" she asked.

"I'd just as soon have everything – the checks and the cash – in fifty dollar bills or less. Maybe most of it in fifties and a thousand dollars of the cash in twenties."

Again she looked at him with curiosity. It wasn't her place, she realized, to inquire why he needed so much money in cash – surely an unsafe way to keep it – or why he needed it in such small denominations. Her quizzical frown, however, betrayed the unspoken question.

"I'm buying a new car," he explained, "and I said I'd pay cash. So… I'm getting the cash." He ventured an unconvincing laugh. The young vice-president continued to regard him disapprovingly. "Also… of course… I'm, ah, going on a trip… as you guessed."

Yep, she thought, *a real weirdo. Well, it's none of my business.*

"Please wait. I'll be back in a moment."

She rose and walked briskly into a back room. The dean viewed her departure with apprehension. He glanced around, but all seemed normal. The bank guard was lounging with apparent unconcern by the door.

In a short time, she returned. With practiced precision, she handed him the travelers' checks to sign, then slid them neatly into several black booklets before her. "Keep your transaction record in a separate place," she admonished, "in case you lose them." With equal precision, she counted the cash, cracking the new bills as she did so. Finally, she pushed three coins toward him across the desk.

"May I have an envelope?" he asked.

"Certainly."

The envelope was provided, and the dean placed the stack of bills inside it, then tucked the envelope and its contents into his inside jacket pocket. The coins he deposited in his trouser pocket as he rose to go.

"Thanks very much. You've been very patient. That was

much easier and speedier than I had thought it might be. I assume the accounts are closed."

"Yes, if that is your wish. Have a good day, Mr. Ansari... and please don't hesitate to do business with us again."

She pulled some papers toward her and began to study them. He had been dismissed. Awkwardly, the dean turned, fastened the top button of his slicker, and walked past the guard and out the door. The driving rain had turned to drizzle, and he turned up his collar. With a quick, but he hoped unruffled, pace, he returned to the garage and his automobile. The engine started; he paid the parking fee. In the glowering, gray light of late afternoon, he swung onto the freeway and headed east. Two hours later, headlights on, the car crossed the state line.

* * * * *

Lieutenant Walsh had finished interrogating Mrs. Ackerman. She had told a puzzling story, and he was uncertain what to make of it. Her distress and obvious sincerity, plus the requirements of her position as secretary to the dean, suggested strongly that she was being truthful. What motive could she have to fabricate a hoax?

Yet he did not totally discount the possibility, nor was it inconceivable – even though highly unlikely, given the evidence at hand – that she had, to use his vernacular, flipped her wig. Lieutenant Walsh had never received formal training in psychology, but he had acquired a wealth of experience from 'the street.' Perhaps, for some reason, she was being hysterical. Or maybe they had been lovers, although the likelihood of anyone in an amorous entanglement with Mrs.

Ackerman seemed remote. But who can dispute taste? Maybe this Dean Ansari had a penchant for elderly, addled maiden aunts. He had seen stranger liaisons. Maybe she killed him in a jealous quarrel and then concocted a wild story about a murder that may never have taken place.

Conjecture followed upon conjecture while he sat, fingertips together under his chin. Occasionally, he raised his hands and pressed his touching forefingers against his pursed lips, a distracted scowl on his features. Certain lines of inquiry would need to be pursued. If not a homicide, possibly a murder, then at a minimum he seemed to have a missing persons case on his hands. And under highly unusual, suspicious circumstances. The blood on the carpet – if it was blood – would have to be analyzed. Perhaps it could be matched against the blood types of the dean and the alumnus who, according to Mrs. Ackerman, had been paying a visit. Probably it should be matched against Mrs. Ackerman's blood type also.

In addition, search warrants should be obtained immediately to examine the living places of the dean, the alumnus and Mrs. Ackerman. Additional witnesses, if any, should be located, and the office and other areas would need to be dusted for fingerprints.

One of the patrolmen approached Lieutenant Walsh as the latter was completing his preliminary list of actions to take.

"We've been through the whole building, even closets and places like that. We gotta have keys for some rooms and a few of the offices. Also a classroom. We finally found a janitor who's got a whole bunch on a ring, and he's helping us."

"Find anything?"

"Nope. Not yet. Not a person, not a body, not nothin'."

Anything, thought the Lieutenant. *Do these guys get*

special training to learn their brand of English, or is it an innate skill?

"Keep looking," he said. "Particularly look where someone might have tried to hide a body. Try that back staircase outside the dean's office. And keep an eye out for bloodstains or signs that someone was in a hurry – like a knocked-over chair or something like that. I don't think we're going to find Dean Ansari, but if you see anyone, ask if they've seen him… And for God's sake, if they have, get their name and address."

"We've already run into a couple of people," the patrolman replied, "but no one's seen him. I asked already. Even three of the profs."

The guy's gone. Shit! Lieutenant Walsh was baffled. *What the hell's going on here?* Reacting to his instincts, he reached for the telephone on the dean's desk. Mrs Ackerman was still seated in her usual chair, sniffling, an expression of acute anxiety on her features.

The desk sergeant answered. "Ray?" Lieutenant Walsh queried. "Yeah. Listen, Ray, we got a really strange situation here. No… no, I'll tell you later. I don't have time. Listen, get McCallister. We need to send someone over to the place where the dean of this law school lives. See if he's there… What?… No, don't worry about a warrant. There's no time, and we can claim hot pursuit. We'll catch him first and explain later… I said, there's no time."

Turning to Mrs. Ackerman, Lieutenant Walsh asked: "Where does he live?"

"Where does who live?" she responded dully.

"Santa Claus," he answered sarcastically. "Who do you think? The dean. Where does he live?"

"Oh." Mrs. Ackerman looked miserable. "Don't be angry.

I'm sorry. She rose unsteadily and went to her desk, returning moments later with a card from her battered Rolodex.

Lieutenant Walsh swiveled his head back to the telephone's receiver. "Be right with you. I'm getting the address."

Mrs. Ackerman placed the card on the desk in front of him.

"Is that an apartment?"

She nodded. "I think so. I've never been there."

"Okay, Ray, he lives in an apartment, and it's right near here. Get a squad car over there and let's see if our friend's at home… Yeah, better tell them he might be armed and may be dangerous. If they find him, bring him into the station house. I need to talk with him."

The lieutenant paused. A question crackled in his ear, and he laughed. "Sorry about that. The name… "

He turned to Mrs. Ackerman. "What's his full name?" She pointed, and he resumed speaking into the telephone. "Oh, Christ, I should have remembered it. It's right here on this card. The name's Massoud Ansari. Yeah… strange. Some kind of Arab or something. I'll spell it. He lives at 432 Chestnut in apartment 3."

The desk sergeant dispatched a black and white cruiser to the apartment and then contacted Lieutenant McCallister, who also departed immediately. He arrived at the same time as the squad car. Another tenant had come home, and she opened the front door for the lieutenant and two patrol officers. In response to Lieutenant McCallister's inquiry, she explained that Massoud Ansari lived one flight up, the first – and only – door on the landing. Antwan McCallister found it as it had been left – slightly ajar. No one responded to his knock. He nudged the door open slowly with his foot and stood aside. There was no sound or movement. After a long pause, one of the patrolmen entered, gun in hand, and looked around. He motioned to the others to follow. A dining room chair was lying on its back. Cautiously, they opened closet doors, then looked in the kitchen. Finally, entering the bedroom, Lieutenant McCallister found the evidence of disordered flight. Clothes were scattered on the bed and floor. A dresser drawer was open. The occupant, Massoud Ansari, was nowhere to be found.

* * * * *

Lieutenant McCallister radioed a report from the squad car. The suspect had apparently fled. The disarray in the bedroom could be evidence of violence, and thus further checking would be necessary, but it seemed more consistent with a hurried departure. There was no indication where the suspect had gone, or how, or with whom.

Lieutenant McCallister returned to the police station and requested an immediate check at the state's Department of Motor Vehicles to determine whether Dean Ansari had a car and, if so, its year, make, color and license plate number. When, in due course, this information was furnished, he sent out an all points alert to stop any automobile answering the description. He also alerted security personnel at the bus station to be on the lookout for any departing passenger who resembled Dean Ansari.

By the time the all points bulletin was released, however, darkness had fallen. Visibility, already masked by rain, was severely diminished. Without hindrance, the dean drove on for several hours and entered the outskirts of Chicago.

Where to go? His thoughts were jumbled, ricocheting from the events of the afternoon to plans for concealment and further flight. What had happened? Over and over, he relived the scene in his office, trying to understand. Had he done the right thing? He did not know, and more than once panic seized him. Perhaps he should have turned himself in, but now flight seemed to confirm his guilt. Everything had happened so quickly. There had been no time to reflect. Where was he to go? Could he go on forever, a fugitive?

As he had done earlier, Dean Ansari forced himself to think one step at a time. He would need a place to sleep, then dispose of his car. He would have liked to keep it, but he assumed the vehicle could be traced, improbable though that might be in such a large metropolitan area. All his life he had succeeded through meticulous preparation and attention to detail. The habit did not leave him. He was applying it, however, in circumstances different from any he had ever known and in a state of high anxiety. A more relaxed appreciation of the difficulties faced by his real or imagined pursuers would have stood him in good stead.

Locating a bed for the night was not difficult. He chose a seedy motel, its vacancy light still on, and woke the drowsy proprietor. After registering under an assumed name, he parked the car in the rear. *A hot pillow joint,* he thought as he entered the room, reminding himself to check the sheets. But he did not. Exhaustion overcame him, and he slumbered soundly.

Anxiety, however, propelled him to wakefulness at the first blush of dawn. Trucks were already on the road, headlights still on, rumbling into the city. He decided not to shave. A beard alters appearance, and even being unkempt might help if someone were looking for a tall, well-dressed lawyer and educational administrator. Donning slacks and a sports shirt, he walked to a diner near the motel for a greasy breakfast. Before entering, he purchased a newspaper from a nearby stand to read while eating. It contained a brief inside story about him – about the possible murder and the fact that he had vanished. Puzzled, he read the article several times. With most local homicides not reported in national papers, the inclusion of this item, together with a photograph, alarmed him. A possible murder by a law school dean, followed by a dramatic disappearance, was apparently national news. He sat hunched over his food, holding his hand to the side of his face, then paid the bill and departed quickly.

He needed to dispose of his car. After renting his room for another night and leaving his luggage, the dean decided to drive into the city. He reasoned that stolen and derelict cars could be no novelty there. It took him some time to find a district of warehouses and factories with a small parking area on a side street. Surely, he thought, an abandoned car in such a place would not be noticed or reported for several days. Removing all identification, he furtively unscrewed the license plates, certain that someone would observe him from a nearby building and report him as a thief. But they did not. He tucked the plates under his arm, walked to a nearby main street, hailed a cab and returned to the motel.

Two days later, his beard now a dark stubble, the dean checked out of the motel. By this time he had decided to leave the country – go to Canada by way of Detroit. Without so much publicity in the Canadian press, he reasoned that he would be safer there. He packed carefully, tucking the plates into his clothing because he could not think how to dispose of them. He was wearing his rain jacket, and he jammed his brown slouch hat onto his head, giving himself the appearance of a down-on-his-luck man who had known better times.

Thus attired, he took another cab to the Greyhound bus station on the near South Side. It was a long, low building, thronged with people traveling to nearby cities and distant points throughout the country. A public address system, announcing times and locations of arrival and departure, blared continually. The dean blended without distinction among the crowd of ethnic poor, unkempt students with knapsacks and elderly women with battered purses clutched to their sides.

He purchased a ticket to Detroit and boarded the next bus without mishap. Hours later, cramped and uncomfortable, he arrived at a terminus on Howard Street similar in type, if not configuration, to the one he had recently left in Chicago. The bus operator opened the side luggage doors and dumped suitcases unceremoniously onto the pavement. Without difficulty, the dean retrieved his bag and, pulling his slouch hat down over his eyes, walked out of the building.

His destination: a small, not too disreputable, hotel somewhere near the bus station. He had asked a gruff, elderly fellow passenger who sat next to him on the bus about lodgings in Detroit. The man's criteria of desirability appeared to be propinquity to bars and the availability of 'broads' or, as he phrased it, 'broadies.' Almost with disgust, apparently suspecting a different sexual orientation, he had grasped finally that the dean was interested in neither.

"Oh, if it's that sort of place you want," he had said

reprovingly, "try the Saint Andrews. It's not far from a neighborhood that you kind of people like." He had then returned to reading the sports section of his newspaper and deigned to notice the dean only once more when, arising to go, he cast him a pitying glance.

The dean made an inquiry on the street and, after crossing a highway, found the hotel without difficulty. It was neat and unpretentious. The clerk was polite, although he seemed to hesitate slightly at the appearance of his guest. I'll have to trim this beard, the dean thought. He checked into a modest room, the second leg of his escape completed without discovery.

* * * * *

"So he went to Chicago."

Lieutenant Walsh was seated in the chief's office, a corner room in central headquarters on the second floor. A metal desk graced one end, and an upholstered couch with three chairs surrounding a coffee table took up the other. Two large windows, unadorned by curtains, occupied each exterior wall. The room had been designed originally to convey an impression of authority, but too many budget cuts and freezes had blunted the effect. The carpet was worn, the desk dull from age, and the couch faded and lumpy. Instead of the crisp efficiency of command, the impression conveyed was of frumpy respectability.

The chief had been speaking. He was a beefy, heavyset man who looked more like a corner cop, which he had once been, than an administrator. Both he and Lieutenant Walsh were seated in chairs by the coffee table.

Lieutenant Walsh cleared his throat. "To be precise, Chief, his car went to Chicago. It wasn't found for several days. By the time it was reported, the wheels and radio were gone. Vandalized. The plates were missing too, but we know it's his from the vehicle identification number. Alert work on Antwan's part."

"Did anyone make a check of the car?"

"Yeah. No blood stains. Nothing. No sign that anyone else had taken it. We're guessing he was in it."

Perplexed, the chief's eyebrows nearly connected. "At this point he's a person of interest, not a suspect. I wonder why he ran away."

"Probably 'cause in fact he did something," Lieutenant Walsh answered. "But what? According to the old lady, his secretary, there was a dead body in the room. All we found was a bloodstain and a pistol with his fingerprints on it."

"Where was the gun?" the chief asked.

"On the desk – his desk in his office."

"And no one's seen him since?"

"Right. We're still checking. It looks like he went home – got out of the law school somehow, although it beats me how – and packed his stuff and took off." Lieutenant Walsh paused. "Oh, we also know he went to the bank and took out all his money. Some in traveler's checks. We've got the numbers."

The chief looked intently at the lieutenant. Removing a pipe from an ashtray, he sucked on the stem. Smoking was no longer allowed in the building, but the chief used the pipe as a prop, imagining that it conveyed an air of thoughtful intelligence. It also gave him time to reflect during conversations in his office when, too often, he had difficulty grasping what people were saying.

After a few moments, he brightened. "Did you check out the other guy, the one who got killed or, I guess, may have gotten killed?"

"He was a graduate and a young lawyer. Also, he was gay – a homosexual."

The chief raised an eyebrow. "Really? Any connection between that and Dean Ansari? Maybe we've got blackmail as a motive here."

"Already thought of it, Chief," the lieutenant replied. "It doesn't look that way, although sometimes with closet types it's pretty hard to tell. From what we can find out, the guy likes women. He's been married once. His ex-wife lives now in Oregon, and he's had a few girlfriends."

The chief looked puzzled. "Which guy?"

Lieutenant Walsh laughed. "Dean Ansari. No, the other guy, the one who got shot, he only had boyfriends."

"And you haven't found him?" the chief queried.

"Found who?"

"The guy with the boyfriends."

"Oh," Lieutenant Walsh laughed again. "Not a trace. We got a lead on him from the secretary, and also found out – through a number on a message slip in the dean's office – that he was staying at the Harvest Inn. It was easy to trace him once we got his hotel registration card. He also left a rental car in the hotel parking lot, and the rental agreement was in the glove compartment. He lived in Omaha, but no one's seen him since he left over two and a half weeks ago to come here, and at his office they don't know where he went. He's vanished into thin air."

"Jesus! We've got a dead person – maybe – but no body, and a suspect who's running from a crime that maybe never happened, although both the dean and his secretary saw what they thought was a corpse and there was blood on the rug. What a mess."

"Well," Lieutenant Walsh ventured, "at least we know the dean probably made it as far as Chicago. That doesn't help us much, but it's something."

"Keep at it, Walsh." The chief frowned, and his jowls hardened with determination. "I'm sick of these reporters bugging me for information. I don't need to tell you this is a big case in this town, even if it's died down a bit in the national news. Let me know when you get a break… and pray to God you do."

* * * * *

Shortly after he arrived in Detroit, Dean Ansari concluded that, in order to enter Canada and avoid being followed, he would need a false passport under an assumed name. But how would he get one?

For a respectable lawyer and academic, seeking anonymity, it was difficult finding an entrée to the world of those who live close to or on the opposite side of the law. He tried asking an elevator operator, who rebuffed him with a glance of incomprehension and scorn. His approach to a bartender achieved the same result. The latter, however, slightly misconstruing the nature of his inquiry, gave him the telephone number of a woman of no virtue whatsoever.

She had been perplexed when he offered to pay, not for her usual services, but for information. Once she understood, albeit after probing his background to make sure he wasn't a cop, she said hesitantly that she might be able to help. But she had only been forthcoming after the dean paid for and engaged in sex, thereby demonstrating his bona fides as someone outside the law. Thereafter, as they were dressing, she volunteered the name of Larry and the name and address of a motorcycle repair shop. Throughout their encounter, she chewed gum.

"Larry who?" the dean had asked.

"Just ask for Larry," she had said. "Everyone knows Larry."

So, with more than a little trepidation, the dean took a bus and then an afternoon walk to a neighborhood of ramshackle brick and wooden houses, bars and dingy convenience stores. It was a lovely spring afternoon when he arrived at the repair shop. A couple of grease-stained men were in front, working on a motorcycle. Its parts were strewn across the concrete paving.

"Is Larry here?" the dean asked tentatively.

"Whadda you want him for?" one of the men replied. "You a cop?"

The question took Dean Ansari by surprise. "No… no, I, uh, I just want to talk with him." Unhelpfully, he added, "It's something personal."

The man with whom he had spoken stood up, wiping his hands on his pants. The dean noticed a large, ornate tattoo on his forearm. "Talk about what?"

"About… well… about maybe giving me some advice where I can get… well… maybe some identification papers."

The man, after stooping to pick up a wrench, looked at him evenly, his eyes squinting. A slight, unpleasant smile crossed his features, showing gaps in his teeth. "He's in there." The man jerked his head toward the rear of the repair shop. Then, as if the dean had never existed, he squatted down and resumed work on the motorcycle.

Larry was a large man, with beefy arms protruding from a sleeveless shirt covered by a black, leather vest. Scraggy blond hair hung to below his collar, and a droopy mustache graced his upper lip. His neck was nearly as thick as the head it supported. Unlike his compatriot at the door, however, he was happy rather than sullen. He could beat a man insensate while saying, "Have a nice day."

"What can I do for you?" the voice boomed out, cheerful and powerful.

"Are you Larry?"

"Yep. Been that all my life."

"I was told you might help me."

Larry looked at Dean Ansari steadily, a smile on his face. "By who? Some friend of mine?"

"I guess so," the dean answered. "She knows you. Her name is Doris, and she said I should ask for you."

The smile never left Larry's face. "What's she look like?"

As best he could, the dean described her.

"That's her all right." Larry laughed. "She's some piece of ass, ain't she? Fuck you all night, you let her."

The dean looked away, then back again. His fumbling encounter with Doris was not enough to provide detail if Larry asked him to describe any of her particular favors. But he did not. "Just checkin'." Larry chuckled at some private recollection. "What can I do for ya?" The sentence came out as if it were one long word.

"Well... " The dean cleared his throat. "I wanted to find out who might make me a passport so I can get into Canada and then, maybe, go overseas."

"What country?"

Dean Ansari groped for an answer. "Not right away. I'm

not sure. Africa maybe, or Brazil… or India. Would that be a problem? Probably to Bombay. You know, it's like the gin." He laughed nervously, then corrected himself. "It's Mumbai now, but I guess you know that."

"I don't know shit about India or whatever that place is called." Larry spat. "And I really don't give a damn where you're goin'. You're runnin', I guess, and I don't ask no questions. What country you want to be *from*?"

"Well, Canada, possibly. Or America."

"Hey man, they're both America."

"Oh." The dean blushed. "I meant the United States."

Again, Larry laughed. Then he squinted, trying to size up his customer. "It'll cost ya, ya know. This ain't so easy. I can probably get it done for a grand and a half. American dollars." He emphasized the word *American*.

Dean Ansari gulped. He had hoped it would not be so expensive. In a tremulous voice, he asked: "Is that the usual price?"

"Nah," Larry said. "Less. Part's for me and part's for the guy who'll do the job. Nice work. You'll never tell the difference between yours and a real one."

For a few moments, the dean surveyed his options. It was pay or rot in Detroit. With a sigh, he said, "Okay."

"I want $500 now," Larry said, "and $1,000 when the job's done. Any bullshit and I'll break your arms." He smiled genially.

"Okay. Certainly. Of course you will. I'll have to get the money. Will you be here in an hour?"

"Yeah. Oh, by the way, if we can do it, we'll make a passport for a real person with a name sorta like yours. Easier to remember. So what's your name?"

That detail had never occurred to the dean. He groped, then blurted the first thought that entered his head.

"Honky… My name's Augustus Honky."

"Honky? You gotta be kiddin'. Come on."

"No, no. That's my name. Really." The dean's face reddened, but once committed, he did not know how to retreat. "I'll see you in an hour. And like I said, the name's Augustus Honky." He smiled weakly. "And, you know, if you'd like, you can call me Gus."

"Hey Johnny," Larry shouted out the wide door. "This guy here says his name's Honky. Shit. He ain't no cop. No cop would be that dumb… or smart."

"So we let him go?" the one named Johnny shouted back.

"Yeah, he'll be back with five hundred *American* dollars." Again the emphasis. "Soon. Why dontcha take a walk with him. Just kinda make sure he stays safe."

"Sure," Johnny answered. He was the man who had been holding the wrench. He smiled crookedly and humorlessly, and the gap in his teeth showed again.

The dean glanced apprehensively from one to the other.

"We goin' huntin' later?" Johnny asked.

"Hey, asshole, the truck's been ready a week."

"This afternoon," Johnny snarled. "I ain't drawn no blood this year. Get me one of them deer so's I can gut it."

* * * * *

It had been ten days since the dean secured his false passport. He was in no hurry to leave Detroit, reckoning that the passage of time was his ally. His plans changed abruptly on a day when he took a stroll after lunch. For several previous days there had been nothing to do in his room but watch television – an endless progression of soap operas and the recycling of twenty-four-hour news. He had seldom watched television in the past, and compelled now to do so or stare vacantly out the window, his mind had wandered naturally to recent events at the law school and his current predicament. That activity, however, was worse than watching television, and he had finally rebelled.

I can't just sit here, he thought. *I've got to do something. Maybe I'll buy a couple of books. Anything.* He looked with distaste at the unblinking, plastic monster, now shut off, that sat stolidly on a small table near the foot of his bed. Almost reflexively he moved to the door, but he did not become insouciant in the face of imagined danger. The day was unusually warm, but he nevertheless donned his old blazer and again pulled his brown slouch hat about his ears. His beard he had trimmed, and it made a dark, neat outline across the lower half of his face. Retrieving his sunglasses from his luggage and putting them on, he surveyed his image in the long mirror on the back of the bathroom door.

Not bad, he thought. *Not bad at all.* To the objective observer, the image was nondescript, a trifle seedy and possibly menacing. To the dean, who had heretofore never envisaged himself as a desperado, his reflection conjured romance. He needed saloon doors to kick in, or perhaps six-shooters strapped to his sides as he strolled into town. Two Gun Massoud, that was it. Setting his hat at a rakish angle, he ventured forth. His loping stride would never be called jaunty, but as he left the hotel, it came as close to that description as his jerky movements could make it.

After two or three blocks, Dean Ansari concluded that

Detroit was neither beautiful nor safe – that, in fact, it was a sump for the urban poor. He felt that he had exhausted its possibilities. Moreover, his appearance, far from conjuring the romance of the Wild West, made him feel uncomfortably vulnerable and alone. When he stopped at a crosswalk, a man behind him said, "Move it!" The tone was not unfriendly, but neither did it inspire a sense of belonging. His ruminations, never far from the surface of active thought, crystallized in the moment of time when the apparition in the Donald Duck mask had spoken to him. *It called me a honky,* he reflected again. *A honky! Or was it a turkey? Why? How dare someone call me a turkey.*

Abruptly, he turned back to the hotel. There was no point in walking farther. But he decided to stop at the bus depot where, he was sure, there would be a newsstand and, quite possibly, magazines and a rack of paperback books. He was not disappointed. He stood, oblivious to the disgruntled stare of the proprietor, for nearly a half-hour while he leafed happily through books and magazines.

However, just as he was about to leave, while he was paging through a national news magazine, he made an ugly, frightening discovery. In a section labeled 'Crime' he came across a brief article about his escape. For a moment a passing reference to a possible homicide puzzled him. Had he not seen the corpse with his own eyes? His attention focused instead on a statement that a person of interest and potential suspect had fled eastward. How did they know? Was someone on his trail? Nervously, he replaced the magazine, purchased a paperback book, and walked quickly past the cash register. He pulled his hat over his eyes and glanced furtively behind him as he walked out onto the bright pavement.

Within minutes he was at his hotel, clutching the book in his hand. No one, apparently, had followed him.

He strode rapidly past the registration desk on his way to the elevator. Startled, the clerk asked, "Is something the matter, Mr. Pilabosian?" calling him by the name he had used when he registered.

"Uh? No... no. Nothing's the matter." A scowl spread across Dean Ansari's features. *Good God,* he thought, *I can't stand this hotel. I can't stand this city. I'm going crazy in this place. Could they have traced my car already? Was that it? Maybe I've been recognized, and the police are just waiting to close in and make an arrest. I've got to get out of here.*

Again, he glanced nervously behind him. The clerk, who had been observing him intently, dropped his eyes and pretended to sort through papers on his desk.

Dean Ansari cleared his throat. "I'll be checking out in a half hour."

"You have the room through tomorrow morning," the clerk answered, clearly startled. "Check out time is twelve o'clock."

"That's okay. I know. Something's come up. Why don't you prepare my bill. I'll be down shortly with my luggage."

* * * * *

"Put me through to the chief."

Lieutenant Walsh drummed his fingers on his desk. He heard the chief come on the line and grunt a greeting.

"Yeah, it's Walsh. I've got a new development. The Ansari case."

"Put them over there, on top of the file cabinet." The voice was muffled.

"What?"

"Sorry," the chief chuckled. "I was tellin' Helen to leave some files. Why dontcha come up? Grab some coffee on the way."

Lieutenant Walsh hung up the telephone. Shutting the door to his cubby-hole of an office, he walked to a hotplate near a bank of file cabinets and poured black coffee into a Styrofoam cup.

When he entered the chief's office, the chief was already sitting on his worn, faded couch reading some papers. He waived Lieutenant Walsh to a chair.

"So," he said, looking up, "what's new? Have we found him?"

"Nope, nothing that good."

There was a moment of silence. The chief, impassive, waited for more.

"We have a pretty good idea where he's been," Lieutenant Walsh continued. He paused. "Well, maybe I shouldn't be that definite. We're fairly sure it must have been him, but until we've got him, I guess we can't be one hundred percent certain."

"What have you got?"

"License plates. The license plates to his car. They were found rolled up in some newspaper in the wastebasket of a hotel room in Detroit. They might have been thrown out by the maid, but the clerk was suspicious, and he went up and looked through the room after he checked out."

"Suspicious?" the chief asked. "Why suspicious?"

"I guess he thought there was something strange about

the way he left. In a big hurry... and pretty anxious. Looking around him all the time, the clerk told us."

Pondering this new information, the chief nervously flipped a pencil in the air. Finally he said, "Dija check the hotel registration? That would be an easy way to find out if it was him."

"It wasn't, as it turned out." Lieutenant Walsh looked evenly at the chief. "The name was Roger Pilabosian. It's an alias. We checked the home address he gave, and no such place exists."

"Well, dija get a description?"

"Sort of. We talked to the clerk – by telephone, of course. He described the man as tall with dark hair... and balding. A big nose and wide mouth. So far so good. But he had a short beard. Apparently he looked pretty dirty when he arrived, and he wasn't wearing a coat and tie or anything like that. He neatened up before he left, but he was still wearing casual clothes. And he had a reasonably large, cloth suitcase. Standard kind."

"Any idea where he was goin'?"

"Nope. No forwarding address. Farther east, probably. Or maybe Canada."

* * * * *

From Larry, for one thousand five hundred American dollars, Dean Ansari obtained a United States passport of flawless quality. On this document his name was Augustus Honque, a naturalized American citizen from Quebec and now a resident of Maine.

Crossing into Canada had been a simple task, much

simpler than he had anticipated. The Canadian customs agent had examined his passport and then peered at him through the taxicab window. He was well dressed with a neatly trimmed beard, and so passed muster. The official then inquired about the length of his stay in view of his bulging suitcase. His response was satisfactory – that he was there on business and for tourism. Apparently his name was not on some sort of watch list, and the cab was waved through.

After successfully crossing the border, he took a bus to Toronto. But then what? Get an obscure, low-paying job? And wait for eventual exposure, arrest and imprisonment? He had not been a prominent person, but his face and physique were familiar to many hundreds of former students. Even with his sprouting beard, recognition would come one day in a store, on the street, in a bar or on a bus. And, if he were given luck and time, he would then be forced to flee again.

No, thought Dean Ansari, *I've got to go where I won't have to run again.* He had already pondered the matter deeply without reaching a conclusion. Europe, particularly the south of France or Italy, seemed the most appealing. But he spoke neither French nor Italian. *Where,* he wondered, *is the farthest, most crowded place on the face of the earth? A place where I can wait until the true culprit is found? Where some people speak English.*

He might have chosen Belize or perhaps Nigeria or Kenya, but a conclusion had come to him in an Indian restaurant. It was a conclusion he had toyed with for some time. Why not India? First, however, he had to deal with a problem that arose as he was about to pay his bill: how to deal with acute indigestion. Indian food, he decided, is spicy and dangerous, an observation that nearly inclined him against his choice.

Within a few days he purchased a one-way Air India ticket from Toronto to Mumbai. Reluctant to take traveler's checks into India for fear that he might have difficulty negotiating them, he converted them to American and Canadian dollars. Some he then used to pay for the ticket, and he kept a substantial reserve of cash that he secreted on his person and in his luggage to pay for living expenses and emergencies.

Chapter Five

Augustus Honque Arrives in India

The first assault on his senses was the smell, a mixture of heat and sweat and incense and urine and flowers and garbage. The next was the din, the cacophony of voices, shouts and automobile horns. The third was the heat, a moist, oppressive envelope that surrounded his every movement. It stuck and cloyed. Last, of course, was the mob of people, sitting, walking, riding bicycles here and there, bronzed faces and bodies accentuated by their light-colored clothing.

The fabled East! *Fabled to whom?* the dean mused. On inspection it seemed more like a run-down version of the worst tenement district in a decaying American city. Except that instead of sullen apathy – figures moving silently against a gutted urban landscape – there was color, laughter and surging vitality.

Augustus Honque had arrived in India – in Mumbai, formerly and otherwise known as Bombay, to be exact. It had been a long and tiresome journey. There had been a stopover of five hours in New York's Kennedy Airport followed by an overnight flight of many hours in a cramped coach-class seat. Sleep had been intermittent, and his legs ached when he finally debarked the plane at the Chahatrapati Shivaji International Airport in Mumbai.

* * * * *

"It is a significant pleasure to have you with us in India. I shall be most honored to be at your convenience."

The speaker was a small, dapper, brown-skinned man in slacks and an open-necked shirt. He seemed about forty years of age. His features were aquiline, and, like the rest of his countrymen, he had jet-black hair. Ramrod erect, with incongruously muscular arms, he wore round, metal-rimmed glasses that he removed from time to time to polish with a soiled handkerchief.

Because he had appeared more reputable than most in the scruffy crowd that was importuning the arriving passengers at the airport, Dean Ansari had approached the man for advice about lodgings, and the obliging fellow had generously suggested that the dean join him in a taxi ride into the city. With equal generosity, he had also allowed the dean to pay the fare. When they arrived at a small hotel, instead of proceeding on his way, the man exited the dilapidated taxicab with the dean and accompanied him inside. In what seemed an act of gracious hospitality, he conferred with the clerk and assisted in carrying the dean's bag to his room. Refusing a tip with an air of offended respectability, the little man departed. But when the dean walked downstairs a half hour later, his new 'friend' was waiting for him in the cramped lobby.

At this point, the dean began to realize that, in place of a fellow passenger in his taxi, he had acquired an intrusive guide and companion.

"I am pleased to be showing you our city. It is not, of course, rich like the United States of America. We have, however, our exciting spots."

The small, dapper man chose his words with care. He

smiled frequently and ingratiatingly, but he nevertheless retained an attitude of dignified reserve.

Dean Ansari was puzzled and ambivalent. On the one hand, he welcomed assistance in a strange – indeed, very strange – city. On the other hand... who was this person? It was unlikely he had nominated himself to be, free of charge, a one-man hospitality committee. People, reflected the dean, rarely do something for nothing.

The desk clerk, who had overheard the offer to be a tour guide, remained impassive.

"That really won't be necessary," the dean said. His instinctive civility did not depart him. "I was just going to take a brief stroll and acquaint myself with my new surroundings."

"Begging your pardon?" The little man stood stiffly before him, a slight smile on his features.

"I'm going to take a walk."

"Ah," the small Indian said, removing his glasses and polishing them fussily. "The city is large. It is unnecessary to be reminding you, a person of obvious intelligence, I am sure, that there are many streets where danger may accost you by misfortune. A wrong turn... pffffttt." He made the noise, somewhat like air escaping rapidly from a deflated tire, and snapped his fingers at the same time.

"You're very kind. But really, your help won't be needed. I'm not going far."

The little man continued to stand before him, carefully and pointlessly rubbing one of his lenses.

"Is there pleasure you would enjoy?" he said after a pause. "There exists in Mumbai nothing that money cannot buy. You like gambling? Ah, or the racing of horses? We have very good."

"No, no. Really, that won't be necessary. Thank you very much."

His cajoling host dropped his voice to a conspiratorial whisper. "Perhaps sexual gratification. Anything, we have. You like boys?" He grinned and shrugged, raising his eyebrows. "Or beautiful young women. I can find you, from any part of the world, maybe two or three. Your wish," he grinned again, "will be, I am assuring you, as a command."

The dean longed for the companionship of a sympathetic woman. No image came to mind, just the unfulfilled, persistent hunger for comfort, warmth and safety. He would not find it, he knew, in the manner suggested. Yet for a moment he paused. And in that moment he betrayed, through a soft exhalation of breath, his inner need.

"Thank you. Thank you for offering to show me Bombay… er, Mumbai. Your help won't be necessary."

While the small Indian shrugged and spread his palms at his sides, the dean walked deliberately around him and out of the hotel. In the stifling heat, the door was open, and he emerged from the interior shade onto a crowded, bustling street.

Where, he thought… *where in God's name did all these people come from?* Cars moved slowly amid a throng of human beings, cows and an occasional goat ambling among them; bicycles, bells ringing, occupied the road with the automobiles. Some of the people, an old, shoeless man in particular, seemed extraordinarily thin. A few lay, exhausted or asleep, near to the walls in the shade cast by the buildings. The tide of indifferent humanity swept by them without so much as a glance.

Mopping his brow – the heat was oppressive, and, it being just before the monsoon season, the moisture content of the air seemed near the point of precipitation – he set out down the street. He noted a store at the corner, a kind of combination market, drug store and variety store rolled into one filthy room that opened like a dark cavern from the street. A large Coca-Cola sign, bent and rusted by age, hung askew above the door. Here he turned right and proceeded up a broader thoroughfare for several blocks.

He decided to walk in a circle. Counting the blocks, he turned right again at the tenth corner. The street he selected was narrow, with overhanging balconies jutting haphazardly from flaking, stucco walls, and it was necessary to thread his way around sidewalk vendors and dodge bicycles and running children. His shirt by now was sticking in moist patches to his body, and he picked at it, pulling the clinging cloth away from his skin. Again, he wiped his brow, regretting that he had not donned his tennis hat before journeying forth.

The road curved slightly, indeed imperceptibly, away from a perpendicular, ninety-degree angle to the thoroughfare from which he had come. The dean was too busy avoiding obstacles and observing the fantastic scene before him to notice. He marched along, wondering how such a hive of activity supported itself to eat and sleep and engage in the pleasures of life. Several more stores displayed signs advertising Coca-Cola and offering a variety of household and personal items for sale: Seiko watches, Nestlé canned milk, eyeglasses, American T-shirts and an array of cheap-quality kitchen goods. Occasionally he passed clusters of men gathered at rickety tables before grimy cafes to sip tea and talk. They watched the dean idly as he meandered by.

He had been counting again, and at the fifth corner he turned right. Ten blocks, he calculated, and he would be back on the street that housed his hotel, the Balfour.

This street was wider but no less crowded. Was there any street, any place, not occupied by throngs of humanity? The men, he noticed, usually wore slacks, sandals and light, open-necked shirts. Women seemed to dress in more colorful apparel; their dresses flowed around them in multi-colored, diaphanous material. Often, he noted, they wore gold costume jewelry with, occasionally, a gold ring in a nostril or ear lobe. Children, barefoot and rag-a-tag in shorts and shirts, were everywhere. About him was a constant hubbub, a babble of voices and ringing bells from passing bicycles.

The dean had not walked three blocks when he felt an insistent tugging at his sleeve. He turned to see a gaunt old woman, who immediately desisted and held out her right hand. Her beaked nose seemed to droop over her mouth, now contorted in a toothless grin as she stared up at him.

As much to remove the spectacle as to be generous, Dean Ansari groped in his pocket and handed her a coin. His generosity did not go unnoticed, and he had not walked more than fifty feet when he felt the same importuning tug on his shirt. This time the beggar was a child.

"Good morning, sir." The words were spoken in singsong. It was mid-afternoon. "You give? You give?" A ragged urchin of a boy was speaking and simultaneously pointing toward an old man propped in a sitting position against a wall. The man's frame was emaciated, and a crude crutch, its top covered with strips of dirty cloth, lay at his side. The ancient figure stared at him impassively from eyes deep in sunken sockets.

Again, the dean fetched a coin from his pocket. As he stopped to do so, he became aware of people staring at him and of the contrast between his clean, well-tailored clothes and theirs. The child took the coin and scampered away, but to the dean's puzzlement, not in the direction of the old man. A woman standing nearby burst into a rude cackle of laughter.

Dean Ansari resumed his walk – now, however, with a feeling of unease. What kind of neighborhood was he in? Did any of these people speak other than limited English? A sense of his own vulnerability began to gnaw at him. And he had not walked, at a somewhat quicker pace, more than a block farther when, once again, he was accosted. The beggar this time, however, did not pluck at him beseechingly. He stood, a slender young man, directly in his path with eyes that stared directly into his own.

"Money? You have?" the young man asked in faltering English. His tone, however, was steady and demanding.

What is this? the dean thought. *The fellow is able-bodied. He can work. And I do not like his manner.* "I have no more," he answered.

The young man's unflinching gaze did not waiver. Not comprehending the dean's response, he repeated: "Money. Money. You have?"

"No… no money."

A frown creased the young man's features. In a quick, stooping motion, he crouched down and to the side and slid his hand into the dean's side pocket. Pulling it out, a handful of change showered upon the muddy street. The young man instantly picked up two of the largest coins and fled into an adjoining ally. A group of children gathered around the dean, but did not move forward, as he groped in the dirt and retrieved the remainder. Ruefully, he pocketed the coins despite the longing stares around him, grateful the man had not filched the wallet in his back pocket. He shook his head angrily and marched away.

As if a hidden telegraph signal had flashed along the street, he was approached no more.

The dean had gone only a short distance when he realized that, in his befuddlement over the incident, he had lost count. Had he walked five blocks or six? Or was it seven? He could not retrace his steps without encountering the same people again. And that, on no account, would he do. He decided to walk another four blocks, then turn right again. If he did not encounter his hotel shortly thereafter, he would know he had guessed wrongly. It would then be a simple matter of walking to the parallel streets on either side. He would, he was sure, be back in no time.

Striding briskly ahead and avoiding eye contact with those about him, he turned right at the appropriate corner. It was soon apparent that his lodgings were not on this particular street. Thinking that he had not gone far enough, whereas in fact he had gone too far, he turned left on a narrow road to his left that he thought would lead him to his destination. He rapidly became conscious that he was in no more than a dark, urban alley surrounded by dirt and flies and stench and gawking urchins. Thoroughly lost and confused, he started to panic. He paused to mop his brow again and stared wildly about him. He thought: *I need to find someone who can give me directions. But not here. These people don't even speak English, and God only knows where they'd send me. I'd get robbed.*

Clueless as to his whereabouts, perspiration beading on his brow, he stood and stared up and down the alley. The dean moved forward several paces, craning his neck and standing on tiptoe, and at this point he spied light at the far end of the street and, farther on, the shimmering Arabian Sea. At a fast walk, he headed in that direction, and with relief he emerged onto a broad thoroughfare, similar to the one he had walked along only a half hour or so before. He did not, however, recognize his surroundings, but he was comforted to find himself in a neighborhood with western-style architecture. Many buildings appeared to house business or professional offices or apartments. *I'll walk a few blocks to the right,* he thought, *and see if anything looks familiar.* It did not, but he soon came to an intersection with another major thoroughfare, and there, off to his right on the opposite side of the street, he saw a hotel – a properous hotel, with a regular entrance, another entrance for automobiles and a gleaming lobby.

The dean nearly ran to it and then pushed through a revolving door and went inside. He was conscious immediately of a chandelier, a thick carpet and cool, non-humid air. A squat bell captain in a blue and gold uniform stood near the door behind a podium.

Dean Ansari fell on him like a vulture upon a dead zebra.

"Excuse me."

"Yes." The squat man turned toward him, a deferential smile on his features.

"Do you speak English?"

"Of course." The man smiled again. "What is it I can offer in the way of assistance?" He spoke in the precise manner of the Indian subcontinent, the cadence and emphasis falling in unaccustomed places on Dean Ansari's ear.

"How do I get to the Balfour Hotel?"

"The Balfour? You do not know how to find the Balfour?" The bell captain seemed puzzled, almost offended, as if he were the butt of some joke.

"No. I mean yes. I do not know how to find it."

"My dear sir, it is only across the street, although around the corner. You are, in a manner of speaking, directly on top of it. Permit me to point."

The bell captain abandoned his podium and walked to a large, plate-glass window, circumventing a grossly overstuffed chair and a heavy, standing floor lamp. Abashed, the dean followed behind him.

"There. Behind that building." With outstretched arm and finger, the bell captain indicated a building farther up the thoroughfare by, approximately, fifty yards. It occupied a corner to a narrow side street. And sure enough, across the way from it, Dean Ansari saw a portion of a Coca-Cola sign hanging haphazardly at an angle on the wall.

With profuse thanks and a feeling of enormous relief, the dean departed and made his way to his hotel. By this time rain had smothered the city. *It's time for a nap and then dinner,* he thought as, dripping wet, he entered the small lobby. The same clerk was there, regarding him impassively from behind his desk. Off to one side, seated beneath a potted palm, was a slight Indian man with metal-rimmed spectacles, a wry smile on his narrow face.

Chapter Six

Lieutenant Walsh Picks Up the Trail

"So? Whadaya got?" The chief had settled back in one of the chairs opposite his couch, his bulk nestling into its receptive contours. One of his jowls twitched.

"Like last time. We got information. We know more about where Dean Ansari's been, and we got an idea where he's going… or went, by this time."

Lieutenant Walsh had entered the room a few moments before, and the chief had abandoned his sanctuary behind his desk and had walked over to one of his stuffed chairs. Once he had nestled himself in it, the lieutenant had likewise seated himself at the end of the chief's battered couch. There any similarity ended. The chief's tie was pulled down from his collar, he was in shirtsleeves, and he was slumped into a weary, curled position of repose. Lieutenant Walsh, on the other hand, sat uneasily erect, his discount department store tie knotted in a broad windsor beneath his Adam's apple.

"I'd a thought you'd lost that turkey once he got outta town," the chief said. "You guys surprise me. Or he does, for bein' so stupid. First he's smart and gets away from us. God only knows how he got outta that building – flew out the window, maybe. Then he practically leaves us bread crumbs on his trail to Detroit. What's with this guy? Most criminals are dumb, but not him. Dean of a law school? You know,

Walsh, be careful. Maybe you're followin' the wrong guy. Maybe it's not him."

"Oh, we think it's him," Lieutenant Walsh responded evenly. "We got pretty good evidence, enough to convince me."

The office windows were open; the clarity of the openings contrasted with the grime on the panes of the upper and lower sashes that were now next to each other. It was a warm day, and a pleasant, gentle breeze wafted into the room. Some papers rustled on the desk, and a car horn sounded down the block. Two police officers, standing beneath the window, had commenced an argument.

The chief's head swiveled in their direction, creasing the folds on his neck. "You two assholes want to knock it off," he shouted. "Some of us got work to do!"

The voices stopped abruptly. Smiling, the chief returned his gaze to Lieutenant Walsh.

"Yeah. Like what?" he said.

"Well… " Lieutenant Walsh hesitated. He was confident of what he had to say, but the chief's interjection had startled him. "Well… first, like you said, we traced his car to Chicago. And maybe you're right. Just because it was his car don't… " he corrected himself "… doesn't mean it was him. Someone else could have taken it, although that doesn't seem likely."

The chief nodded his head, happy to have his sagacity recognized. It was, in his view, a much too infrequent occurrence.

"That took us that far," Lieutenant Walsh continued. "And then we found the plates in Detroit, and it seems like he left them there. But the guy checked out of his hotel, and we didn't have any other leads or place to go. So dead end, right?"

The chief looked at him intently. "I guess not, or you wouldn't be tellin' me this story. Why dontcha cut the drama and get to the point."

The bluntness of the comment took Lieutenant Walsh by surprise. He wanted recognition, and he was feeling pleased with himself. Pleased enough for a small, dramatic flourish. *Talk about being an ass*hole, he thought. *The damn chief's got no couth.*

"Sorry, just thought I'd bring you up to date," the lieutenant said. "It looked like we'd hit a stone wall, like I said. I guessed maybe he'd gone to Canada, because it's right next-door. That or home, which we found out was originally in Connecticut. No trace of him there, though. I mean, in his hometown. We checked the relatives who hadn't seen him for a couple of years. And so we figured Canada, but it's a big place. There's a lot of room to hide.

"And then what do you know. About three weeks after he disappeared for good we got information that he'd used a passport to enter Canada and that he'd cashed some traveler's checks. You may remember. He purchased some at the Union Bank just before he disappeared."

The chief's head had been resting to one side on his jowls while he drummed his fingers on the arm of his chair. He looked up, and one of his eyebrows inclined upward.

"Yeah," Walsh said. "He crossed over from Detroit to Windsor, like I guessed he might. Then he went to Toronto. At least that's where the checks were cashed. And right after that – maybe a couple of days later – he cashed some more and bought an airline ticket out of the country."

"No shit?" the chief sat up straight in his chair, now clearly interested. "To where? Could you find that out?"

"Sure. Easy. We asked the Toronto police to check with the airline. They had a record of the transaction – you know, how much he paid, the change they gave. And also, of course, the ticket he bought with the money; it was for a one-way, coach-class ticket to Bombay, India."

"Jesus, Walsh, good work! But India? For Chrissake. How do we deal with that? Interpol, or something?" In his small midwestern city, the chief was unfamiliar with international crime, although drug trafficking, even if occasional, was bringing the problem closer to home.

"Let's back up." Lieutenant Walsh was pleased, and he was now in charge of the unfolding story. Confidently, he continued: "We still can't be sure it's him. Like you said." He observed the chief's faint, lop-sided smile. "I mean, his countersignature is on those checks. Probably his, but it could have been forged. We're still checking. And the ticket was not to Massoud Ansari. It was for some guy with the absolutely ridiculous name of Augustus Honque."

"Honque? You gotta be shittin' me."

"Nope. That's it. Really weird. No one could describe who bought the ticket, but I got to thinking. How's this guy going to get outta Canada and into India without a passport? If he used one of ours, it would most likely not be one with the name Massoud Ansari on it. The Canadians, it turns out, have no record of issuing one to someone named Honque, but that didn't mean he didn't have a forged one of ours."

"It usually tells where someone's been," the chief snorted, "but not where they're going."

"Yeah. But if I remember right, if a big, foreign hotel registers someone and keeps the passport and then reports regularly on the ones they have to the local police, what with computers and all… if the name's in the system… you might pick someone up. A big fish, anyway."

The chief sighed. "So this guy got outta the country to Bombay, wherever the hell that is. It's near Turkey, isn't it? In the… in the Mediterranean some place."

It was Lieutenant Walsh's turn to smile, albeit circumspectly. "Sort of. Anyway, I was wondering what to do, and then we got a break. Just blind luck. We think this guy called Augustus Honque has a phony passport. Right? Where'd he get it? We didn't know. But practically on the same day the Detroit police pick up a man passing counterfeit dollar bills. Really good ones. Through him – after a lot of questioning – they locate the person who makes them. It turns out he also makes phony IDs, diplomas, certificates, anything you'd like. The police picked him up too, and sure enough, he remembered making a passport for someone called Augustus Honque.

"But he never saw him. His contact was a mean, smiley son-of-a-bitch called Larry Burkhardt, who runs a motorcycle repair shop. Guy's got a record long as your arm. Strange place for someone like Massoud Ansari to be. When the Detroit cops finally got around to him, he'd split. Must have found out his man was talking.

"But they pick up this sleaze who's a pal of Larry's and works in the shop. Another loser with a record. The cops talked to him, and he finally gets around to saying that not long before some man came to the shop and spoke to Larry. They thought the guy's name was a big joke. You got it – Augustus Honque. Later these two slime balls went hunting or something and were laughing about it, and Larry said Honque was running to some place he couldn't remember.

But it had the same name as a bottle of gin. I went to a liquor store to check. It's gotta be Bombay.

"Larry's pal gave a description of Honque. It sounded the same as the one the clerk gave in Detroit – beard, tall, same body build as Ansari. And a real gentleman. I think we've got enough. He's the man; Massoud Ansari is Augustus Honque."

Lieutenant Walsh stopped talking. He had been gesticulating, and now he folded his hands in his lap. With a faint exhalation of breath, he glanced at the chief, who was staring at the floor. The chief's brow was knotted, and his entire, beefy face was frozen in concentration, as if somewhere in his intracranial interstices of tissue, bone and fat – but mostly fat – he might stumble upon the germ of an idea.

He abandoned the effort. "So now whadda we do?"

"We go get him." Walsh seemed surprised.

The chief's eyebrows began to knot together at the bridge of his nose. "You can't just do that." His tone was hesitant, his expression confused.

"Why not?"

"Well... well, because it's not our country, that's why not. Where you gonna take him into custody? Just drag him to the local jail and tell some raghead to lock him up? 'Who the hell are you?' is gonna be the answer."

The chief raised his eyes. He was staring at Lieutenant Walsh. "For that matter, how you gonna find him? There must be lots of foreigners in India... although I guess maybe they stand out. The Indians are darker skinned than us, aren't they?"

"Yeah," Walsh replied. "I seen some at the university. They got white faces but brown skins... Look, Chief, there can't be that many places where foreigners stay in a strange place. He isn't going to go play native, eat their food, wear a sarong or whatever."

"Suppose he decides to go somewhere else?"

"Go somewhere else? Oh, for God's sake, he already *has* gone somewhere else. Half-way round the world. My guess is he'll stay put for a while and try to figure things out. He's going to be feeling pretty dislocated, and he'll wait for awhile."

"So then if we catch him, or get them to catch him," the chief interjected crossly, feeling slightly put out that Walsh had corrected him so bluntly, "we'll still have a problem. We'll have to go through a lot of extradition proceedings. I don't even know how those work or who pays for them. Do we? It's sure not in our budget."

The budget! The chief fretted about it constantly, convinced that his reputation in law enforcement would improve if only he had more resources. How would the mayor and Board of Supervisors react to spending money in India? He winced inwardly. On the other hand, this case had become a sensation, with national publicity. If Massoud Ansari had indeed crossed state lines, or fled the country, then the FBI could get involved. That might solve his budget problem, but it would also effectively end his chance to have his department get the credit for solving the crime. Accolades, so rightly his, would go elsewhere. He winced again.

Peevishly, the chief spoke before Lieutenant Walsh could interrupt. "It looks like we've hit a dead end."

"But… but, Chief, wait a minute. Now we know where he is, we can find him."

There was silence.

"I'm sure of it," Lieutenant Walsh added emphatically.

More silence.

"Look," the chief said finally, "why don't we face it. He's gotten away." Privately, he thought: *and I'll be damned if someone else is going to arrest him.* "He'll come back, though, and when he does, we'll get him." Frowning, the chief shifted his bulk in his chair, as if to rise and return to the work on his desk.

Lieutenant Walsh's eyes seemed almost to bulge outward, and his face reddened. Agitated, he sat bolt upright, frozen like a pointer who has just flushed a bird from hiding.

"I'll go get him."

The chief settled back quickly in his chair and stared at him.

"You'll do what?"

"I'll go get him. I'll go to Bombay and find him. I'm sure I can do it."

"Your assignment is here, or have you forgotten? And I'm not spending this department's money to send you on some Goddamned fishing expedition half-way round the world."

"No one asked you to." Lieutenant Walsh spoke in a tone of irritated, flat finality. "I'll go on my own nickel."

"What the hell are you talking about? Go on your own?" The chief mimicked the phrase derisively. "Are you off your nickel, I mean your rocker?"

"No, I'm not. I'm scheduled to go on vacation in three weeks. You approved it. I haven't taken any time off in over two years, and I've got a month."

"To go to India?" The chief was flabbergasted. "Aren't there elephants there? And monkeys and snakes? India?"

"Well, why not?" Lieutenant Walsh's voice became gentler. "What was I going to do anyway? Sit on some beach and feel sorry for myself? Come on, you know why I haven't gone before now. There was no point. I've saved money. Antwan will be here to fill in. It would be really interesting and would give me something to do."

"You can't… " The chief stared at his subordinate. "Are you serious?" He answered his own question: "You are serious… aren't you." Less strident – and less concerned about the budget – he grappled with the idea. Compressing his lips, he cleared his throat. Of course he knew the private circumstances, the personal anguish, the unflagging work his lieutenant had devoted to the office in a desperate effort to forget. The suggestion, in its peculiar way, made sense.

"Okay, let's think about it. Give me time to mull it over."

"You don't need to. It's my vacation, and some ideas just grab you. This is one of them."

"An adventure," the chief murmured. "Sure. A real adventure. It fits. I kinda envy you, except for bein' around all those foreigners and snakes." He paused, fiddling with a pencil, twirling it between his fingers and thumb. "Tell you what. What you do on your own time is your business. Like I always said. But maybe we could give you a little leg up, seein' as you'll be partly doin' your job. No transportation. We're not payin' your way there, but maybe… " his eyes rolled up to the ceiling, "… maybe some room and board. Hell, during the times you're workin', we don't even hafta call it vacation. I'll hafta think about it… even if you don't… just maybe we can make a deal.

"But I gotta warn you," he concluded, "even if you catch him, I don't know how we get him back here. He's only a person of interest. Hell, we don't even have a body, just some crazy old woman tellin' us she seen one, a missing person and – we know it now for sure – some blood stains."

Chapter Seven

Honque Meets a Beautiful Chinese Woman

Raji Rau was seated on a metal chair, with a twisted, floral design for a back, at a small, round table outside an establishment advertised on a large sign over the entrance as the Karma Kafe. The faded lettering on the sign was in Hindi with English beneath it. The chair on which Raji Rau was seated was old and rusted; a stained, russet-colored tablecloth disguised the table; and the establishment consisted of a dark, smelly interior room, where overly spiced food was served at cut rates, and a small, outdoor seating area near the street where beverages could be purchased. These last came in all types from tea to soft drinks to beer or wine. Raji Rau was sipping a beer.

The Karma Kafe was about a half-block from the Balfour Hotel. Raji Rau often sat at a table there, and frequently during the day he was joined by female companions. The women did not seem particularly fond of his company. There was rarely laughter or a convivial gesture of greeting or farewell. Rather, his dealings were in the nature of business transactions. Often there would appear to be an exchange of information, and equally often, and furtively, money would pass hands, always from the woman to the man.

On this steamy day, under a bright sun but with storm clouds billowing in the southwest, Raji Rau sat with his gaze fixed on the street leading to the hotel. Two young women were with him. Both, in their separate ways, were strikingly beautiful. The one seated opposite him, her short, buxom form draped in a sari, was mostly Indian and perhaps part Thai or Chinese. She had large rings in her ears, partially disguised by flowing black hair, and a half-dozen additional rings graced her fingers. Almond eyes and dark but soft features betrayed an admixture of genes from lands farther to the east.

Her companion, by contrast, was wearing a western-style dress, the skirt slit up each side, that clung to her body like a stocking. It was a luminescent green. She was devoid of jewelry, it being unnecessary to accentuate her beauty. Unusually tall for someone Chinese, she had long, dark hair that fell straight to the middle of her back. Small-breasted and slender, she possessed. a vivacious face that broke frequently into a smile when she spoke. At this moment, however, she was silent, waiting and watching with the others at the table.

It was about one o'clock, too soon to rest in the heat of mid-afternoon. The ideal time, Raji Rau thought, to take a stroll after a filling, midday meal. He had begun to fidget, however, and his normal imperturbability was on short tether. The women had been chatting gaily with each other, occasionally giggling behind an upraised hand, until he had silenced them with a curt, icy request to be still. Through bitter experience, each knew enough not to annoy him further.

So they were quiet until, after several minutes, the woman in the sari spoke in a hesitant, sibilant murmur.

"How is it, you say, he is looking?"

Raji Rau looked at her, not bothering to mask his contempt. The woman wilted and cast her eyes down.

81

"Were you not listening?"

"Yes, but I wanted to be certain."

"I shall repeat," Raji Rau said in a low, rasping voice. "He is American. Tall. With a beard." Here he moved his fingers across his upper lip and along his jawbone, roughly indicating the location of facial hair. In a characteristic gesture, he then removed his round glasses and polished them. "Possibly he is cultured – an educated man. More important, I am thinking he has money. And he wants a woman, I am sure." Raji Rau smiled. "Yes," he drew out the word, "very sure."

"Why he come Balfour?" the Chinese woman broke in.

"Because I brought him there. A nice hotel where no questions are asked. I watched him pay the taxi driver, too."

"He know what kind place it is?"

"Of course not, you fool. And you are not to tell him. Not yet."

"What he do in Mumbai?" the Chinese woman asked, persisting in her questions.

"It is impossible for me to be answering your question," Raji Rau shrugged irritably. "One of you must get to know him. Find out. Perhaps we can use him. Or perhaps, if he is not dangerous and not able to complain, we can take his money. If he tries to contact the police, he will not be the first tourist," he spat out the word, "who gets lost and no one is hearing from him again. It is a difficult city in which to find one's way."

Get to know him. Each woman knew what that meant. *And when he is asleep, steal softly from bed, remove the wallet from his trousers, and slip silently from the room. Or, discovering where he hides his valuables, enter the room during his absence and steal them.* It had been done before.

Raji Rau lapsed into silence, but he continued to stare down the street. He squinted through his glasses, then removed them and passed his soiled handkerchief over one of the lenses. When he returned them to the bridge of his long nose and looked again, he involuntarily clutched the arm of the Chinese woman.

"It is him. I am nearly certain," he said quietly. "Only… only… where is the beard? He is wearing shorts? Only boys wear shorts!" He uttered a guttural, derisive grunt. "But I am thinking it must be him. Now remember. Ask if you can help him. Is there anything you can be doing to make his stay in India most pleasant? He will, I am guessing, surely be liking one of you, or perhaps both."

Mirthlessly, Raji Rau smiled again.

Augustus Honque, formerly Massoud Ansari, was making his way through the jostling crowd on the street, and he spied the small group at the table just as the man seated there looked up and, with apparent surprise, caught his glance. Raji Rau waived his hand in happy greeting.

"Ah, sir. This is a gracious – and, may I say, most unexpected – moment of pleasure. I am seeing you again with utmost happiness."

The dean did not reciprocate the sentiment. Neither did he dislike the little man seated at the table. A feeling just outside conscious awareness bade him be careful, but that unarticulated instinct did not prompt him to be rude. He paused in the street a few feet from the table.

"It's nice to see you again," he said.

"But sir," Raji Rau said with a broad grin, "you have changed. I see that India has already had an effect on you. A most becoming effect, I can assure you."

It was true. The dean had changed, even though he had been in Mumbai only a few days. After his initial foray, he had not ventured far from the hotel, but he could not bear to stay in his room or the small lobby as if cooped in a cabin. Often he returned to the modern hotel around the corner to enjoy its air conditioning or sit, sipping a drink, on the verandah that surrounded an interior courtyard.

These excursions, while neither daring nor lengthy, had exposed him to the heat and discomfort of much of his clothing. He was glad he had stuffed summer clothes and his tennis hat into his suitcase. After a couple of days he donned shorts in spite of local custom and purchased a pair of sandals. These he had on, along with a loose-fitting short-sleeve shirt and his tennis hat. In addition, he had decided that his beard, finally respectable in length, was uncomfortably hot and no longer necessary as a disguise. Only that morning he had shaved most of it off, leaving a mustache, long sideburns and sickly, pale cheeks.

The result was an oddity. The sandals flapped on his feet, appendages at the end of thin, stork-like legs with knobby knees. The chicken-white skin on his arms and legs, covered with dark body hair, was red from recent exposure to the sun. And at the top of this assemblage of body parts and clothing bobbed a head that was graced by a floppy white hat and adorned with sunglasses and a budding handlebar mustache. This last item, curving slightly upward at its tips, reinforced his smile, making the dean seem particularly jolly. Although he remained tall and slightly stooped, the entire effect, unplanned and unbeknownst to its possessor, was a transformation and near perfect disguise.

"Would you honor us by joining our humble gathering?"

Raji Rau added after a moment. "Perhaps I can offer you some tea or a bottle of beer – very good, but unfortunately not American."

The dean had been about to resume his stroll. One of the women, the one in the clinging green dress, smiled at him. He hesitated. It had been a long time since he had enjoyed company, even the company of strangers.

"Come," the small Indian continued ingratiatingly. "We can obtain for you a chair. Let me say that you will not regret a moment of respite." He fixed a glance on the woman in the sari, who at once rose and fetched a chair from an adjoining table.

The dean continued to hesitate, uncertain whether he should accept the invitation. But the outcome was foregone when Raji Rau rose to his feet, beaming genially.

"Allow me, sir, to introduce you to my companions. Then it will be my pleasure to purchase for you a beer or other cooling refreshment." With a grand sweep of his arm, he indicated the empty chair at the table.

The dean, no longer uncertain, approached the table and stood awkwardly by the chair. He removed his hat and stuffed it in a pocket.

"Well… yes… a beer would be very nice. I'd be happy to sit down and join you for a few minutes." He smiled, and the women smiled back.

"This, sir, is Barbara Chu." Raji Rau, palm upward at the end of his extended arm, indicated the woman in the sari. "And this is Lin Fei." As he spoke, after nodding in the direction of the Chinese woman, he turned toward the dean. "And I… I have not had the honor of making your formal acquaintance. My name is Raji Rau."

"Very nice to meet you, Mr. Rau," the dean responded. "Or rather, it's nice to see you again. My name is… uh… Gus. People… ah, just call me Gus."

There was a moment of awkward silence. Raji Rau squinted slightly. He removed his glasses and examined the lenses, then looked up, again smiling.

"Will you be enjoying English beer? Sergeant's?"

"That would suit me fine."

"Pardon?"

"Oh," the dean blurted quickly, "yes, that would be very nice."

Raji Rau turned and entered the building, his small, lithe form disappearing into the interior gloom. The dean seated himself and glanced shyly at his new acquaintances. Reflexively, in the heat, he ran his hand across his perspiring brow.

"Your name," he inquired hesitantly of the woman in the sari, "is Barbara Chu? Do I have it right?"

She nodded her head in affirmation.

"And yours," he said, turning to the Chinese woman, is Lin?"

"Yes," she answered with a warm smile, "Lin Fei." The dean nearly blushed at his frank recognition of her beauty.

"You long time India?" Lin Fei asked him. Her voice was low and softly modulated.

"No, no, I've only been here a few days."

"What brings Mister to India?" Barbara Chu asked.

"Oh, nothing. Well… actually, not nothing. I mean, I'm here on business. Ah… personal business. It will… ah… require me to be here for a time. That is why I… I'm… staying at the Balfour."

Both women looked at him, as if hanging on each word.

"You see Mumbai? You enjoy sights?" Lin Fei inquired.

"Yes… I mean, no." He was flustered by her steady gaze and half smile. "I went for a walk a few days ago. But I got lost. Very easy, I guess." He laughed unnecessarily and nervously.

To his relief, she laughed with him – a tinkling, merry laugh – and clapped her hands. "I show you Mumbai. Have you seen the Gateway of India? Other sights? You want, Gus? Okay?"

He started at the sound of his new name.

"Well, sure. No, I haven't seen… I mean, yes, that would be very nice."

"You go now?"

"Yes, well, not this very minute… I was just going to take a short walk. Around the block." In response to her quizzical expression, he drew a circle in the air with his finger. "Then I was going to stop at the Excelsior, the large hotel around the corner."

"I go with you," Lin Fei interjected eagerly. She touched his arm as she spoke, and he had to consciously refrain from pulling it away. Even such slight contact was too overtly sexual in the presence of such a lovely woman.

Barbara Chu looked slightly discomfited. Lin Fei had captured the attention of the stranger so quickly, and so effortlessly, that she had not had time to entice him herself. No matter. There would be other men, and perhaps other opportunities with this one. Life, she knew, took strange turns. Her concern was directed toward Raji Rau's reaction and not toward remote feelings of personal disappointment.

As Lin Fei was concluding her offer, the small Indian returned to the table, a bottle of beer in one hand and a glass in the other. He placed these items on the table before the dean and sat down, his erect posture partially compensating for his short stature.

"So," he said, "it appears you have already secured the company of one of these beautiful women. You Americans! You are always so lucky." He shook his head appreciatively. "It would take me, I am assuring you, one whole year to do what you have done in five minutes."

Dean Ansari blushed, his white cheeks turning as red as his arms and legs. He was not sure exactly what he had done. In his experience, it was the woman who usually decided and the man who thought that he had, but in this instance he did not experience that sense of false, masculine gratification.

"Uh… thanks… thanks for the beer," the dean said, pouring the liquid into the glass and taking a sip. "This is very nice of you."

"My deepest pleasure," Raji Rau replied. "I hope we shall have many more such fantastic meetings. Perhaps… perhaps if you are staying in India for some time, Gus," he spoke the name slowly and carefully, "we may even have an opportunity to discuss business. I should be enjoying to know what you do."

Barbara Chu relaxed. It was obvious to her that Raji Rau was pleased.

"And now," Raji Rau looked at Lin Fei, his eyes shining brightly, "where will you be taking our new friend?"

"We go shop?" she answered demurely, glancing at the dean. "You like? Okay?"

A response seemed appropriate. He was flattered but slightly befuddled. A short stroll had somehow turned into a shopping expedition. But with such a companion!

"Do you know the way? I do not."

"Lin Fei," Raji Rau interrupted, "has lived in Mumbai for two or three years. Any fears, I am assuring you, are unjustified. She will be a delightful guide." He turned to Lin Fei. "May I suggest you stay away from Dharavi. I am suspecting our new friend has already seen enough of back streets and alleys."

Raji Rau settled back in his chair. The dean, continuing to blush, looked first at him and then at his new companion. Barbara Chu nodded in evident affirmation. Lin Fei continued to gaze at him, the same slight, enigmatic – or was it tempting? – half smile on her features.

* * * * *

What a curious little man. Oily. Are all Indians like that – only taller? The ones I've met always seem to have moral pretensions, but not this one. I wonder what he does, that he can sit drinking in the middle of the day with two gorgeous women. And go to the airport. Maybe he's in the export-import business, and I could get a job with him. He said something about business. Why is he always fussing with his glasses? There's something about him not quite… I wonder, is he what the British used to call a wog, or was that the Chinese? If he is one, am I one too? Surely people of Persian descent weren't wogs, but then what were they? Themselves, I guess, but the damn English certainly have a way of making everyone else feel ill at ease. Except maybe the French, who probably don't know, anyway, that they're called Frogs. Frogs and wogs.

The dean was seated, musing, in one of the overstuffed chairs in a lounge at the Excelsior. It was early evening, and a torrential shower had ended. He had changed to different apparel: slacks, shoes and a clean, well-fitting shirt. The sunglasses were gone, but the budding handlebar mustache remained.

As his mind wandered, he reached into his pocket for the card that Raji Rau had handed to him before he and Lin Fei departed on their shopping expedition. Casually, with a faint smile, he read it again.

Raji Rau
Department of Political Economy
University of Lucknow
(almost graduated)
Vishnari Road, 38
Mumbai, India

No wonder he speaks English, and not badly, too. He also seems to have some understanding of the world. But there was something… something he could not put his finger on. *Oh well.* Through him he had met Lin Fei, and wasn't it really good luck that she also lived at the Balfour. He would see her again… in fact, this very evening, in a few minutes.

Had the dean known, which of course he did not and could not, Raji Rau was also thinking of him. He had just finished talking with Lin Fei in her room, trying to glean hard facts about his potential quarry. Was the gangly American truly as absent-minded as he seemed? Did he, as Raji Rau suspected, have money? How much, and where did he keep it? What did he do to get it?

In Raji Rau's opinion, the dean was an enigma. A strange enigma, possibly dangerous, but then possibly an easy mark.

He needed to know more. From his manner of speech, the man had to be educated. That much he surmised correctly. From his mode of dress and general appearance, he could tell virtually nothing. Those shorts! Was he trying to ape the British? If so, it was a typically American effort, a bungled attempt by the garish mongrels of the world to mimic those with a pedigree. Americans, to his taste, were much too genial, deferential and unsure of themselves. And that mustache! Even Raji Rau could recognize a pathetic imitation of Lord Kitchener. Altogether, a very strange man. But possibly useful. For the time being…

Lin Fei was not helpful. Her ungainly companion had been charming – far more charming, in fact, than she had anticipated. The shopping expedition was, as he said at the end, "really good fun." They had gotten along, enjoying each other's humor, to the extent they could communicate. Gus, as she quickly learned to call him, had bought her a colorful silk scarf that she had admired. When she first saw it, she had picked it up and draped it over the back of her head and across her shoulders. She had laughed as she looked at him. His expression in return, so frankly admiring, had made her feel good – not afraid, as she was of so many men, but comfortable in the affirmation of her femininity. And then, sensing that she genuinely liked it, he had purchased the scarf and made it a gift.

She had, to be sure, tried to gain information from him about himself. It was quickly obvious, however, that this time together need not be the last, and she was in no hurry. The questions were innocuous, the kind any man and woman would ask as they got to know each other. Where was he from? What work did he do? Why was he in India and did he like it? And even, near the end of this afternoon together: was there a woman in his life?

To all these inquiries, he had been invariably polite and uninformative, in an informative way. That is, in saying a lot, he revealed very little. Only to the last question did he reply with an unequivocal no, a rueful smile and a shake of his head. In response to the others, she had learned only that he had lived somewhere in the middle of America, that he had once worked in education, position unspecified, and that he was in India on personal business. And yes, he found India fascinating although, to his taste, with too many poor, and much too hot.

Not far from the Balfour, as they were walking back, he had asked if she would care to join him for dinner. Normally she might have been otherwise occupied, but Raji Rau had asked – indeed, commanded – that either she or Barbara "find out about our visitor." How better than to continue their budding friendship. Besides, she had, to her surprise, most enjoyed his company. It would be a pleasure to have dinner with him.

Thus she had little to report, much to Raji Rau's disappointment and annoyance. Because she had said she would be delayed, although naturally omitting the reason, she and Gus agreed to meet later in the lobby of the Excelsior. She walked there with a growing sense of pleasurable anticipation. Lin Fei had changed her dress, putting on one with a high collar and a skirt with only a modest slit up the sides. This time, the color was a subdued blue. Again, she did not apply makeup, and she had brushed her hair so that it hung in iridescent black across her shoulders and down to the middle of her back.

Upon sight of her, he rose with a smile that wrapped across his lower face. "Ah, you've come. I was beginning to get just a little anxious." He looked at her with frank admiration. "Don't you look beautiful… I suppose I shouldn't have said that… but it's true."

All the time, he kept his lopsided smile, and a blush suffused his now ruddy complexion. With his hands hanging loosely at his sides, he had the demeanor of an awkward schoolboy.

Lin Fei was pleased, and she looked without embarrassment into his eyes and returned his smile. The plan was working. That was good. But she had to recognize that her pleasure was also personal, an affirmation of herself.

"Again see you also very good, Gus."

He continued to blush and stood rooted by the overstuffed chair in which he had been sitting. Then he moved his right foot forward and simultaneously swung his right arm in an arc, much as if he were a wind-up toy.

"Let's go directly into the dining room. I've already reserved a table."

Lin Fei could not restrain a giggle. "Okay, Gus. I follow you."

"No, no. We're going together. None of this following; this isn't ancient China."

He moved forward, and together they walked through the lobby to the dining room that overlooked the interior courtyard. Neither saw the plump bell captain shake his head disapprovingly after they had walked by, and both were oblivious to the hesitation of the maître-d' before he seated them. His action was indiscernible, a pursing of his lips and fluttering of their menus before he led them to a table in the corner by a screened window.

For them both, the dean ordered a gin and tonic. It seemed the thing to do when in India. They were comfortably seated. He slouched in his chair, but Lin Fei sat erect, ready to listen, it seemed, to anything that was spoken.

"So... isn't this nice," he said. "We'll order in a little bit."

Lin Fei smiled.

"I suppose we'll have to eat their Indian food. I'm not sure I like it. Too damn hot, and it all tastes the same. How about you? Do you like it?"

"It okay. Why you not order English? You like leg of lamb? They have."

"Do they? Then I'll order it." *She's been here before,* he thought, slightly disappointed. *It would have been nice to be the first to treat her to the opulence of these surroundings.* After a moment, swirling the ice in his glass, he said: "Well, while we're waiting for the waiter to come back, tell me something about yourself. I did the talking this afternoon."

Lin Fei seemed disconcerted. She had expected to encourage him to speak, to listen and to laugh or smile.

"Me? Nothing to say."

The dean – Gus – cocked his head. "Of course there is. Let's start with where you're from."

"Where from? You mean hometown?" Her voice was low and hesitant. It had been a long time since anyone had cared about her background. It had become irrelevant.

"Yes." Gus smiled, then chuckled. "Hometown. Where you're from. I want to know where you're from."

"Hong Kong."

"How interesting. You grow up there?"

"No."

"Come on, Lin. I'm not going to bite you. You're from

Hong Kong but not from Hong Kong. Where did you grow up?"

"You really want know?"

"Yes. I really do. I want to know."

Lin Fei looked at him. She dropped her eyes and looked down at the table. She looked back at him. Her hands played nervously with the corner of her napkin.

"Okay, Gus. I tell you. Where you want I begin?"

"At the beginning," he said. This time they both laughed.

Softly, hesitantly, Lin Fei told her story.

"I born in mainland China. I not sure. I think in village by Beijing. My father professor in university." Lin puckered her brow, straining to recall. "I think we live in big house. I very little, and I not remember so good. I remember, though, many people in house, lots of noise. Shouting and glass breaking.

"My mother and father, they go away. Those people – you say Red Guards – they take them. They beat drums. I remember. They say my mother daughter of landowner. In China before big war with Japan, her father have much money. They say we have too much… pictures, good furniture, rugs. They break furniture and throw rugs in street. My father, his family not so rich, but they say he… he stinking, bourgeois intellectual.

"Neighbor woman who live near, she take me and younger sister. After long time… many, many days, my father come back. He look very bad, and he very frightened. We go away… my father and me and my sister. Many days on train. We hide, get on and off many time. It dark and cold. My sister sick, and we have no food. Little bit, first two, three days. Then gone. I very hungry, I remember."

The dean interrupted gently: "Your mother did not go with you?"

"No." Lin Fei reached for her gin and tonic. "I never see mother again. My father say she die." She swallowed; her expression was blank.

"One day," she continued, "we leave train and hide in… in… building. Place where are animals. It warm, I remember, and man bring rice. Two, maybe three days later, we leave at night. We told not make noise, but my sister crying. My father angry. We get in boat. It very dark and we are in bottom of boat. Must lie down. I not know what happen, but I think we cross Pearl River. After long time… I very sick, we told to get off. No moon. I remember, no moon. Just woods. We walk, on road. My father carry sister.

"Man in car, white man," Lin Fei smiled, "stop by us in morning. I never see before. Think he may be devil, have big nose, also blue eyes, maybe green. I frightened, but my father very happy. We go in boat again to big city. I never see so many buildings.

"We in Hong Kong. Safe. But my father… he not same as before. All time he shake and cry. For long time, no job. Then he work as tailor… he make clothes. Not so good like before, but we have two rooms. And food. My father work all time, but he make my sister and I go school. There I learn English… how I speak, Gus? Okay, or not so good?"

"You speak very well. Remarkably well. You should hear my Chinese." He laughed at his own joke.

"We very poor," Lin Fei continued, "but my sister and me, all time we talk what we do, how we make money. Be movie actress, I say, or dancer. It time to leave school, and I think, what I do? Then my father get sick. Every day bad. He stop work… cough all time. Worse… it get. He stay in bed. I at school, come home… he dead."

Lin Fei looked bleakly at the napkin she was twisting in her hands, oblivious to her outward manifestation of distress. "I ask, what I do? Not be tailor, for sure. Sister stay in school… she very good student. We need money.

"Then I see advertisement in newspaper. It say, come to India for year, make good money, learn to dance. Not to worry. I see man who buy me ticket, and I come to Bombay – now we call Mumbai. Raji Rau meet me at airport. Job very different. I not learn to dance. Not send money to sister. Not have money. I in this place for three year."

An expression of unutterable sadness passed her features. Conscious of it, she ventured a wan smile.

"So, Gus, that my story. I no face look at you. But now you know me."

"What does Raji Rau do? I'm curious."

Lin Fei stared at the dean blankly. "He in business," she faltered. "Sell things, maybe."

"Like what? What does that mean?"

Lin Fei started to twist her napkin again, and she looked down at the place setting in front of her. After a moment of awkward silence, she said, softly: "Like… is that what you say, Gus?… Like? Like… whatever you want." She groped for an answer. "He get for you."

The dean remembered his offer at the end of their drive into the city from the airport. How could a beautiful woman like Lin Fei even be acquainted with such a man? Still, in a city like Mumbai, with so many miserably poor people, he surmised that most of them scrambled for survival in any way they could. *You make yourself useful. Is that it? Maybe,* the dean thought, *I could help Raji Rau out for a while; it would be something to do, if he needs someone to look after some aspect of his business.*

"And how about you? After you got here, if you didn't dance, what did you end up doing?"

This time Lin Fei was prepared. "I went into hotel work. Also, I greet visitor, sometime show them city. Give tour." She laughed. "Like you, Gus, only you no pay."

Her description was accurate, if condensed. But it invited an interpretation at variance from the truth. Misled, and wanting to suspend disbelief, the dean imagined a respectable profession, and he therefore probed no further. The conversation drifted to Lin Fei's sister; where she lived, what she was doing. She and Lin had communicated by letter, and he learned that the sister had graduated and had started work for an export-import firm in Kowloon. Recently, it appeared that she had married and was living in the New Territories. Lin Fei expressed great hope that her sister would soon be pregnant.

They also talked of Mumbai, its attractions and problems. They ordered dinner, and it was served. Feeling expansive, the dean purchased a bottle of French wine. The conversation drifted to America and comparisons between it and the two parts of the world that Lin Fei knew: Mumbai and Hong Kong. She was fascinated by his descriptions of football games, national elections and New York City.

The speed of time's passage can seem rapid or slow, depending on the pleasure or boredom of the occasion. For Lin and Gus, it was the former; the evening sped in light conversation to its conclusion. Dinner was served and eaten. The wine warmed them in the process. After declining dessert, they ordered two cups of tea, and, in the mutual glow of each other's company, after dinner liqueurs. Those, too, were consumed, and finally, no further excuse available, it was time to depart.

The dean scraped his chair back. Rising, and placing his napkin on the table, he stood behind Lin's chair, assisting it backward so that she could stand. The gesture, so natural to him, was noteworthy to her. She had seen it in the movies but had never experienced it.

They walked through the lobby to the street. Once outside, Lin put her arm through his, and he winced in inward pleasure at the touch. He imagined her movement was special to him and the happy intimacy of the evening.

Rounding the corner, the entrance to the Balfour clearly in view, he glanced down at her. "Lin, I had a wonderful evening… I didn't expect that something so nice would happen to me."

"Also, I enjoy myself very much, Gus. It special evening. Did I say that right?"

"Yes," he laughed. "Couldn't have been better."

Lin gave his arm a small squeeze. He held the door open for her, and together they walked toward the elevator.

What would happen, he thought, *if I asked her to come to my room? Would she be offended? Better not. She's much too refined, and a question like that would ruin everything… But God, she is beautiful.*

"I stay here in lobby a few minutes, Gus, then go to my room."

"Well then, I guess it's time to say goodnight." He smiled and blushed slightly at his unspoken thought. "It would be… ah… awfully nice to see you again if… if that would be possible." He paused. "We might even… as long as you give tours, see more of the city… Would you do that?"

"Yes," Lin giggled. "Tomorrow?"

"Tomorrow?"

"Yes, Gus, tomorrow. I meet you in lobby ten o'clock. Okay?"

"That would be wonderful." The smile warped across his features again. "So I'll see you. Ten o'clock."

"Goodnight, Gus." She shook his hand.

"Goodnight, Lin." He turned and entered the old, cranky elevator.

Chapter Eight

Back at Crabshaw (Where Eagles Become Beagles)

"Now hear this! Now hear this! This is your captain speaking. All students – and any members of the faculty who happen to be around – wait one minute for an important message." There was a dramatic pause. "The Registrar's Office is now accepting pre-enrollment forms. I say again: the Registrar's Office is now accepting pre-enrollment forms. For that regrettable ten percent who never seem to get the word, your last name comes first on the form. Also… tonight the library will be open until ten o'clock." There was another pause. "Over and out."

"What's that asshole talking about?" one student muttered to another as they were leaving the building. "He's our dean, not our captain, and the library is always open until ten o'clock. Its hours are posted at the entrance."

The second student sighed.

Two weeks after Dean Ansari's departure, upon recommendation of the faculty, President Zo had appointed an acting dean. There were some on the faculty who expressed surprise at the absence of meaningful debate at their conclave to recommend the interim successor. Dean Ansari had, apparently, vanished. There was an unsolved mystery – a possible homicide – that had generated national publicity. Not all of it, in the eyes of the university's Public

Relations Department, had been favorable. Adjectives describing the school, such as 'mediocre', 'struggling' and (worst of all) 'dreary', had stung. It was important to regain a posture of obscure normalcy as quickly as possible.

So the faculty had convened in an air of crisis. For some, a lethargic air, but an air nevertheless. No such momentous decision had confronted the school since the raging debate about whether to convert the path in front of the school from gravel to concrete.

Those who expected a full discussion, however, were disappointed. There was a Stalinist cast to the proceedings. First Junker, then The Duchess, rose to extol the merit – indeed virtue – of nominating Boomer as acting dean. A few members present were taken aback, if not aghast. But they had not come prepared to suggest an alternate candidate, nor were they a coalesced voting block. Another name was proposed and received a tepid second. Then Aaron, after nervously adjusting his glasses, also spoke warmly in favor of Boomer.

At this point, Duxbury intervened. In view of the strong sentiment for their colleague Boomer, it seemed appropriate, he said, to call the question. He thereupon made a motion to that effect, which was seconded promptly by Junker. Duxbury further urged that the vote for Boomer be unanimous to demonstrate faculty solidarity during this trying time.

Every year the dean recommended each faculty member's salary to the president. These recommendations were always accepted. The dean also drafted the course schedule for each year and made teaching and committee assignments. To vote against the obvious favorite in open meeting, therefore, could be risky, but a few stalwarts held out. When the vote was counted, however, Boomer prevailed by a narrow but convincing margin. Duxbury revived his suggestion for faculty solidarity; a second vote was taken, and this time the choice was unanimous. The meeting, which might have dragged on for an entire day, lasted less than half an hour.

President Zo, though surprised, acquiesced in the faculty judgment. Boomer was installed as acting dean, his appointment to end either when Dean Ansari returned and demonstrated his innocence or when a permanent dean was hired. As neither of these events was likely to occur for some time, Boomer took office as if he were the permanent successor.

Within days, he ordered a public address system for the school with speakers throughout the building. The microphone rested on the side of his desk in the office formerly occupied by Dean Ansari. Vice-President Caribe, the chief financial officer of the university, questioned the cost, but President Zo overruled him in an effort to establish good will at the beginning of the new dean's administration. Caribe prevailed, however, in turning down the additional request for a bos'n's whistle, and in any event it was unclear who would blow it prior to the dean's afternoon broadcasts. The harried Mrs. Ackerman had firmly rejected the suggestion that she add this skill to her limited repertoire.

Eyebrows rose further when, a month after the broadcasts began, the new dean ordered a company car.

"What do you need it for?" Vice-President Caribe had asked.

"I've discovered," Boomer replied haughtily, "that a car at the disposal of the law school administration is essential for attending alumni luncheons and… and placement conferences with partners of law firms."

"How come Dean Ansari never needed one?" Vice-President Caribe inquired. "And a Lexus? Surely you don't need a Lexus."

"You're missing the point," Boomer thundered, so that Caribe's head jerked back several inches. "This law school must give the appearance of being first-class. Massoud Ansari never grasped that point. Success breeds success. When students see the Lexus, they'll take pride in the school... tell their friends, applications will go up... we'll get more selective, the bar pass rate will improve... and" – here he added the clincher – "and five more students at $30,000 tuition for each will pay for the Lexus and more."

The vice-president caved in, more to stop the noise than in agreement with Boomer's argument. Shortly after delivery, the director of Career Services asked to use the car to attend a conference with the hiring partner of a major law firm. "Of all the impertinence," Boomer had fumed. "That car is obviously for the dean. When I said it would be for use by the law school administration, I was naturally thinking selectively. If everyone drives it, the image of importance we are striving to cultivate will be lost. No... no, I'm afraid only the dean can have the keys to the car."

The attitude lurking behind these purchases was not lost on the law school staff. Their relative importance in the new order became quickly apparent. Had the new dean demanded that they wear livery in Crabshaw colors, no one would have been surprised. In fact, he did say, on one infelicitous occasion, that staff members should rise to their feet when he entered the room. Instead, several resigned, to be replaced by obliging toadies, and this daring concept in employee relations was shelved.

Mrs. Ackerman, however, remained at her post, doggedly determined to outlast the pretender. Somewhere, in some corner of her heart or brain, she clung tenaciously to the belief that Dean Ansari would return. Then all would be well once again. Increasingly, she went outside during breaks for a cigarette, regardless of inclement weather, as if she were a squid scuttling behind a cloud of protective smoke, and the butts on the pavement multiplied.

The faculty remained indifferent. Like the Chinese peasantry, they preferred an emperor who was far away. Boomer, who had been a faculty member himself, understood this state of mind, and he acquiesced to it. To reinforce his hands-off policy, he appointed Bathroom Bob the new academic associate dean. With this bold stroke, the new dean assured his hitherto somewhat nervous colleagues that his administration would be more a source of amusement than intimidation.

Only Duxbury retained an active involvement with the new Maximum Leader. In view of his prior ascendancy over his colleague, he treated Boomer initially as an eager, bumptious and rather inept pupil. Old habits die slowly. Yet there was a change. When Boomer had suggested – tentatively – that faculty members should be in their offices on Monday mornings and Friday afternoons, Duxbury openly scorned the idea.

"That would be ridiculous," he said reprovingly. "It's important to be able to read at home, and prepare for class, without being interrupted by some idiot student. Monday mornings away from this place are essential. And Friday afternoons… why, you know as well as I how hard faculty members work. We are all exhausted by the end of the week. Nothing gets done on Friday after lunch."

That was true enough. Unfortunately for Duxbury's argument, however, Boomer did know how hard faculty members worked. He was understandably suspicious. In former days, before becoming acting dean, he would have lapsed into uncharacteristic silence. Now he sat at his desk, frowning.

"No," he said finally, "I might buy what you say about Monday. *Might.* But I don't buy Friday. It seems to me there's no good reason why professors can't work to the end of the work week. Is that too much to ask? They already get the whole summer off."

And he prevailed, to the muted astonishment of both. Shortly thereafter, Boomer broadcast his decision to the school. He chose to deliver his edict on a Wednesday afternoon to achieve a maximum listening audience, and he calculated that, by also informing the students, he would bring subtle pressure to bear on his colleagues.

In this respect Boomer was, as was so often the case, mistaken. For two or three weeks, there was compliance. But then, with appropriate excuses – an ill mother, a board meeting, a trip to a conference – the faculty began to absent themselves. Doors on the faculty floor were shut and locked. At first, only a few. After a couple of months, nearly all. The familiar stillness returned.

Duxbury sensed his loss of authority, but through subtle manipulation, he usually had his way. He did convince Boomer, for example, that there should be an open period in mid-afternoon in the class schedule. The time, he argued convincingly, could be used for student activities and faculty committee meetings. He solidified his recommendation by noting that biorhythms are at a low ebb during this time.

Appealing to the goal of academic excellence, he pointed out that teaching and learning are least effective when people feel like napping.

"The Mexicans take siestas," he argued. "They're smart. They've never been infected by the Protestant work ethic. It's their way of storing energy so they can do whatever it is they do for the rest of the day." *Womanizing and eating*, he surmised, but that was no concern of his.

Boomer was convinced. He issued the necessary edict. This time, because the idea perfectly matched the proclivities of his listeners, there was instant and enthusiastic compliance. A siesta became a claim of right. Only Duxbury, tending to his own affairs, continued to labor diligently throughout the afternoon.

Chapter Nine

Intermission

"What a mess!"

"I beg your pardon."

"I said: what a mess!"

"To what are you referring – Massoud Ansari's predicament, the faculty, the plot or the general caliber of writing in this book?"

"Do I have to choose?"

"Of course not. And if there is a mess, whose fault is that? You could intervene, you know, and make the story come out any way you want. Mortals have no right to choose what happens to them. Long ago we decided that they should live in fear and die alone, although I've always admired the ones who grasp that they are part of a cosmic joke."

"Existence is not a joke, even if a sense of humor helps, and you should know that as well as anyone. And if you don't, you should never have been made a guardian."

"All right, all right. I'll amend my comment. I've always admired the ones who grasp that they are a fragmentary part of a vast interconnection among things and across time. Those few understand that they are not alone but part of a larger whole... Is that better?"

"Yes, although vague, pretentious and not particularly helpful – certainly not helpful to Massoud Ansari, Lin Fei or even Joe Walsh."

"Anyway, let me get back to my point. You can choose an ending to this story, but you don't seem to care. You're just letting it drift forward, and I have an uneasy feeling that everything is coming together – sort of like fusion in their sun – and there's going to be an explosion. Something terrible may happen."

"Not necessarily. Something interesting, for sure, but as far as Dean Ansari in concerned, everything could work out in his favor… or not. That's the way life is. He certainly is in a strange predicament, and it has been getting stranger with each revolution of the earth – or, as they say, with each passing day. I think I'll stay on the sidelines, not interfere, and just see how everything works out. I haven't had so much amusement in centuries."

"Nor I. Everything seemed to be returning to normal – if such a word can be applied to Crabshaw School of the Law – and now look what's happened. I'll join you."

Chapter Ten

Dean Ansari Greets a Visitor

"So... what kind of place is it?"

"Huh?" The man's reverie apparently had been interrupted. "What kinda place? You speak English?"

"Yes... yes. Of course I am speaking English."

"You American or an Irishman or somethin' else? I can't place you."

"No... I am from South Africa, and we speak English. Well, maybe not all of us." Dean Ansari was doing his best to imitate Raji Rau, and the result was a strange amalgam of American English, an Indian accent and an Irish brogue. He had quickly detected that the man facing him was an American, and so he had adopted this partial disguise.

His interlocutor was a middle-aged man of average height, a mesomorph with a solid build, graying hair and open, friendly features. In appearance he differed substantially from the slovenly, paunchy individual with unkempt hair whom the dean had encountered briefly over two years before at the law school. Only minutes before, the man had debarked from an aircraft, stiff and tired from hours cramped in a coach class seat he had first occupied in Frankfurt, with only sporadic trips to the airplane's bathrooms to stretch his legs. He had joined a jostling, babbling crowd as it made its way to a baggage retrieval location, thence to customs and finally to a large concourse filled with waiting relatives and hawkers of every description.

Measured against the fashion of the day on Madison Avenue, his attire was tasteless. His brown polyester slacks were far too heavy for the climate he was about to encounter. Above them, he wore a yellow shirt with broad green stripes, open at the neck; a mismatched tan jacket was slung across his arm. Dark wrap-around sunglasses with a heavy plastic frame concealed pale blue eyes.

He was addressing another man who was holding a sign, with bold lettering on it in English, which the man had hoisted over his head by means of a crude stick. The sign advertised lodgings in the city at moderate rates. The resplendently incongruous figure holding this advertisement was tall, slightly stooped and wearing shorts and a floppy, loose-fitting shirt. Since his arrival in India, he had lost twenty-five pounds due to the change in diet and the heat. Large feet, attached to the ends of long, bony legs with knobby knees, were enclosed in floppy sandals. A magnificent handlebar mustache, sunglasses and a crumpled, dirty tennis hat completed his ensemble.

Despite his occupation, which might have suggested a degree of alertness to gull the unwary and weary traveler, the sign-holder had been lost in contemplative thought: nothing abstract and certainly not speculation about an inward journey to enlightenment and at-oneness with the universe. No, he was wondering rather about the peculiar twist of fate that had made him a sign-carrier. How was it that his offer of assistance in business had resulted in this menial occupation?

Boredom, he thought. *Something to do, instead of take walks and drink endless cups of tea.* And then he had been interrupted by this... this hideous, cheerful amalgam of middle America.

"So... like I said... what kinda place is... uh," the recent arrival craned his neck backward, "the Balfour? Reasonable rates? How reasonable?"

"For Mumbai… yes… very reasonable."

"Is it clean?"

"Yes."

"Big place, or small?"

"Well… not tiny," the taller man replied. "Not like a rooming house or, maybe, some kind of bed and breakfast inn as you might find in the States. It's more just a small hotel… like you'd find in a small city or big town. I am estimating maybe thirty rooms."

"Sounds good. Got its own restaurant?"

"No, but there's a large and most nice hotel around the corner that has one."

"Okay." The man pursed his lips. "I think you've got a customer. One last question… " he paused and looked at the sign again. "What's with the massage?"

"Massage?"

"Yeah. Your sign says it's a place to enjoy pleasure in the atmosphere of a relaxing massage… whatever that means."

"It does?" The tall man looked perplexed; he lowered the sign and turned it around to peer at the lettering. Exactly as he had been told, the sign read:

BALFOUR HOTEL
Very Reasonable Rates
Convenient Location
Gentlemen and Ladies
May Enjoy their Exquisite Pleasures
In the Atmosphere of a Relaxing Massage

The tall man's brow furrowed as he read, and then reread, the sign. "Well," he said after several moments, "I'm not sure. I am thinking the Balfour has a masseur or masseuse. Maybe there's a sauna room or a steam bath… yes… yes, that most assuredly must be it." He hesitated. "It's a very nice place."

"I'll take your word for it," the shorter man said genially. "How do I get there? Take a bus?"

"N . . o." The monosyllable was drawn out, while the sign-carrier's head swiveled as he looked around. The surge of passengers from the airplane had dwindled to a few late stragglers. None seemed interested or about to stop to make an inquiry. Their eyes were fixed forward, or they were in animated conversation with family or friends, oblivious to their surroundings.

"No," he repeated himself. "I'll join you, if you don't mind, and take you to the hotel in a taxicab… we can split the fare, if that's all right with you." He lowered the sign and, for ease of transportation, unfastened it from the stick.

The two men turned, and the taller one tucked the sign under his arm. Sandals flapping on his feet, he proceeded to the exit with the recent passenger walking briskly by his side. Conversation ceased. They were in a building like any major airport in the world, but the newly arrived man's attention was absorbed not by the architecture but by the appearance of the people passing by on every side. Many had on European clothing, and indeed a fair smattering were European or North American. Many more were Indian, and the tide of dusky faces was the first, and most obvious, difference that assaulted him. The second was the swirling colors of the cotton fabric draped upon the women. He was intrigued, also, by the number of men wearing some kind of fore-and-aft cap, as well as the ragged poverty of the seemingly limitless number of porters and handlers bustling about with baggage.

Which was why, he reflected with growing excitement, it was a good idea to come. But he could not erase anxiety as he contemplated the days ahead. If he needed clothes – and the stifling heat already prompted him to reappraise his wardrobe – how would he purchase his kind of shirts, his kind of underwear and his kind of shoes, without access to a discount store? He certainly did not want to be reduced to the footwear of his new companion – sandals, for God's sake! Everyone would think he was some kind of California beach bum.

As the two men stood near the curb, the taller of the two scanning a line of waiting vehicles, the shorter man spoke: "You know," he said, "I should introduce myself. It sounds like you stay at the Balfour, so we might be seeing each other. My name's Joe."

The tall man stretched out his hand. "People call me Gus," he said. "It'll be nice to have you around. From what place are you from?"

No response was forthcoming, because at that moment a cab pulled up in front of them. It was dilapidated but serviceable. The heavy-set driver, his jowls greasy with sweat, leaned across the front seat to ask their destination in heavily accented English. Satisfied, he opened his door, got out, and waddled around the vehicle to pick up the bags. Joe noticed that his clothing, once white, had become stained and soiled from years of use. The man's eyes surveyed his prospective passengers without expression. He lifted the luggage into the trunk – or boot – and returned without uttering a sound to his place behind the wheel.

There he sat, impassively, while his riders clambered into the back seat. The door squeaked violently as it was opened, and it groaned loudly as 'Gus' pulled it shut. The dean leaned forward. "As I said, the Balfour Hotel, near the Excelsior."

If the driver heard, he gave no indication. But he promptly threw the automobile into gear, grasping a worn shift that hung haphazardly from the steering column. The cab lurched forward into traffic and gathered speed. As they entered the sprawling city, however, their progress slowed as they threaded their way past carts, auto-rickshaws, bicycles, swarms of people, an occasional wandering cow, old, rickety trucks heaped with bales of goods, and shops of every description in a mélange of bright colors. It was Mumbai, formerly Bombay, one of the great entrepôts of India.

* * * * *

"Well, this is it."

Joe Walsh stood outside, surveying the establishment skeptically. Its small verandah lacked fresh paint; the short bench, table and two chairs on it had seen better days. They were scuffed and worn. Being a new arrival, he did not realize that their condition was the norm for a modest hotel, not the exception.

"You say it's an okay place?"

"Yes," Gus answered. "Take my word. And if you are not liking it, just stay a night or two and then leave. My guess is you should not be wanting to be searching for a room at this point. In your shoes, I'd be wanting to take a refreshing nap."

The dean picked up the two bags that had been deposited with a grunt by the taxi driver in front of the hotel. On receiving a tip, that factotum had displayed his first sign of sapient life by inclining his head in appreciation. He then departed in a swirl of dust. Gus marched into the hotel and deposited his burden before the clerk's cluttered desk. More precisely, he dropped the luggage with a thump. One reason was to gain the clerk's somnolent attention. Another was his surprise, and pleasure, at seeing Lin Fei across the small lobby.

She was talking with a tall, good-looking man, and Gus was aware of a tinge of jealousy. Perhaps it was the hint of flirtation in the way her lips were parted. He noticed that she seemed somewhat disconcerted to see him. He had not been expected back from the airport so soon.

In a barely concealed fluster, she broke off her conversation and ran to him. The man with whom she had been chatting knitted his brow, evidently displeased but uncertain what to do.

"Gus, how good you seeing. I thought… I thought you be in airport."

A question glanced across his mind. How did she know where he would be?

She detected the subtle puzzlement in his expression. "Raji Rau, he tell me. He say," and she laughed, "no need today you go shopping."

"Does he order you what to do, or not do?" His puzzled expression remained. "I mean, what… "

"No… no, Gus, he not tell me. He… just friend. He just making joke."

There was a pause. His features softened. "Lin," he said, turning to the man standing to his side and slightly behind him, "I want you to meet a new guest. Joe… it's Joe, right?" He looked first at Joe Walsh, and then at Lin. "This is Lin Fei. Lin is also living here at the hotel." As the dean spoke, he continued using his newly acquired accent. Lin cocked her head to one side and peered at him but said nothing. For a moment, Joe Walsh looked bemused, an expression he did not conceal. Seriously, and somewhat stiffly, Lin held out her hand.

"It is nice you meeting."

"My pleasure," Joe responded warmly and with a broad smile.

"Tell me something," the dean interjected. "Joe noticed something funny on the sign I was carrying at the airport. It says something about… " he stumbled, "about getting a massage. You know what a massage is?"

Lin started. Her eyes flickered, then she looked downward. "A massage?" she said slowly. "What you mean, Gus?"

Joe Walsh was looking at her intently.

"I mean… well, let me see. A massage is when someone rubs your back, usually someone who you pay, a man or a woman. They squeeze your muscles, sort of… it's supposed to be very relaxing."

"You say here in hotel?"

"Well, sure… I mean, lots of hotels… well, maybe not lots… have a steam room, or a sauna… something like that, and you can also, sometimes, get a massage. I am thinking." He had slipped back to an American accent but quickly corrected himself.

Lin had not looked up. She said nothing.

"So," the dean bumbled onward, but with more resolution, "I was experiencing a moment of surprise when Joe noticed that you can get a massage at the Balfour. I have not seen any sign for a steam room or exercise room and no one was informing me… it might be nice to get a massage some time. Where are they?"

"Where is what?" Lin raised her eyes tentatively, but her composure was returning, and she wore a baffled, scrunched-face expression.

"The rooms. I don't know how to get to them or where they are."

"I not know, Gus," Lin replied. "Maybe downstair. I never ask. Maybe outside somewhere." She smiled encouragingly. "Maybe you ask clerk. Or better, you ask Raji Rau. He give you sign, so maybe he know."

Joe Walsh had watched this interplay with interest. Was the woman holding something back? He wasn't sure. He had noticed the evident pleasure with which the woman and Gus had greeted each other and her apparent embarrassment at his question. Somewhere he had heard that Asian women are modest and deferential, and he wondered whether his recent acquaintance's inquiry had been tactless and too straightforward. Perhaps that was the problem.

If so, the damage was clearly not permanent. Both Gus and Lin were now smiling.

"Are you, by any chance... free for dinner?" the dean asked.

"Tomorrow, Gus. We go tomorrow, you want. Today I have customer... that man, over there." She inclined her head in the direction of the tall, good-looking man across the room. "He pay for tour. We go now, and I not sure when return."

"Lin gives tours," the dean said brightly to Joe Walsh. "Good ones, too. I've been on several. She took me once on a ride in an auto-rickshaw outside the central city. The traffic was chaos, particularly at the intersections. At one there were other rickshaws right next to us. I mean, maybe only an inch or two away. You have to see it to believe it… you should sign up."

Lin glanced at Joe, a shy smile crossing her features. "Sure," she said. "I show you Mumbai big time, you want. Maybe we go tomorrow, day after sometime. You see all sights."

"Only if you get him back in time for us to go to dinner," the dean added cheerfully.

"Okay, Gus, you got date." She had turned back to look at him, and then she swiveled her head in the direction of Joe Walsh. "You want tour?"

"Maybe," he answered. "Let's see how I feel tomorrow. Right now I'm going to get some sleep. I feel like I could sleep for ten hours."

Joe stretched his arms over his head. The man across the room was beginning to look annoyed and impatient, and Lin turned to go.

"You seeing, Gus," she said softly.

"Oh, one thing," Joe Walsh added hastily. "You give tours. Where's the police station? Is there one near here? If it's not too late, maybe I'll walk over to it after I've rested."

"Not near here," Lin replied. "I not sure."

The dean, in an attempt to be helpful, interrupted: "I'll ask Raji Rau. I'm sure he'll know. You may have to take a taxi to get there."

Why the police station? he thought with a flicker of fear, but then dismissed the inquiry from his mind.

Chapter Eleven

A Dinner Conversation

The day had been miserably hot. Through the haze that hung like a miasmic cloud over the city, the sun had beaten relentlessly upon the wood and concrete and stucco and metal and flesh below. It sought every corner, every cranny, until even the insects and crawling things shriveled in their hiding places. The swirling dust of the streets was subdued. All colors were reduced to pastel. In the vast darkness of space, the sun might be a mere speck of glowing coal; in the sky above Mumbai, it was a living, pulsating orb of luminous intensity, a burnished shield – set in a pale, sickly field of blue – that scorched and burned.

Relief of a sort had come with twilight and with the recent, and still sporadic, monsoon rains. Waiting for Lin in the lobby prior to their date for dinner, the dean had encountered Joe Walsh. The latter was descending the stairs, stepping carefully over the frayed carpet at the edge of each step. He had changed to a light, open-necked shirt with short sleeves, but he still wore his polyester slacks and leather shoes.

"My God," he said, "I had been told it would be hot, but I never expected anything like this!" A trickle of perspiration ran down the side of his face.

"You need to wear shorts," the dean remarked, inwardly wincing at sight of the leather shoes.

"Is this do as I say, not as I do? Why don't you?"

"I had them on all day. Tonight I'm going to dinner with Lin, so I thought I'd dress up." The dean paused, slightly irritated that he was offering an unnecessary explanation. "Which reminds me, how was it going for you today?"

"Oh… great. We really had a good time… or I did, anyway. I guess it's old stuff to her, but she's such an enthusiastic person that she made it seem as if it was all new to her."

"Where did you go?" the dean asked as they walked to the sitting room. He sat on the edge of a wicker chair and casually leaned forward. "What did you see?"

"We went first past a huge oval in the middle of the city where men were playing cricket. Funny game – really slow. There's a museum nearby called the Prince of Wales but we didn't stop. Instead, we went to the Oberoi Hotel where there's a walk by the sea called Marine Drive. It was very pretty – lots of people walking and jogging."

"Anything else?"

Joe Walsh wiped his brow with the back of his hand. "Yes," he said, "but while I know what I saw, I'd never find my way back. Shops and a temple and a really interesting outdoor market with lots of stalls and people haggling over things. I got some stuff to take back home, and I'd like to go back… Lin said she took you there, too. I tried to buy her something, but she said you'd already done it." He hesitated a moment. "She certainly seems to think well of you. Every place we went, she mentioned the fun you and she had being there together… Anyway, I had a terrific time, even when it rained, and I'd like to go out again… to that market, especially."

"Maybe we could all go," the dean replied enthusiastically. "That is," he added impishly, "if you're not going to feel like the odd man out."

For a moment they both fell silent. No one else was in the sitting room, dimly-lit due to rattan shades that had been drawn to shield the interior from the heat outside. The clerk, standing behind his nearby desk with an air of resigned inattention, rubbed the back of his hand across his mustache and wiped his brow.

Walsh finally asked: "Are you meeting her here in the lobby?"

"No… we're meeting at the Excelsior. I was waiting for this man called Raji Rau to see whether he had any other jobs I might do."

"Lin mentioned his name a couple of times. Does he own this place… or what? From the sound of it, she doesn't seem to like him very much."

"That's cause he's an ingratiating little… " the dean snorted, then thought better of what he had intended to say. "I shouldn't speak ill of him. He's different, though… and I'm not sure how much I trust him."

"Why not?" Joe Walsh was curious. A professional career in police work had sensitized him to nuanced judgments of character. Moreover, he noticed that for a moment the dean no longer spoke with a slight Indian accent.

The dean realized it too. Frowning, he scratched the back of his head nervously, then resumed his affected manner of speech. "I am not knowing. Something… he's almost too friendly. Why was he meeting me at the airport? Was that just an accident?"

"Why did you meet me?"

"That was different. That was business."

"So… maybe he made it, like, his business to meet you, particularly if he owns this hotel. Or has some arrangement with the owner. It seems like somethin' like that is goin' on." The clerk, who had appeared indifferent, cocked his head in their direction. He smiled thinly.

"Well, anyway," the dean continued, "he is usually here in the late afternoon. In the lobby or on the porch. But I've not seen him, and I've got to go."

"You want me to keep an eye out for him?" Joe Walsh volunteered.

The dean raised his chin and smiled. "Don't worry, he'll be most keen to be meeting you. If this little man comes up to you, wearing eyeglasses and always cleaning them, and very formal in the way he talks, that's him. If he's the way he was with me, he may even tell you he can fix you up."

Joe Walsh's eyes narrowed for a split second. "Is that right?"

"Yes. His business is any business that you are wanting help with. That is what he will tell you."

"Including finding someone? Can he do that?"

"He seems to know a great many people, so yes... yes, probably." The dean's tone was cautious. "Are you looking for someone, if it's any of my business?"

Joe Walsh's expression did not change. "Just wondering what all he could do. I do have one question, though, and that's where most Americans hang out." He paused. "It might be nice to meet some attractive, middle-aged tourist... you know, some woman over here like me, just lookin' around, who'd like some company."

"I guess he could answer that," the dean responded with a laugh. "And if it's company that you want... although not so interesting or exciting... don't forget we're going to have dinner together."

His friendly tone did not match his feelings. There was something about Joe Walsh that made him uneasy – maybe his intrusive comments, maybe his tacky apparel, maybe a vague feeling that they had met before. *Perhaps,* he thought, *it's simply that if we were at home and not strangers thrown together in a foreign land, we'd have little in common.* "How about we go to the Excelsior tomorrow night or even we get Lin to tell us a nice place and we go there? Nothing too expensive. My odd jobs don't pay much. I could meet you here in the lobby the same time as right now."

"Should I wear shorts?" Walsh teased. "You seem to be the only man who does… just joking. I'll be here."

"Okay, good," the dean said. "I hope you meet Raji Rau… I guess. I'm on my way."

* * * * *

They were seated at the same table where they had eaten dinner the first time. Indeed, it was the same table on every occasion they had met for dinner at the Excelsior – by the window, at one end of the room, slightly removed from the other tables. Only a smattering of other guests were present. The staff stood smartly, if idly, in their uniforms by the entrance to the kitchen, waiting for a flick of the maître-d's finger to summon them to duty. A slight breeze wafted through the tall windows. Ceiling fans, whirling in their posts, were emitting a low thunk-a-thunk noise as background – enough to disguise conversation, had that been necessary.

Lin, as on prior occasions, was wearing a close-fitting dress – this time, an iridescent green – with a high collar. Her long hair hung loosely down her back, although a few strands had strayed across her shoulder. She was looking intently at the dean and playing casually with the stem of the glass before her. A mai tai. The dean, as was his habit, had ordered a gin and tonic. He not only enjoyed the drink and the relaxation that attended it, the addition of tonic lent a pukka-sahib air to this evening ritual.

The preliminary, animated chatter of first greeting was behind them. Lin spoke: "How come, Gus, you speak funny around that other American? He ask me to call him Joe."

The dean was unprepared for the question, and he fumbled for an answer. "I just… ah… don't want to get too friendly with other Americans. I'm not here… to meet people I could meet at home." His response was misleading, albeit close to the truth, and he was not sure Lin believed him. He started to elaborate, thought better of it, and said: "For a second I forgot you took him around today… how did you like him?"

"He very nice, Gus. Ask many questions. We see many things, and I think he pay go again." She smiled playfully, looking at him directly in the eyes. "All you men from middle of American country very nice."

"You told him I was from America?"

She detected the note of alarm in his voice. "No, Gus, no, I not tell."

"Well, best to leave it that way. Anyway," he exhaled, "I saw him in the lobby, just before coming over here. We're going to have dinner tomorrow night. I was waiting for Raji Rau, and Joe asked about him."

Lin arched an eyebrow. "Ask what, Gus?"

"He asked what does he do. And, you know, I don't really know. Joe seems to be a shrewd observer. He said, maybe Raji Rau owns the Balfour… or, at least, has some arrangement

125

with it. He must. Does he, or why would he have given me that stupid sign to carry around? Better than sitting around all day, but I felt pretty silly."

"So what you want to know, Gus?" Lin continued to play with her glass, rocking it back and forth between her slender fingers.

"I guess… what does he do? Does he own the hotel?

"No, Gus," Lin answered, "he not own hotel. I pretty sure."

"Well it certainly seems he has something to do with it. What kind of person is he?"

Lin looked at Gus for a few moments of silence. "What kind of person?" she repeated softly. "That very hard to say. He easy man get meet, very hard get know. Very hard."

"Why?"

"Why?" Again Lin repeated the question. "I not know. He not talk too much. He do many thing, and no need he tell me… I know him only at hotel – like you – or close when we are sitting and have talk."

"What do you mean *close*?" the dean asked.

Lin caught the bare hint of jealousy, and the corner of her mouth curled slightly in amusement. "I mean, Gus, when we close to hotel, like at Karma Café, and sometimes have drink. Then we talk. Since three year, I not learn much, but I am learning some little what he do."

"Do you like him?"

"No." Her voice was emphatic.

"Really? Because I've seen you with him, I thought maybe the two of you were friends."

"He send me business," she said slowly, "so we talk. That's all." Lin studied the dean intently, no longer fingering her glass but, with one hand, twirling a loose strand of hair that had fallen over her shoulder. Her eyes cast down, she swallowed hard before starting to speak again in a low, tremulous voice.

"I tell you now something, Gus. You promise never to say who told you. Promise?"

"Why should… ?" She clutched his arm. "Okay… sure, I promise."

"Raji Rau… Gus, he very bad man. Very bad… I tell you, now you ask me, you better not working for him. Better for you."

He stared at her, not mouth agape but with a look of concerned, gathering concentration. "This is getting interesting. Now I've got several questions, not just one. I mean, how is he a bad man? How do you know? What's he done?"

Lin looked behind her with an alert, worried expression. "Gus, you not tell anyone. Please! You tell anyone, it very bad for me, I think." Looking forlorn, her voice dropped to a whisper. "He hurt people sometime very bad, and he not care. It make him laugh. You not see. He very strong and quick. I think, maybe, he even kill some people sometime somewhere. I not sure, but he speak of it."

"You've got to be… " His voice trailed off in the face of her unwavering, frightened gaze. "Kill someone! My God… that makes him a murderer!" He supplied the unnecessary legal conclusion.

"Yes," she said simply.

"Why? Now I really am interested. To do that means he's into some pretty bad business. It must be drugs. Is that it? What else does he buy and sell? Boys… or women? Is he an arms dealer? Do you know?"

"Most of that, Gus, I think," she said, again simply and softly. "I… I not sure."

"So I guess that's why he had me go to the airport with that sign. Get some suckers… Oh, for Chrissake, I could have been some kind of courier and not even known it. I'll bet that was it."

"Not yet, Gus, not right away. That not his way. You go many times again, once you get arrested. He tell police. Something very bad you not know. Then… he pay someone, he get you out. Or maybe not really police. You not know. Afterward, you do whatever he want, next time take drug to America. You not do, you just disappear. You never see again."

"Is this the little bit you learned?"

"No, Gus. I not know. But I think. I think you stay away from Raji Rau before too late and you very sorry."

* * * * *

By unspoken agreement, they did not discuss Raji Rau again. The dean made an attempt, but Lin ignored his comment, and he understood that the topic was closed.

The waiter, with interminable lethargy, took their orders for dinner. The chef was apparently afflicted with the same malady. They did not care. The conversation, once the forbidden zone had been defined, danced backward and forward. Lin spoke more of Hong Kong and her fragile remembrances of the Mainland. The dean – now Gus – spoke of America. Dinner, eventually and almost superfluously, was served. The waiter ostentatiously lit a low candle on the table. Its suggestion of heat was unwelcome, but in the gathering dusk, the light cast a soft glow on their animated features.

At length – considerable length – the dinner concluded. Both were slightly giddy from their alcohol consumption, both before and, after a bottle of wine had been ordered, during the meal. *Why not ask her,* he thought. *She must like me, or she wouldn't be having such a good time. Or is it an act? That's her business, isn't it? Oh come on, if it were just business, she'd be pleasant and polite, not so personal about herself and her past. But what if she turns me down? I'll ruin everything. No, I won't; women like to be asked, at least by the right man. It's kind of a compliment, isn't it? Or is it? Which is it?*

His stomach was in a knot. The natural result was that he said nothing. Instead, he rose, a trifle unsteadily, and walked behind her chair to assist her from it. Lin glanced at him, a frowning question in her eyes. She shared qualms with him for reciprocal reasons, but she knew her assignment. And she knew, too, the penalty for failure.

They walked together from the dining room, through the lobby and out to the street. A hot breeze tugged at their clothing. Lin slipped her arm through his, and together, silent now, they traversed the short distance separating them from the Balfour. Night had fallen, but the streets were still clogged with people.

Does it ever cease? he thought. *Where are they all going? And why, at this hour?* They came to the front of the hotel, its small verandah directly before them. To enter was to say goodbye, and he did not want to. But what to say here?

"Lin… I really had a nice time. Like always."

"Me also, Gus. I very happy."

His stomach constricted again in a knot. *Now… now, or probably never.* "Lin… I'm very fond… I really like you."

She said nothing. Neither did her clasp on his arm weaken. Her face tilted upward, but her eyes did not seek his.

"Well, I was wondering," he cleared his throat, "whether you might... well... maybe come to my room with me. I thought," he blurted a weak joke, "that you might rather kiss me there than in the middle of the street." He laughed awkwardly and unconvincingly.

For a long moment, Lin said nothing. But her eyes found his, and she broke into genuine laughter. It was so warm and lively that his nervous discomfort dissolved, even if rejection should follow.

It did not. "Of course, Gus," she giggled. "We not kiss here in street. Much better in room." She added, more shyly: "Perhaps I stay with you, you want." And with that, she squeezed his arm, half pulling him forward toward the hotel.

However, he did not see her frightened, distraught face as she entered his room after he had opened the door. Later, naked and spent, he fell heavily asleep in her arms. He did not stir, and again did not see, when she slipped quietly from the bed in the middle of the night. He might have been dimly aware of her rising, but his awareness did not extend to her hurried, furtive search of his suitcase and personal effects.

In the morning, when he woke, she was gone. Opening his eyes, for a few moments he did not recall the events of the preceding evening. Then the remembrance flooded consciousness. Where was she? Why not wake to find each other? In perplexity, he rose and slowly dressed. Ruefully, he realized that he did not know her room number or how to locate her. They had always just seemed to meet in the lobby or at a pre-arranged place.

Still bleary-eyed, he descended the stairs to the clerk's desk. That worthy was gazing vacuously at the front door as he approached.

"Excuse me," he said.

"Sir?" The clerk turned to observe him, his drooping mustache giving his countenance an appearance of weary resignation.

"Could you tell me the room number of Lin Fei? I need to get in touch with her." And, he thought, hug her, and kiss her, and arrange a time to meet again.

"The room number is twenty-three," the clerk responded in a precise Indian accent, after glancing at a roster in front of him. "The lady has gone out."

"Did she possibly say when she would return?"

"It is not possible to know," the clerk shrugged. "But… it is Mr. Honque, is it not?… She left this note for delivery to you."

The dean took the proffered envelope, ripping it open as he walked into the sitting area. A brief note was inside.

Gus –

Thank you. I never forget. It is better, I think, we not meeting again.

With love,

Lin

Chapter Twelve

Another Dinner Conversation

Lin did not return. For much of the day, he loitered in the sitting area adjacent to the lobby, hoping to intercept her. Once or twice he knocked on the door of her room, but there was no response. It occurred to him that on other days he had neither asked about nor known her whereabouts, but somehow that had not seemed important. That oversight, he reflected, had now cost him the possibility of locating her.

In the heat of the early afternoon, he strolled to the Karma Kafe, trying to appear unconcerned. His deception was not worth the effort. No customers sat at the battered tables, and the dark interior was empty, save for one man – a customer, possibly, or the proprietor – sitting in the gloom with his elbows on a table and his chin resting on top of his interlaced fingers.

He had been pleased by the closing words of her note, but her joint declaration of affection and departure baffled him. He had to see her, convince her she was making a mistake. Why did she not return? His anxiety increased with the passing hours of the day. Eventually he wandered out to the verandah, a book in hand, and tried to read. It was a disjointed effort, interrupted by his thoughts and his restless scanning of the street for her familiar figure and face.

Preoccupied, he had forgotten his dinner engagement with Joe Walsh. Even when he caught sight of him walking slowly toward the hotel, he did not remember. After their mutual greeting, it was difficult to feign pleasure upon being reminded of the obligation. He would be forced to abandon his vigil. On the other hand, telling Joe about his predicament might elicit information or, at a minimum, a potentially insightful observation about the vagaries of feminine behavior.

With barely concealed reluctance, the dean abandoned his post and retired to his room to don slightly more formal clothing. Not having seen Lin, he of course had not had the opportunity to inquire about alternate places to dine. It would have to be the Excelsior again – a not unwelcome prospect, in view of the faint possibility that he might encounter her there.

Nothing of the sort happened. Arriving before Joe in the lobby downstairs, where they had agreed to rendezvous, he asked the clerk if Lin had returned or had been seen. If the clerk was aware of his anguish – and his repeated inquiries throughout the day would have alerted the most doltish observer – he betrayed not the slightest hint of sympathy or interest.

"The lady has not returned," the clerk said curtly, turning his back to stamp some papers.

Joe Walsh joined him a moment later, and they walked to the Excelsior. There was no sign of her on the street. At their destination, the two men were ushered to a table in the dining room close to where the dean and Lin had sat the previous night.

Again the dean ordered a gin and tonic, and again the service was leisurely to the point of interminable slowness. He had ample time to savor his drink's bitter, pungent taste. Mostly silent, he listened as Walsh described his travels of the day with annoying embellishment. Apparently he had also attempted to find Lin and employ her services again as a guide, but without success. This morsel of news elicited a flicker of close attention from his companion. Left to his own devices and the plodding, mechanical advice of the clerk, Joe had set out on his own. The effort had not been entirely successful. More alert than the dean to his surroundings, he had not gotten lost. Nevertheless, he had seen nothing in particular and everything in general – the teeming life of a giant metropolis, strange to him in so many ways, but no sight of compelling interest.

Throughout this discourse, the dean listened with varying degrees of attention. He was aware of a widening pit in his stomach, a signal of bereavement and loss. But the events of the last twenty-four hours were too close at hand to compel an abandonment of hope. Even if Lin was absent, she would presumably return. What would they say to each other? His mind strayed to the note, its words engraved into instant recall.

"You seem rather preoccupied," Walsh ventured. He looked around for a waiter. It was time for dinner to be served or another drink. Not experienced, he did not realize the choice must inevitably be the latter. "Is something wrong?"

"No, not really," the dean lied. "I was looking for Lin earlier in the day and couldn't find her. I was just wondering where she might be."

"Probably out giving a tour."

"No," the dean paused, "I don't think so."

"Maybe she had to do some business for that fellow Rau… By the way, I never saw him, and I hung around for awhile after you left."

"That's all right," the dean said slowly. "I don't think I want to go on working for him. I've… uh… changed my mind about him."

Questions and thoughts tumbled upon each other in his mind without resolution. *Lin doing some business for Raji Rau! What kind of business? Is that it? Did she decide it was too dangerous being with me after she told me about him? Is she in trouble? Is she another person who has disappeared?*

Joe Walsh had responded, and in his distraction the dean had not heard him. "Excuse me. I'm sorry. Would you repeat that?"

Walsh surveyed him with a questioning look. "You really are preoccupied. I was just agreeing… saying that I didn't think carrying signs seemed to be exactly your kind of work."

"Yeah… " The dean smiled wryly. "You are most correct." It was time to change the subject and regain his strange accent. "So," he took a sip of his drink, "it sounds like you had a day half-way interesting. India is such a fascinating place, isn't it? Just about everywhere you look, something is most different. What people are wearing, or what they are eating, or just their way of saying hello. You are not needing to see a temple. Walking around is an education by itself."

"It sure is," Walsh answered. "I sat for a while and had a cup of tea – me, of all people – in the middle of the afternoon before it showered, and just watched the people walking by. Short, tall, fat, thin… you name it, it was all there."

"Did you find the police station in your travels? Or where Americans get together?"

"No," Walsh smiled. "I just played tourist."

"Why were you wanting the police station? It seems like a most odd thing to ask for the minute you arrive."

Joe Walsh hesitated. "Professional reasons."

"Professional? Why… you know, I have never asked what you do – or did – for a living back in the States. Are you an FBI agent or something?"

Walsh smiled again. "Nothing that exciting. I'm an ordinary detective. You know… police work, help solve crimes, that sort of thing. Sometimes it's interesting, but a lot of the time it's pretty routine."

The dean's interest quickened. *Good God, could this be Joe Walsh, the detective I met over two years ago?* "You are having a case all the way to India?"

"Not really. I'm here mostly on vacation. But, yeah… I'm also looking for someone in my spare time. Thought I'd check with the police, find out if they know anything. It's not likely."

"Why not?"

"It's not public enemy number one I'm looking for or anything like that. You wouldn't know, living over here. Still, the case got a lot of publicity, and we've got a continuing interest in it."

"What kind of case?"

"A homicide. Thought I was going to say an international crime syndicate running drugs, or something like that, didn't you? Nope. A probable murder in a small city in the Midwest… but a funny one."

"How so?" Suspicion had escalated to alarm. The dean managed, with effort, to keep his tone politely curious and detached.

"I probably shouldn't talk too much about it," Walsh answered, "although I don't know why not. I'll take leads wherever I find 'em. It was a strange kind of homicide in a law school, if it was one, and we think the dean did it. He disappeared."

"And you think came to India? Why all the way to India?"

"Seems unlikely, I know. We got some good people in the department, and they picked up some evidence of his whereabouts… and I needed a vacation. Since my wife died, I've been living my work, and it's good to get away from it."

"That's a good idea. As far as possible, that's my motto." The dean attempted a hearty laugh.

"So that's my story. A bit of it, anyway. Now you tell me what brought you to this part of the world."

The dean's chin tucked in, and his head inclined backward. The effect, and his expression, was what one might expect on observing someone swallow a goldfish.

"… Ahhh, yes… " he managed to say.

"Ah yes?"

"Yes, what brought me to India? A good question… but easier to ask than to answer."

Walsh observed him expectantly. The dean twirled one end of his mustache and cast his companion a bleak eye. He was thinking rapidly, uncertain if he might stumble in a lie, unaware until too late of an internal inconsistency.

"It's such a long story," he ventured, improvising wildly, "and yet… and yet so simple, really. The usual things. A long romance… I thought we would marry… then she met another man, an American, and ran off with him." He attempted a forlorn look, and, in view of his inner turmoil, largely succeeded. "I inherited some money; I was sick of my job; and I'd always wanted to travel. So I followed her to the States like a hound on the scent, as it were, but it was no use. She wouldn't come back."

"Where were you?"

Better not say I was in the Midwest, he thought frantically. *Where I grew up, that's it.* "I was mostly in Connecticut, and I stayed for three years, even picked up an American accent. You may have noticed."

Joe nodded his head in affirmation. "What did you do all that time?' he asked.

"I did a little photography in Hartford, but there wasn't enough money in it. I finally secured a very satisfactory position in the purchasing department of a company making parts for helicopters."

"No kidding. Outside Hartford? Which one?"

The dean clutched at a name from distant memory. "Pantronics."

"My brother-in-law works for Pantronics! It's such a small world! My wife used to say everyone is only seven handshakes away from knowing everyone else. Nice company. Small. If I worked in industry, that's the kind I'd pick. You must know him – Kevin O'Connell."

"Kevin? Yeah… I think so. Sounds familiar."

"Sounds familiar? Hey, Gus, he's the Executive Vice-President. You gotta be kiddin'. Everyone knows him."

"Sure… " the dean groped. "Like I said, I think so. When did he get there?"

"Christ, Gus, he's been there forever. Whad are ya talkin' about? He grew up with the business… started when there were only a half dozen guys. He told me he made it a point to meet every new employee. And you wouldn't believe the guy's memory. Like an elephant. I can't wait to tell him I met one of the guys in his purchasing department – who can't remember him."

"No… no, I didn't say that. I was there only a few months. What is he looking like?"

"Come on, Gus. You really don't remember? Kevin's a cue ball with a bushy beard. He hasn't had hair since he was twenty-five."

"I… yeah, I remember. Vaguely. Must be getting old, but it's coming back to me. Like I said, my girlfriend left me… it was a bad time. Then I got some more money. Came here."

"You've been here quite a while, I gather."

"Yeah… did some traveling in Europe first." *I've got to make him believe I've been out of the country for the last couple of years,* he thought. *And I've got to change the subject.* "It's getting time to move again. Any ideas where I should go next?"

"No. I used 'em up when I came to Mumbai. How about Africa? Or New Zealand. I've always wanted… "

"Maybe I should go to Europe."

"I thought you just said you'd been there."

"Yes… yes, of course. Other parts, I meant."

The conversation, on a new tack, drifted forward. Dinner was served. Lin was forgotten. It was indeed time to move again, and with haste. *But,* he thought, *make it look right. Natural. Don't lose my cool. New Zealand would be a good choice. But don't tell him that. Leave a farewell note. No more questions.*

He nodded at appropriate intervals. Smiled. Made innocuous inquiries. Eventually the meal concluded. Painfully aware of his predicament, wanting to flee, the dean asked casually if they should retire to the bar for an after-dinner drink. To his dismay, Walsh accepted. It was late when the two diners finally emerged and retraced their steps to the Balfour Hotel.

* * * * *

They said good night, and with elaborately concocted casualness, the dean strolled to his room. He shut the door with a soft click, listening as Joe Walsh's footsteps receded down the hall to a stairway at one end. *Stay calm. Don't do anything hasty.* His frightened expression, which he glimpsed in a cloudy mirror over a sink at one side of the room, belied these thoughts. His fingers twitched nervously in his palms. *I've got to get out of here. One more question about that damned brother-in-law and it would have been all over. For Chrissake, I can't even remember what I said. I've got to get out of here.*

With a quick stride, he crossed the room and opened his suitcase that was sitting precariously on top of a battered chest of drawers. Reaching within, he unfastened a hidden interior compartment and groped inside; then groped again; then frantically rummaged within the entire suitcase. Finally, in panic, he dumped the contents onto the floor. Dropping to his knees, he hunted among his scattered effects, brushing socks, underwear and sport shirts aside. In a moment, with a sigh of relief, he came upon the object of his search: a plastic billfold that, for some unaccountable reason, had been stuffed under his clothing instead of being secure, where he was sure he had left it, within the bag's secret compartment.

Taking the billfold in his hand, he opened it to quell still present fears of theft. Relief, so momentary and fragile, dissolved in ragged disbelief. Empty. He opened it again, stared, then in frenzy and anger threw his personal belongings this way and that in a vain hope that, somehow, his money had fallen out and lodged within his clothing. Calming himself, he patted and shook each article, then checked the chest of drawers, his trouser pockets and the pockets of his jacket. To no avail. His money – nearly all the money he possessed – was gone.

Chapter Thirteen

A Dual Departure

If fear has a temperature, it is probably cold. If calculation has a temperature, it is cool. The dean experienced a chill. For several minutes, his fruitless exploration concluded, he sat on the edge of his bed, collecting his thoughts. The money, no doubt, had been stolen. Perhaps a professional thief had taken it, or perhaps an employee. While unlikely, the thief may have been apprehended, the money found and recovered. He should report his circumstances at once. Flight was imperative, but flight without funds was impossible.

The hotel clerk, he recalled, did not quit his post until midnight. Somnolent and surly during the day, his alertness and demeanor were barely affected by evening hours. *I should try him first*, the dean thought, *then make an inquiry of the police in the morning. Perhaps, possibly, the money is even now in the clerk's possession, having been turned in by someone who found it.*

In a corner of his mind, he knew the improbability of this happening. Even if the money had been found, why would the clerk return it? He was undoubtedly a scoundrel, if his flinty replies to simple inquiries were any indication. Nevertheless, asking would cost nothing, and not asking might, just possibly, thwart his means of support and escape. He was alone, a foreigner without friends, and delay might result in arrest, extradition, a trial, imprisonment and – oh,

God! – execution. Somehow, in his worst fantasies, the cold, metallic electric chair was always in a green room, and for a ghastly, fleeting moment the vision returned.

Locking his door behind him, the dean left his disordered room and descended to the now unoccupied lobby. No one was there, although a half-hour remained until midnight. A glaring fluorescent light illuminated the space, accentuating the flaking paint on the white walls. Without hesitation, the dean knocked briskly on the door at one side of the desk which led to the clerk's sleeping chamber. He knocked again.

There was a muffled sound within, much like a grunt, and faint rustling. In some embarrassment, the dean stepped back. Perhaps he had interrupted an amorous interlude in the clerk's dull existence. That worthy now opened his door a half-foot and peered around it, his mustaches enclosed and swept backward by cloth sleeves designed to retain their shape during the night.

"What are you wanting?" he snarled.

The dean was taken aback. "I... I," he stammered, "sorry... I thought you did not go off duty until midnight. I need to ask you a question."

"At this hour of the night? I hope, sir, that it is an important question." The clerk eyed him contemptuously.

"Yes, yes, it is," the dean entreated. "Did you by any chance find money? My money... in the hotel, or in my room. I mean, it's been stolen. Has it been returned to you?"

"Your money, returned to me? At this hour?"

Was it the dean's imagination, or did one of the cloth sleeves rise slightly in a sneer? This was not the first theft at the Balfour reported by a distraught guest. The clerk's task was to deal with such occurrences with firm indifference.

"We are not being responsible for personal articles in rooms," the clerk said without sympathy or interest, preparatory to closing his door.

"But… my money… "

"Is not, I assure you, my concern." The door was nearly closed. However, loud thumping at the front door, which burst open, interrupted his practiced, curt rudeness.

A figure staggered inside. It was a woman, and when she lifted her face, the dean recognized Barbara Chu. But barely, because her features were contorted by fear and pain. She was sobbing and moaning in a language he did not understand, and her entire right shoulder, and the front of her dress, was drenched in blood. It flecked down onto her skirt below. She was holding the right side of her head with her hand, and he noticed that her hair was wet and matted with blood that oozed between her fingers.

"My God," the dean cried, "what happened?" He moved quickly forward, barely aware of the clerk, who emerged from his room, struggling to put on a pair of pants. "What happened?"

With a start – an involuntary convulsion – Barbara Chu seemed to see him for the first time.

"Raji Rau," she sobbed.

"What?"

"Raji Rau… Raji Rau, he hurt me!"

She was nearly at the desk, and for the first time the dean noticed that she was holding something in her left hand. He noticed also that she had been beaten. One eye was nearly closed, and her lower lip was cracked and bleeding. As she groped forward, she dropped the bloody object in her hand onto the desk blotter.

For a second, he did not recognize what it was. Then, in horrified astonishment, he saw that it was a small, shrivelled ear – her ear, with a gold earring still attached – that had been brutally sliced from her head.

Barbara Chu now stood before him, cowering, shaking and gripping the desk with one hand while she held the other to the gaping wound at the side of her head.

"Help me," she sobbed.

The dean did not know what to do. His eye fell upon the clerk, who was scurrying about with a towel trying to clean blood from the floor. The tension of his predicament, coupled with this new development, exploded in wrath.

"Get fully dressed, you idiot," he bellowed, "and get some water and a bandage. Use a sheet if you have to – and, damn it, make sure it's clean."

The clerk vanished inside his room. Gently, the dean gripped Barbara Chu's arm and led her to a wicker chair at one side of the lobby, where he indicated that she should sit. She stared at him, slowly nodding her head, and slumped down.

"It's all right. It's all right," he murmured in a meaningless incantation. "We're going to help you."

The clerk, having added a light shirt to his trousers, emerged and ran to a closet at the end of a short corridor leading from the lobby. He still had on the cloth contrivance to protect his mustaches. There was a brief sound of running water. When he returned, he had a bucket half full of water, not particularly clean, and an armful of towels and a sheet. As he stood before him, the dean observed that the man, so recently supercilious, was shaking with fright.

"Now, call an ambulance, if that's possible in this God-forsaken place," the dean said through clenched teeth. "Or if it's not, get a taxi to take her to a hospital. Get out on the street. Go to the Excelsior if you have to. You're taking her… I'll pay." He recalled his lack of funds. "No… no, this damned hotel will pay. Hurry!"

"But… but, sir, the blood! The blood! I shall be up all night. The hotel, it must be clean." The man continued to shake. He grabbed the dean's arm. "You will not tell Raji Rau." He was babbling. "You must not tell the police. You must not tell Raji Rau that I helped."

The dean had taken a towel, dipped it into the water, and was slowly washing Barbara Chu's hair from the wound.

"Tell? No… yes… no, of course I won't tell. God damn it, hurry!"

Barbara Chu seemed to faint. The dean held her upright, blood slowly staining his fingers, palm and wrist. The clerk ran onto the verandah. When, within minutes, he returned, the dean had already wrapped the sheet tightly around Barbara's head. It was stained red at the place where her ear had been, and she was slumped to one side.

"I have secured a taxi," the clerk cried. "It is outside."

"Good. You are going with her to the hospital. Help me carry her."

"But the blood. I must clean the blood."

"I'll do that and throw this stuff behind the desk. You see that she is cared for. I don't care what story you tell. And here – take this." With that, the dean picked up the severed ear, placed it in his handkerchief, and handed it to the terrified clerk.

* * * * *

It did not take long to clean the lobby. Only the wicker chair, where blood had seeped into the interstices between the caning, gave him trouble. These places he rinsed thoroughly with water, and he removed the fresh, red spots on a pillow with ample scrubbing. The floor he mopped with a damp towel. His task accomplished, he deposited the bucket of muddy, reddish-brown water behind the desk and threw the soiled towels in a heap beside it.

The lobby was silent. The sound of an occasional taxi, car or truck sounded through the front windows. The curtains rippled softly in a night breeze. The dean pulled the cord to the overhead fluorescent light, so that the only illumination came from a bare bulb hanging by its wire from the ceiling of the adjacent corridor.

For several minutes, he stood by the desk, thinking. It was long past his usual bedtime. What a strange, disruptive twenty-four hours he had experienced. Once again, unexpectedly and suddenly, his life had taken a violent turn. And as before, his circumstances were perilous.

He walked into the small sitting room next to the lobby. Arms akimbo, he stood in the dark by the window. More minutes passed. Then, slowly and deliberately, he walked out of the room and ascended the stairs to room 23.

To his surprise, a faint glow of light was visible beneath the door. It shot out onto the frayed carpet in the hallway. He knocked softly. There was no sound. But the light went out. Again he knocked, low pulses of sound into a hollow void. Again there was silence, not even a faint rustling of clothing or muffled breath.

The dean placed his mouth next to the doorjamb. "Lin," he whispered, "it's me. It's Gus." Was it his imagination, or did he hear a noise, a soft scraping. "For God's sake," he continued urgently, "open the door."

He waited. "Lin, open the door. Please, it's Gus."

He heard a low murmur. "Gus. Gus, is it really you?"

"Yes. Please let me in. It's really me."

The door opened tentatively – a crack, then more. Foolishly, or wisely, he stepped into the blackness within, and the door shut behind him. He heard a movement, and the light went on.

Lin was standing next to the bed, fully clothed, holding a table lamp in her hand. She had been crying. Taking a step forward, she collapsed onto him, requiring him to support her quickly in his arms.

"Oh Gus. I feeling so bad. I missing you so bad."

About to kiss, he drew back and removed the lamp from her hand. As he did so, he looked around the room. "What...? What is this suitcase doing? You're all packed."

She nodded. "I running away."

"Running away?" He was befuddled.

"Yes, but I very frightened. I waiting for clerk to go bed."

He stared at her in astonishment, releasing the arm he still had around her as he stepped back.

"You must take me with you."

It was her turn to stare, incredulously.

"What you say?"

"I must go with you. Lin, don't ask why. You must take me with you... if you can. I... I went to my room tonight, and my money... my money, almost all of it, it's been stolen. Can you help me?"

Lin hesitated. "Yes... yes, Gus, I can."

"Where are you going?"

"To home town, Gus. To Hong Kong. If Raji Rau not catch me."

"Do you?… That's a long way. Do you have enough money? And for me, too?"

"I… " Lin hesitated again. "I have several thousand dollar, Gus. You not asking how. It enough, I think, maybe help us… We must leave tonight," she clutched him, "or Raji Rau, he find out… he find out I not do what he say. He kill me."

"He hurt Barbara Chu," the dean blurted. "Just tonight. He… he cut off her ear."

"Oh, God, no." Lin's hand fluttered to her mouth. "I knew something bad happen. Today he very angry, say she not give him money." Her grip on him tightened. "Gus, you get suitcase too. You come back quick, knock three time. We go together." For the first time she smiled. "I like that very much."

* * * * *

Noiselessly, he left her room. His packing did not take long. He had arrived with little, he would leave with little. Just as before, on the first day of his flight, he threw his belongings helter-skelter into his bag. The task took only a few minutes.

On his third knock, Lin opened her door. She was ready. Stealthily, they crept down the corridor and began to descend the stairs. But the dean, who was in the lead, heard a low sound, possibly a footfall. He held up his hand. The sound recurred. They froze. Without question, someone was in the lobby. The clerk? Could he have returned so soon? Motioning Lin to go back up the stairs with their suitcases, her footsteps mercifully muffled by the carpet on each tread, he continued onward to reconnoiter the problem.

It was not the clerk. The small man was standing by the desk, staring at the pile of bloody towels. He had removed his glasses and was wiping them with a soiled handkerchief. When he heard the dean, it was too late for the latter to retreat. The man turned with a scowl and adjusted his glasses to the bridge of his nose. As he did so, he also adjusted his features to an obsequious smile.

"Ah, Mr. Honque. What an unexpected pleasure. What keeps you up at this hour of the evening?"

"I… I could not sleep. I thought, perhaps, it might be cooler in… in the sitting room." It was not an artful falsehood, but it was the best he could contrive. In the dim light, it was difficult to gauge the response, but it seemed as if the other man smiled – with his mouth, not his eyes, which in any event were partially veiled by his spectacles.

"I might also ask," the dean continued with fake joviality, "what brings you here in the small hours of the morning."

"A business engagement… concluded satisfactorily." Abruptly, Raji Rau changed the subject and pulled the cord to the fluorescent light. "It appears that the clerk has met with an unfortunate accident."

And, indeed, that was the appearance. The red-stained towels were where the dean had thrown them in a disheveled heap next to the bucket of water. The door to the clerk's room had swung open, and his quarters were obviously unoccupied.

Again the dean feigned his response, wondering as he did so if the other detected his deception. "Why," he cried, "what happened? Where is the clerk?"

"He has, perhaps, fallen against the desk," the small man responded with a thin smile. "It is unfortunate, a problem with people from the villages. I should venture that he has been drinking to excess. Not for the first time."

The explanation, which both knew was false, seemed appropriate. Raji Rau opened his hands in mock resignation, as if to say "what are we to do with these people?" and shrugged. "The poor man may need help," he added with seeming solicitude. "I am, as you might well imagine, most concerned. We must search for him, and I had thought to look upstairs."

"Upstairs? Oh… I think, I mean I don't think, you'll find the clerk there. As… ah… as I said, I couldn't sleep, and I'm sure I would have heard him. Particularly if he was hurt. And drunk."

Raji Rau looked at the dean with curiosity.

"In fact… " the dean stumbled forward, rapidly formulating his thoughts, "in fact, now that you mention it… you did mention it, I think… I heard a noise. Maybe the front door shutting and… and some banging, and I looked out."

Raji Rau was staring at the dean intently. "And what," he said softly and evenly, "did you see?" His expression was opaque. The glaring light reflected off his lenses.

"I saw a person," the dean answered. "It was a man, I'm fairly certain, and he was bent over. Yes… it was hard to see at night, but maybe that was the clerk. I couldn't really tell. He was holding his stomach as if he were sick."

"And in which direction was he going?" Raji Rau asked without emotion. "I cannot stress too strongly that it may be necessary to obtain immediate help for him."

The dean looked about him. "That… that way," he said wildly, pointing in the direction opposite to the Excelsior Hotel. He walked to the front door, Raji Rau closely following, and gestured into the darkness. "Toward... toward the Karma Kafe."

At this delicate moment a small, nocturnal insect, attracted by the illumination within, flew through the open door and, for some private reason of its own, decided to find sustenance within the dean's ear. The dean hopped back from the opening, nearly landing on one of Raji Rau's feet.

"Ech... ecch," he cried, tilting his head to one side and banging its top side. He shook his head violently, only he being privy to the loud buzzing within. "Ecch... eccch."

Raji Rau surveyed him with astonishment and barely concealed disgust. *American buffoon*, he thought.

"Ecch... oww!"

The insect, having ascertained that foraging was poor, or perhaps ill at ease with the violent shaking in its new quarters, crawled forth and resumed flight. The buzzing stopped.

"You appear distraught," the small man said indifferently, peering along the poorly lighted street, "and of course you do not know the city. I shall conduct a search myself. It is not necessary," he concluded in a firm tone, "that you join me. I shall deal with the clerk on my own. Go get some sleep."

Raji Rau slipped around the larger man, crossed the small verandah and began walking briskly up the street. As he brushed past, the dean noticed spots on his trousers – spots similar in color to those on the towels behind the desk.

* * * * *

For a few moments, the dean observed his departure. In terrified haste, he wheeled about and ascended the stairs two steps at a time. Pressed into a doorway, the suitcases beside her, Lin was at the top. He could not know – but would be told later – about the wild thumping of her heart as she listened to the conversation below and, misinterpreting, heard the sound of the dean attempting to evict the unwelcome tenant in his ear.

"Quickly, Lin," he whispered. "We must run to the Excelsior with these bags."

"Through the front door?"

"We'll have to take the chance. We'll find a taxi there."

The dean lifted the suitcases. In jumbled flight, they crossed the lobby, pausing briefly at the door to listen and espy, if possible, a returning figure. There was only darkness. Nearly at a run, they proceeded in the opposite direction to the one taken by Raji Rau, rounded the corner by the store with the lop-sided Coca Cola sign, and crossed the large thoroughfare still crowded with people. The liveried doorman seemed startled by their arrival, but a generous gratuity subdued his qualms. In a few minutes he secured a taxi, and with elaborate, painful care, he placed their luggage inside. *Perhaps,* thought the dean, *he is trying to earn his tip. Or perhaps the cheeky beggar wants more.* None was forthcoming. They tumbled inside, and the cab pulled away, its taillights slowly winking to small red dots in the distance. The two fugitives vanished into the night.

Chapter Fourteen

The Journey

Their flight across India took many days. Avoiding the airport, the most likely point of embarkation, the fugitives instructed the taxi driver to take them to the Bombay Central Terminal – called Victoria Terminal or VT by the local inhabitants..

Late at night the sprawling, gothic station was cavernous and dark, and they finally found places on a bench in the gloom of a corner to await the dawn. Neither could sleep, and they huddled next to each other, tensely surveying each entrance. Their vigil was undisturbed, however, and as the light of the next day filtered into the building, the terminal gradually swelled with people in various states of wash and unwash. Soon taxis and auto-rickshaws began to choke the adjoining streets. The silence of the night dissolved into a hubbub of blaring horns and shouted commands and curses.

Most of the tattered throng of passengers – men, women and children – had purchased third class tickets. They waited anxiously, the women in colorful saris, often holding children while other children clung to the descending folds of cloth. Each family seemed to guard a pile of battered luggage or possessions tied in cloth parcels, and each seemed to have brought its own basket of provisions. A strong aroma of pungent food, combined with the odor of sweating bodies, began to fill the crowded terminal.

"Where shall we go?" Lin asked anxiously as the crowd began to swell in size.

The dean furrowed his forehead. Desperately, he tried to remember maps of India from his grammar school days, an odd assortment of unhelpful novels about India from the days of the Raj, most by Rudyard Kipling, and movies like *Gunga Din* and *A Passage to India*. They offered little in the way of a clue. Then he remembered an article that had fascinated him in the *National Geographic* about the ghats in Benares.

"Benares," he said emphatically. "We'll go there and then decide what to do." He had no idea where Benares was located, but Lin agreed, not knowing herself but reasonably certain that it had to be far away. And her goal was to be far away, wherever that might be.

After being informed by a supercilious clerk that Benares was now Varanasi, they bought tickets in a first class compartment to that destination. Lin, who seemed to have some experience, had strongly urged the additional expense. Her judgment was vindicated when soon thereafter the train, empty at the commencement of its journey, entered the station and stopped next to the crowded platform. At once, a jostling surge of humanity moved toward the doors, and the growl of curses and shouts rose to a roar. The platform became a scene of chaos, as families shoved their way forward, lifting packages and children and heaving them into the cars.

This swirling tide of humanity ebbed before the few first class compartments. A porter assisted the two passengers onto the train and helped them stow their luggage in a rack above their seats. Only a fat businessman in a gray tunic joined them, and they sat in relative tranquility, staring out the window, while the bedlam on the platform subsided. The final passengers were herded into their accommodations; the conductors shouted down the line of cars and jumped aboard as the train lurched slowly forward.

Many trains in India have an antique appearance. Battered by years of use and indifferent maintenance, the passenger cars appear more like old, open-air trolleys than modern, sleek passenger coaches. Because of the often-stifling heat, doors and windows remain open, and people lean from every window or cling, in haphazard fashion, to every platform including the roof. Vendors crowd every station, so that the arrival and departure of a train is like an impromptu, open-air bazaar.

But the repetitive scenery grew tiresome to Lin and Gus as the miles ticked away. The view from their windows varied from rolling hills punctuated by stands of forest to hot, flat and dusty fields. Eventually they grew bored and attempted to doze. Villages flashed by, an occasional cow wandering a dirt street; women washed laundry in streams and rivers; children waved; and bullocks straining in harness toiled in the endlessly flat fields. And above it all – above the fields, the mud villages, the clumps of trees – rose plumes of smoke from thousands of cooking fires. These, in turn, paled to insignificance as they approached Varanasi and the Ganges. Funeral pyres burned along the banks, and the dark, sweet smoke cast a dim pall across the sky. To the inhabitants, how diurnally normal; to Lin and Gus, how strange and mystical that so many, countless souls would desire their ashes and charred bones to find a final resting place in the sluggish waters of the sacred river. The train, a tangible, mechanical intrusion from the modern era, could not – and did not –

disturb the ancient rhythm of millennia. Two different thought processes, two entirely different conceptions of reality, coexisted in the same place and time, neither imposing on the other.

The fat businessman in the gray tunic departed. Both Lin and Gus had wondered who he might be, and they were relieved to see him go. By this time they had decided not to journey to Hong Kong by air. Raji Rau knew whence Lin had come, having had one of his agents recruit her there, and he could easily surmise that she would return. The airport might be watched, and so they determined to go by sea in the slowest manner possible, because it would be harder to watch the docks, and the agent would probably weary of searching after a limited period of time.

They concluded that they should travel on to Calcutta, now Kolkata, and after a day of sightseeing, they boarded a first class compartment in a train as dilapidated as the previous one. A large woman in an ochre sari took a seat with them, beaming cheerfully and chatting in Hindi until she grasped that they could not understand. In Varanasi they also acquired an itinerant European student with knapsack, shorts, sandals and an unkempt, scraggly beard. He knew English and insisted on engaging them in conversation. His odor was unfortunate.

At first they did their best to be polite, listening attentively and occasionally asking questions. But they soon tired of the effort and tried pointedly to discourage him by talking to each other or by staring out the window. Their dodges were to no avail. The voluble wretch droned on, his singsong voice reminiscent of the pitch emitted by the moving gears of rusty machinery. Only darkness slowed his interminable monologue.

Lin dozed, her head resting on the dean's shoulder, and, as sleep overtook him, the moving mouth of the student eventually slowed to a stop.

At a bend in the track, or possibly as the train sped through a village, the engineer sounded the horn. It emitted a scream in the night, and the train lurched slightly. Waking, the dean opened one eye to observe their traveling companion hard at work picking his nose. His forefinger, buried in his left nostril, was working actively to dislodge a particularly recalcitrant particle. The dean shut his eye. He had no desire to see how inventively the student would dispose of the fruit of his labor.

To their dismay, their companion continued with them the following day. The sensation was like being locked in a box with a malodorous, sawing cricket. He clung. His voice rose. It subsided. Silence came only when the dean rose stiffly and extracted writing paper from his suitcase in order to compose a letter. The task was difficult. Trains moving down the Ganges valley to the Bay of Bengal do not move swiftly. The roadbed is uneven. It was trying, in the swaying compartment, to hold pen to paper and write legible script.

And the dean realized, when this task had been completed, that he was defenseless. He had brought nothing to read. When he looked up, folding his writing paper, he would be staring directly into the eyes of their insistent interlocutor. The sensation, he knew, would be like standing at the foot of a verbal waterfall; more, as in a bad dream growing worse, his feet would be mired in cloying ooze. He would not be able to extricate himself, despite frantic, unavailing effort. Each tug would sink him farther, until the torrent of words crashed over his mute, supplicating form, his eyes cast upward to an indifferent heaven.

Or at least so he thought. This grim, and unhappily realistic, fantasy caused him to labor over his composition. As a rule, he did not concern himself with the phraseology of a letter. In his circumstances, however, every word seemed to have crucial significance. There were so many choices. And he dared not look up for fear of making dreaded eye contact. His features puckered, therefore, in both real and pretended concentration, he kept his gaze directed downward on his task.

However, despite his lingering efforts, his writing was at last done. The letter, in fact, was brief. He felt – was it just his imagination? – that the student's eyes were on him somewhat the way a vulture, perched on a bough, observes the last, weak flailing of its prey on the ground below. The awful moment could no longer be delayed. He looked up.

The student was asleep. Lin, seated next to him, was staring out the window. The scenery had changed. No longer were they traveling through fields and villages. Many buildings surrounded them on either side. The principal streets were paved, and the ubiquitous signs for watches, soft drinks and cigarettes were once again in evidence, as in Mumbai. Their pace slackened as the train negotiated it way forward, approaching Howrah Station, one of the great railway terminals of the world. They were entering Kolkata.

* * * * *

"Isn't two thousand dollars each a trifle excessive?"

The dean's voice betrayed an edge of puzzled outrage. He was standing on a dock: a crumbling concrete structure protruding into the Hooghly River and half occupied by a dilapidated wooden building. It was humid and hot, and his face was shaded from the glaring sun by his floppy hat. Lin, standing next to him, was dressed casually in slacks and a loose-fitting blouse.

The man to whom the dean had addressed his remark was standing just outside the door of the building. A faded curtain hung limply across the opening. This worthy was not a prepossessing example of humanity. Short, bald and with protruding front teeth beneath a narrow, hooked nose, he resembled nothing so much as a wharf rat transplanted from dockside London – in fact, his place of origin. By occupation he was the master of a rusty freighter secured by creaking hawsers to the pier. In addition to the transshipment of goods, the ship derived income from accommodation for up to a dozen passengers. These were obtained through advertisements hawking the opportunity to visit ports of call in the fabulous Spice Islands, last stop Hong Kong. The passengers were also afforded the dubious opportunity of dining every evening at the captain's table. The quality of the fare was not revealed.

Lin and the dean had escaped the student by a simple expedient. When they departed the train, he had leached along at their side, but they jumped nimbly into a taxicab, slammed the door, shouted a cheery farewell and ordered the driver to move on. Anywhere. At first the driver hesitated, not knowing the destination, until harshly ordered forward. He took them to a hotel much like the Balfour. There they remained for a few days, exploring their options and determined to leave the subcontinent in the least obtrusive way possible. An advertisement to explore the Spice Islands had been tacked to a bulletin board in the hotel, and two days after reading it they had ventured to the dock to make an inquiry. The ship was scheduled to sail the following day.

"With all due respect," the captain responded to the dean's inquiry, "this here opportunity ain't likely to come your way again. Once in a lifetime, I'd call it. And mind, we give you a plushy stateroom – sorry I can't show it to you at this very moment – deckchairs, a little shuffleboard, bridge in the evening, if you like that sort of thing, and the rule against drinking on board don't apply to passengers, if you get my meaning." He winked.

"But is your charge the standard fare? It seems very expensive."

"Expensive?" The captain surveyed them with the eyes of a wounded deer. "Begging your pardon, it's what I'd call a real bargain. Three weeks cruising the loveliest part of the world. And while you two take a holiday snooze, we do the work."

Lin and Gus exchanged glances.

"Who you have, other passengers?" Lin asked.

The captain hesitated. "Well, missus, I expect plenty will be here today – like yourselves, quality people. You're the first, you see, but it's always busy at the last minute. This here opportunity doesn't stay open. You come back late this afternoon, you'll likely be too late."

Again, they exchanged glances, and the dean nodded his head. With all its drawbacks – not least having dinner every evening with this feral apparition – it was what they had been seeking.

"I think we'll sign on," the dean said.

"Good, good," the other replied. He nearly made the mistake of rubbing his palms together. "I'll require half payment in advance, all gear here on the dock by eight in the morning… And whose names, may I ask, shall I have the honor of placing at the top of our passenger list?"

The dean paused. "Ah… why don't you list us as… ah… Mr. and Mrs. Augustus Honque… The Third," he added as an afterthought.

From the corner of her almond eyes, Lin shot him a curious glance but said nothing.

Chapter Fifteen

The Dean's Correspondence

The dean mailed the letter that he wrote on the train several days after he arrived in Kolkata. It was addressed to a professor of law, a former colleague on the faculty of Crabshaw School of the Law. The envelope had no return address.

Uncertain that he was making the right decision, the dean had delayed while he pondered the wisdom of making contact. How could he be sure that his confidence was well placed? Suppose his location was revealed. Yet, he knew, a letter postmarked Kolkata, without his name on the exterior to alert some vigilant postal clerk or faculty secretary, would tell very little. Moreover, by the time it arrived, he would be gone, whereabouts unknown. For all anyone might know, his destination could be Nairobi, Warsaw, Auckland or San Francisco.

Would his colleague betray him? In view of his past help, it seemed unlikely. Presumably, no one knew of the assistance he had rendered. Still, even though he was not likely to be charged as an accessory after the fact, his colleague might have revealed his role to the authorities in order to mitigate potential punishment. In addition, the prompting of conscience, the dean knew, with its corollary compulsion to confess, can work strange consequences. Many culprits have traded the security of silence for an end to gnawing guilt.

So he fretted. Twice he went to a post office, and twice he returned with the letter still in his hand. At last, however, the good sense of his endeavor prevailed. How could he fairly judge his circumstances without more information? His conversation with Joe Walsh, who surely had up-to-date news, made clear that he was the lead suspect. Were there others? John Vandervoort had knowledge that something was amiss. What? Was anything suspicious going on at the law school that was worthy of investigation?

If he was not to remain a fugitive his entire life, he had to find a way to intervene actively in events. Some channel of information and communication would be necessary. And so, despite his misgivings, he mailed the letter on his third attempt.

My good friend:

You are probably surprised to hear from me, and from the postmark, which I assume will be on the envelope – to say nothing of the stamps – you may wonder how I got this far. It's too long a story. Maybe, God willing, one day you'll hear it.

Sorry about my jiggled handwriting. I'm writing this on a train that keeps swaying and lurching so that it's hard to keep my hand steady. There's some idiot foreign student opposite me who talks more than ten people combined. More even than your colleagues at a faculty meeting. Ha-ha-ha. And just to give you an idea how bad it is, he's even less interesting.

Anyway, I'm writing to ask a favor. I'm not including a return address. That's partly because I don't know what it will be and partly because, even though I know you'll be careful, I would hate to have this letter fall into the wrong hands. I know you'll understand that I have to be super-extra cautious.

So one of these days, not right away, I'll call you at home.

I've got the number, and with satellite communication, it's supposed to be easy. In the meantime, please keep an eye out for me. By now you know what was supposed to have happened, except that I didn't do it. You've got to believe me. I need someone to let me know if there are any other leads or whether anything funny is going on that might suggest who really did it.

Please, please don't tell anyone about this letter. I've got to trust someone, and I need your help. I have to rely on you. I have to believe that one of these days the real murderer will be found, and everyone will realize that I'm innocent.

Sincerely,
Massoud

Chapter Sixteen

Meanwhile, Back in Mumbai...

Joe Walsh was puzzled. He was also concerned.

At first, nothing had seemed amiss. Following his delightful evening with Gus, he had noticed the next day that the usually taciturn clerk was not behind his desk. This observation elicited recognition of the fact, nothing more. Clerks in India, he surmised, are entitled to days off or get sick or have an errand to perform or whatever. A stranger was in his place – an evil looking, smelly fellow with a hawk-like face and a dirty turban. It never even flickered across Joe's mind that, from appearances, the clerk and his replacement seemed to have attended the same finishing school. He had no need to do business with the man.

The day was sticky hot – again, nothing unusual. Joe went for a stroll, then sat reading for two or three hours in the small, shaded sitting room off the lobby. In mid-afternoon he observed a person who matched the description of Raji Rau, but he pointedly ignored him. That person, in any event, appeared to be occupied with business and spoke at length with the clerk's replacement.

He was disappointed not to encounter either Lin or Gus, and at length he retired to his room, napped briefly, and then walked to the Excelsior for dinner. Afterwards, as he had done the evening before, he enjoyed a drink in the bar. He then returned to the Balfour and bed. No one, he noted idly, was behind the desk in the lobby.

That post, however, was occupied the following morning when he descended for breakfast. The clerk had returned. But he was a clerk different in appearance from the man he had seen two days before. Apparently he had been on the losing side of a fight and had sustained a vicious beating. His right eye was swollen shut, and his cheek was bruised. He walked stiffly, and a crude sling supported his left arm. Most noticeably, his usual immaculate turban was gone, and in its place was a bloodstained bandage swathed around his head that covered his left ear.

Not wishing to pry, Joe merely nodded in the clerk's direction as he set off for breakfast. But he did not want to spend another lonely day, and so he thought it best, upon his return, to inquire about Lin. He decided to leave her a note suggesting that they meet for another tour and asking her to contact him at her early convenience.

He therefore stopped at the clerk's desk on his way back to his room after breakfast. The clerk was bending over some papers, shuffling slowly through them, and he glanced up with an expression of infinite, suffering melancholy. One side of his face twitched, and Joe noticed that his free hand had a slight tremor.

"May I assist you in some manner?" the clerk said dolefully.

"Yes," Joe answered with affected cheer. "And, say, you look like you were on the losing team in a tag-wrestling match. Must have been a bear on the other side." He laughed heartily.

The clerk, who had not the slightest idea what was meant by tag-wrestling, simply stared at him blankly. *Noisy idiot*, he thought. But he understood the general drift of the comment, and, after a moment's hesitation, said: "May I suggest that your inquiry is most rude."

"Sorry. No offense intended. In fact, if you need a helping hand, just let me know."

"That will not be necessary."

"I just wanted to know if you've seen Lin Fei around. You know, the pretty Chinese woman who conducts tours. She wasn't here yesterday, and I'd like to go on one. Maybe I could leave her a note."

How odd, Joe thought. *Why is this man fidgeting so much? He almost looks frightened.*

"There is no need for a note," the clerk said slowly and carefully.

"How so?"

"She is not here. It will not reach her."

"I know she's not here." It was Joe's turn to regard the clerk with condescension. "That's why I want to leave a note… " Then the ambiguity of the clerk's response registered. "What… what do you mean it won't reach her? You can just slip it under her door."

"She has no door. The lady about whom you make inquiry is no longer a guest."

Joe's cheerful expression clouded, then vanished. "No longer… she didn't say anything about… are you sure? Maybe we're not talking about the same person."

"I am quite certain," the clerk said firmly, for a moment a reincarnation of his former self.

For almost a minute, Joe stood quietly, staring vacantly into space and drumming his fingers on the raised front of the desk. Something was not right. "Did she," he asked at last, hopefully, "go to a nearby hotel? The Excelsior?"

"It would appear not, but I cannot say."

I'll walk over, Joe thought. *No harm in asking. When Gus hears about this, he's going to be pretty unhappy.*

"Just one more question. She told me she had a lady friend. Another Chinese woman, I think. Would that woman, maybe, know where Lin is?"

The clerk started and closed his eyes. "That woman," he said flatly, "has also gone away somewhere. She will not be coming back."

Joe ceased his unproductive questions and walked briskly to the Excelsior. Without Lin, he mused, his tours were at an end unless he checked into a different hotel. That might cost more money. It occurred to him that, of course, Gus might know where she had gone. He would have to ask him.

The Excelsior had no record of a registrant named Lin Fei. And, he was informed, no Chinese woman answering Lin's description had registered the preceding day. Or rather, the helpful woman behind the registration desk explained with a smile, she had not seen such a woman. She assumed that Joe was a jilted lover. A pretty Chinese woman could have registered with someone else, while she was out, perhaps during the evening…

He peered into the sitting area of the lobby, but aside from a pair of Japanese businessmen, no one was there. The men were conferring intently about a paper that one of them had just removed from an open briefcase on the floor. Next he glanced into the dining room where he had just been for breakfast. The delicate Indian hostess, wearing long, filigreed earrings, was surprised to see him again so soon; she inquired solicitously whether he had forgotten something. No, he had replied, just looking for a friend. Had she, by any chance, seen an attractive young Chinese woman or a tall American with a large mustache? The answer was negative.

Disappointed, Joe retraced his steps to the Balfour. It

would, he supposed, be necessary to speak with the clerk again – never a pleasant prospect in the most trifling circumstances. But his curiosity had been roused. Where could the woman have gone – and why in such haste? What had happened to the clerk? He needed to find Gus.

As usual, the clerk was shuffling papers on his desk. The stack before him never appeared to change, but he seemed continually in the process of rearranging it. Needless to say, following his usual custom, he did not look up as Joe approached.

"Excuse me."

"Yes?" The clerk scowled dourly in Joe's direction, his annoyed expression accentuated by his battered appearance. "I see that you are desiring assistance *again*." The impression conveyed was that he had just spied a cockroach or some other noxious pest, and it was now his duty to exterminate it.

"I need to ask you a couple more questions."

"Yes, what now?" the clerk said in a tone of exasperation.

"Have you seen the other American? The tall man named Gus with the mustache? I need to speak with him."

"Ah. You are referring, no doubt, to Mr. Honque."

Joe stared. "Hon… ? Did you say Honque?"

"Yes. Mr. Augustus Honque."

There was a long pause. *Goddamn. Goddamn. No wonder he didn't know my brother-in-law! It was all a story! And I had to be the guy with the big mouth and tip him off. Gus. What a fool I've been; why didn't I realize that Gus is short for Augustus? Cop all my life, and I still screw up.*

"Listen," Joe said quickly, this time with a note of desperate urgency in his voice, "I need to speak with this man." His deferential, I-don't-want-to-be-an-ugly-American tone was gone. "And don't crap around. I've had all the surliness out of you I'm going to take for one day."

The clerk was surprised. As before, the meaning of some words eluded him, but he understood the voice of command. His demeanor changed.

"I have not seen him, sir."

"Not at all, today?"

"No, sir. He has not come down. I would have noticed."

"What's his room number? I've got to find him."

The clerk carefully lifted the papers before him with his free hand and scrutinized a roster on the desk. "Mr. Honque is on the first floor. Room 12."

"Thank you." Joe turned and strode quickly to the stairs. He ascended them rapidly. In a few seconds, the clerk heard a loud, staccato rapping on a door. This noise was followed by stillness. Then it commenced again. Then stopped. Then started yet again.

Not long thereafter, Joe Walsh stood impatiently before the clerk's desk. His mouth was set in a grim line. "No one answers. Listen up. This is important. I need to check that room and make sure no one is there."

"Obviously it is so, sir, as there was apparently no answer to your most insistent knock."

"You must come with me and open the door."

"I cannot stress too strongly, sir, the irregularity of your request. It cannot be done." The clerk shrugged his shoulders and simultaneously winced with pain.

"Take me to the room and open it, dammit," Walsh exploded in wrath. "And don't hand me any shit – or you won't just have an arm in a sling. Your ass'll be in one too." His gaze was steady and menacing. Walsh stepped to his left, as if to force his way behind the desk. The clerk, visibly alarmed, noted his thick neck and hunched, burly shoulders.

"On the other hand, sir," he murmured nervously, "perhaps in this one case I can be permitted to make an exception. I see that we are confronting an emergency of some sort… Of course… I shall accompany you and determine if Mr. Honque is, perhaps, sleeping somewhat too soundly."

The clerk fumbled in the desk drawer and withdrew a large ring of keys, much as if he were a medieval jailor. Unable to hold the ring in one hand while sorting with the other, he dropped them on the desk and riffled through the jumbled assortment until he came to the one labeled 12. He then picked up this key, with the ring and other keys dangling beneath it, and emerged solemnly from his sanctuary. "Follow me," he said officiously and unnecessarily.

Joe Walsh fell in behind, his face still set in a scowl. They brushed past a woman descending the stairs who seemed rather startled by the clerk's bandaged appearance.

"I shall, madam, attend to your needs in a moment," the clerk said as he stepped aside to allow her to pass. With a formal nod of his head, Joe did the same.

Room 12 was halfway down a short corridor one flight up. The clerk knocked gently. As before, there was no response. Inserting the key, he unlocked the door and pushed it slowly open with his foot. Both men stood at the entrance and looked inside. The bed was made. No one was there. The room seemed curiously bare.

"Gus?" Walsh said. There was no answer. He walked into the room, followed by the clerk, and jerked open the closet door. It was empty. There was no suitcase, no clothing, no personal effects scattered upon the top of the worn bureau.

The bathroom door was open, affording a view of an empty room. Joe quickly glanced under the bed. Nothing was there.

"It appears," the clerk said with dismayed surprise, "that Mr. Honque has left."

"As I suspected," Walsh muttered as he methodically opened each dresser drawer and looked inside.

"And now, may I ask," the clerk cried in alarm, "how we are to be paid our bill… Several days now he is owing." He shook his head. "It would most certainly be appearing, as you say in your country, that Mr. Honque has… ah… flapped the chicken house."

* * * * *

Joe Walsh was seated in the small sitting room off the lobby. He was staring gloomily at a frayed, greasy copy of the *International Herald Tribune.* The news section was several days out of date. That did not matter. For the most part, he was sunk in his own thoughts, and the newspaper merely constituted a prop to justify his presence and ward off any garrulous stranger.

Where could they have gone? He was vexed that his pleasure at finding a congenial stranger had dulled his critical faculties. Holding a sign, with those floppy sandals and mustache? The man looked nothing like his photograph. But the name? *Shit! I should have known better. And I was having a good time. Sort of. At least it was interesting having Lin show me around. Now I suppose I'll have to join some goddamned tour group unless I figure out where they've gone. Fat chance of that. How could I have been so stupid?*

The fan in the ceiling above was revolving slowly. Without

looking, Joe slapped at a fly that had alighted on his arm. The Balfour was in its accustomed state of torpor, aside from one or two nicely dressed gentlemen who proceeded directly upstairs without looking to right or left. Safely ensconced behind his desk, the clerk was staring vacuously at the entrance.

Minutes and more minutes passed. For a brief period of time, Joe's head nodded forward in the enervating heat. He became aware, however, of a slight commotion. Someone had entered the hotel, and, as Joe lifted his chin from his chest, he noticed through his peripheral vision that the clerk had stiffened to attention.

When he glanced into the lobby, he saw a small man standing by the desk conferring with the clerk. He was slowly wiping his glasses, and the clerk, who seemed to be responding to an inquiry, appeared to be highly agitated. He was speaking rapidly in a hushed tone.

Lin knew Raji Rau, Walsh thought. *So did Gus – or is it Massoud, or whatever the hell his name is. And that must be Raji Rau. He matches the description. Maybe he knows where they've gone. Didn't they both work for him?*

Joe stood up and, with feigned inattention, stretched languorously. Then he ambled slowly in the direction of the desk in the lobby.

"Say, aren't you Raji Rau?" he said genially. "My friend Gus told me to look you up."

Like a well-oiled doll, the little man turned sideways toward the direction of the voice. He was squinting until, with a slow, deliberate movement of his arm, he adjusted his glasses to the bridge of his nose. Without affect, impassively, he looked into Joe Walsh's face.

"To whom do I have the honor of speaking?" he said quietly.

"Sir, his name is Joe Walsh," the clerk interjected obsequiously. "He is a guest here."

Raji Rau spun in the direction of the interruption with an expression of fury. "You will speak when spoken to – or not at all," he hissed. The clerk quailed.

"As I was saying," Raji Rau resumed, "to whom do I have the honor to address myself?"

"Like the fella said, the name's Joe Walsh. I'm a pal of Gus."

"And, it appears, a fellow American." Raji Rau smiled, but with his mouth, not his eyes, which glittered without visible warmth. "In what manner may I be of assistance to you?"

"Well, I was looking for the Chinese woman, the one called Lin, to show me some sights. But it seems like she's left. And now it seems like Gus has left too."

Raji Rau nodded. "Of this I have just been informed."

"So," Joe continued, "I was wondering if maybe you might know where they've gone. I never got a chance to say goodbye."

Raji Rau stared at Joe intently. "Mr. – you said Walsh, did you not? Or perhaps it was this clerk." He cast that unworthy a baleful glance. "When you spoke, I entertained a momentary hope that you might answer the self-same inquiry. It is indeed a puzzle, where they may have gone. I am making the assumption, of course, that they have departed together."

"Seems likely," Joe said laconically.

"It appears," Raji Rau added, "that you would like to find them."

"Yes, very much."

"I also. Miss Lin was, how shall I say, an investment. Her departure is most unfortunate. Mr. Honque's involvement is, in a manner of speaking, a form of theft." His face hardened. "They should both be severely punished."

"Well, now, I dunno about that. Maybe they eloped."

"Kindly explain."

"Maybe they got married. They sure liked each other a lot. That was obvious."

"Of this also," Raji Rau said in a low tone, "I should have been informed." Again he glanced in the direction of the visibly nervous clerk. "It was contrary to our rules."

"That's human nature for you," Walsh boomed, as if oblivious to the import of Raji Rau's remark.

"And if," Raji Rau continued, "what you inform me is correct, she will obviously not be returning to her assigned work." He reflected for a moment. "It seems most likely that they have departed for America."

"Maybe. That's a possibility," Walsh replied. "On the other hand, Gus didn't want to go back home. I'm… ah… pretty certain of that. Sure beats me." He contrived an air of idle curiosity. "I'll bet they went on a honeymoon. Some other part of India. You'll see 'em again. They'll be back in a couple of days."

"No, that is most unlikely," Raji Rau murmured. "But you have caused me to reflect. If they do not journey to America, then perhaps they journey to Miss Lin's home… Yes, that is most certainly a possibility."

"Where's that?"

Raji Rau seemed startled. The blunt form of the question struck him as impertinence. He removed his glasses and studied Joe Walsh through squinting eyes. "Because you appear to be a concerned friend," he said finally, "I shall inform you that Miss Lin came to us from Hong Kong. She was a worthless woman. No doubt she will continue as before."

He then turned abruptly to the clerk. "Contact Srinivasa in Hong Kong to be alert for their arrival. And this time, do not fail your assignment."

* * * * *

Joe Walsh had the information he needed. He might have wished for more, but he knew that more would not be forthcoming. It was a lead. It was also a guess. Together with Raji Rau, however, he believed that it was the most likely possibility. He guessed, too, that he had better find the pair somehow before Srinivasa found them, whoever he was, or his work would be for naught.

With assumed casualness, he returned to the sitting room and resumed reading. After a while, he stood up, threw down the magazine, and walked through the lobby to the entrance as if he intended to take a stroll. Raji Rau had long since departed.

His walk, however, took him to the Excelsior. Trust no one, he thought, and disguise your movements. The hotel, being large, contained an office for making travel arrangements. He went directly to it and there made a reservation – unfortunately, an available seat at an affordable price was not available for many days – for a flight to Hong Kong.

* * * * *

And so the paths of three travelers – Joe Walsh, Lin Fei and

Massoud Ansari (otherwise known as Gus) – led to Hong Kong. Only Joe did not know if the others would be there; the others did not know that Joe would be there; Lin did not know that "Gus" was in reality Massoud, a law school dean and person of interest in a possible murder; and Massoud did not know that Lin had been a coerced prostitute in Mumbai. He also did not know the origin of Lin's horde of American dollars, but one thing he did know: that he was falling in love with her, if indeed he had not already fallen.

Joe, on a direct flight from Mumbai, was the first to arrive. He rented a room in the YMCA off Nathan Road in Kowloon, and late in the evening on the day of his arrival he called the chief in the United States. The chief had entered his office only ten minutes before the telephone rang at the secretarial workstation, and he was sitting moodily at his dented metal desk. A cup of coffee steamed from a Styrofoam cup in front of him. A stack of files, waiting to be read, lay to one side, their very presence a reproach to the unfrenzied pace of activity in his department.

A careworn secretary – the unhappy, middle-aged flotsam from a disastrous, and penurious, marriage – opened his door timidly and announced that a Mr. Walsh was calling. From Hong Kong, she added with a concerned look.

"Who?"

"A Mr. Walsh. I think it may be Joe, but I'm not sure. What could he be doing in Hong Kong?"

The chief fumbled for the telephone. At least it wasn't the mayor or some alderman with a complaint.

"Chief Pendleton speaking."

"Hi. It's Joe. Guess what. I'm in Hong Kong."

There was no doubt about the voice. The clarity of the

satellite transmission was such that Joe sounded as if he was calling from a block away.

"How the hell are ya," the chief shouted unnecessarily, as if voice projection was required in order to reach China. "You sound like you're calling from next door. Can you hear me okay?"

"Yeah, fine." Joe held the receiver an inch from his ear.

"What the fuck you doin' in Hong Kong? I thought you was in India."

"Listen, this is my nickel, and this isn't a local call. I found him. Well, like I found him, but I didn't, 'cause by the time I knew it was him, he was gone."

"Massoud Ansari? You actually… no shit. Nice piece of work. You got any idea where he went?"

Joe laughed audibly. "Why do you think I came to Hong Kong? I can't say for sure, but he's with a Chinese woman – real nice, believe me – and my best guess is they came here. So I followed. Anyway, Chief, it's on the way home, sort of."

"So now whadda you gonna do? You got any leads?"

"No," Joe answered truthfully. "I need more time. A couple of weeks, maybe three. I'll pay expenses, but this is company business. Whadda ya say?"

There was an interlude of silence. Foreign intrigue was not part of Detective Joseph Walsh's job description. But his journey, apparently and amazingly, had not been fruitless, and a refusal on the chief's part would doom any further chance of success. Certainly he could not send someone else to take Joe's place.

"We're pretty busy here, ya know," the chief pontificated, ignoring his cup of coffee and the unread files on his desk. "It's not as if we couldn't use some help."

"I'm only asking for a couple of weeks."

More silence.

"Well, look," the chief said finally, "suppose I say okay. You're kinda like an investment. If we don't put more money in, we'll lose it all."

"So what do you say? Same deal as before?"

"I say stay and find him. I'll cover… but don't think this is gonna be easy."

"Great! You'll get the credit if it works."

"Damn right. And the blame if it doesn't. But what the hell… that's why I get paid, to come up with this kinda game plan."

Joe Walsh smiled. "I'll call again in a week or so. I'm at the YMCA in Kowloon, which is part of Hong Kong, I think… By the way, any new developments?"

"No."

"Okay. My best to Antwan. Talk to you soon."

"Good luck catchin' that guy."

* * * * *

Approximately three weeks after departing Kolkata, Lin and Gus arrived – but under less attractive, albeit bustling, circumstances than Joe. There were no gleaming corridors leading from arriving aircraft to a baggage area with smart posters decorating the walls. Nor were there rows of automobile rental agency booths, with their prim female attendants in well-pressed attire, officially correct and reserved, to funnel them through the airport and out into the teeming hubbub of the city. Instead, there were shouted commands, hawsers secured to giant cleats on the pier, the rumble of a gangplank and cranes swinging into action to unload cargo in the fore and aft holds.

Their freighter had stopped at the port of Rangoon, but only for a sweltering day to unload and reload its store of goods. They were not permitted to leave the ship, and as a result, their principal impressions of the city consisted of barges, loading nets hanging from cranes, and the sweating, copper-colored bodies of stevedores heaving crates and bales of produce into the nets.

From thence they had proceeded through the Strait of Malacca to Singapore, the greasy captain often at the helm. Not that they minded his absence in the wheelhouse. Their luxury cruise included a few ancient deckchairs, the varnish long since yellowed by the sun and worn from use, and they quickly learned to dread the few occasions when the captain chose to join them while they sat on deck. It was bad enough sitting at his table at dinner, but at least there they could anticipate a predictable end to each meal.

Once, as he was walking by, Gus asked a question.

"How long will it be 'til we get to Singapore?"

"A couple of days, I should think. Mind… that's assuming fair weather and the bloody boiler holding up. That goes and we'll broach and be fair game for the pirates." The captain flashed them a yellow-toothed smile.

"Pirates?" Lin looked at him in alarm. "You saying pirates?"

"Them Malays. Always been thieves. It's in their blood… that and being lazy. We should have made repairs in Rangoon, but you can't trust 'em."

"Can't trust who, Captain?" Based upon previous exchanges, Gus immediately regretted his inquiry. The captain had certain bedrock assumptions about humanity, impervious to reason. These included the natural superiority of the English, with himself as a sterling example of the breed. All others descended to abject inferiority beginning with the French and ending somewhere in the Antipodes, Australia and New Zealand provisionally excepted.

"Those bloody Burmese," the captain answered. "Just like all Orientals. Can't drive a cattle cart, much less run a country."

He caught sight of Lin's curious expression.

"Begging your pardon, ma'am. No insult intended, but you get my drift."

These precious, jewel-like interludes, combined with a lack of diversions, added to a tedious voyage. The shuffleboard court consisted of a few fading lines painted on the deck. Their plush cabin was a cramped, over-heated box with a swarm of overhead pipes. And the other, quality passengers consisted of a grossly obese woman who spent her days smoking on the afterdeck and a taciturn, tattooed man with a gleaming bald head whose furtive glances in port suggested a fear of the law. Under the circumstances, they preferred their own company. And despite the tedium, they were grateful to spend time together and be safe at last.

In Singapore, the ship again stopped to exchange cargo, and this time they were permitted a day to explore the flat, sprawling, gracious city, its old colonial buildings dwarfed by the office towers that bespoke its new prosperity. They visited Saint Andrew's Cathedral, viewed the famous lion statue with its lion head and mermaid body and strolled around the Padang, or cricket field, where the original parliament buildings were located. Late in the afternoon, tired and happy, they enjoyed a drink in the bar of the Raffles Hotel.

The next day the freighter got under way again, steaming

across the bright calm of the South China Sea until, at last, it swung westward toward the Pearl River.

In the West Lamma Channel opposite Lantau Island, almost within sight of their destination, the ship nearly collided with a motor-driven junk that had the right of way. The captain was not amused. Rules of the road notwithstanding, his view was that boats driven by Chinese should clear out of the way. Rushing out on the bridge, he shouted an obscenity that could not be heard over the rumble of the engine. Nor, in all likelihood, would it have been understood. The Chinese man at the tiller did seem a trifle surprised, however, at the captain's uncomplimentary gesture: an upward sweep of his arm, middle finger extended, before turning to shout an order to the quartermaster.

Lin watched this episode without amusement. It was late morning. She had been up before dawn, keen with excitement, and had strained at the rail to catch the first sight of land. When Gus joined her, she clutched at his arm, fairly hopping with anticipation. From time to time she glanced eagerly at his face to see if he shared her feelings, yet knowing that he probably could not. But he did his best to simulate her mood, and both of them stood, intently watching, as the thin gray line on the horizon slowly materialized into land.

For Lin it was a homecoming – a return she had scarcely dreamed possible. She would find her sister and experience the unalloyed joy of reunion. For Gus – or Massoud – the emotional reaction was more complex. He was happy their seagoing journey was at an end, and he looked forward to a new place and the novelty of exploring it. He would be with Lin, or so he hoped, which was a happiness he could not have imagined only a short while ago. But was there hidden, unanticipated danger? He did not know. The incredible shock of meeting Joe Walsh in Mumbai had alerted him to the potential fragility of his position.

Dockside Kowloon, in bustle, heat, smell and confusion, much resembled Kolkata. Without regret the passengers bade farewell to the captain and ship's officers, endured a brief customs inspection by officials in neat, crisp uniforms, and melted into the throng of people who jostled along the sidewalk outside the pier.

More crowds, thought the dean. *Is no place in Asia without them?* He was struggling with Lin's suitcase and his own. Lin signaled to a taxi that pulled to the curb. Somewhat to his surprise, he heard her speak to the driver in fluent Chinese, and the driver then returned her apparent inquiry with a babble of words. She opened a door and entered. The driver pushed open the door opposite him on the front seat for the dean to deposit the bags, which he did. Gus then got in, sitting next to Lin, and the driver promptly and deftly maneuvered into a crowded stream of traffic.

Their destination, he learned, was Nathan Road and a bus to the New Territories. That was where Lin's sister lived, now a mature married woman. No longer possessing her maiden name, the sister, with her husband, occupied an apartment in one of the high, barren complexes of square-towered buildings that dotted the hills to the west of Kowloon. Lin had kept the address on a scrap of paper in her purse. Unnecessarily, she took it out and scanned it again.

It was delicious to imagine the greeting that awaited her. Perhaps she and Gus could stay for a time, if there was sufficient room. Detection in such a situation would be unlikely, as there would be no name through which to trace their location. Despite lingering worries, particularly on the dean's part, neither of them considered hiding important. They had quit India, destination unknown, and who possibly would journey to Hong Kong to seek them? And who, if he – or she – came to Hong Kong, could possibly find them amidst the millions of people who crowded the streets and buildings of the former Crown Colony?

* * * * *

The dean was fascinated by the taxi ride to Nathan Road. The city was clean and obviously prosperous. By a hotel near the Star Ferry terminal, there was a break in the line of docks, and he had a view across the harbor that was crowded with ferries, ships and small craft including, to his surprise, a smattering of junks. At its closest point, only a narrow stretch of water separated Kowloon from the island of Hong Kong. He could clearly see the massive, modern buildings that lined the island's inner shore. And rising above them, its verdant slopes dotted with houses and apartment buildings, rose Victoria Peak. Earlier, still out at sea, Lin had pointed out the mountain to him with excitement as they had steamed toward the entrance to the harbor.

Kowloon also seemed prosperous, although slightly shabby in comparison to the gleaming towers across the water. As they neared Nathan Road, the crowds thickened – Chinese and foreigners of every description thronged the streets. Shops of varying size, and with every conceivable type of merchandise, beckoned. For sale were watches, cameras, clothing, and jewelry; and there were bars, and girls too, for those with an interest. The dean stared intently at an establishment with the provocative name Bottoms Up. Its sign consisted of about a dozen pictorial representations of bottoms – the human, and presumably female (not the ship) kind – seen from various angles. Beneath these wondrous depictions a man was endeavoring to entice customers inside, the advertisement apparently not being a sufficient inducement.

Somehow the scene was as he had always imagined a Chinese city. But it was the signs, often strung in banners across the streets, that interested him the most as the taxi finally negotiated its way onto Nathan Road. Often long and rectangular, they covered the walls of buildings and hung over the sidewalks, a colorful mélange in thick profusion. On the portion of road near to the water, many were in English, no doubt to accommodate foreign tourists, but they rapidly gave way within a few blocks to Chinese characters. And the buildings – a varied assortment of old, new, tidy and dilapidated in the tourist section – gave way also to flaking cement structures latticed with open windows and balconies. From these hung bedding of all colors, adding to the variegated picture show before him.

Lin seemed confident of their destination. Near a busy intersection, the taxi pulled to the curb. She hopped out nimbly, leaving the dean inside, and walked to a small booth in the wall of a building where she exchanged money. Returning, she paid the driver, and the dean once again hefted the suitcases for a short walk to a bus stop. Here nearly the entire throng were Chinese dressed in modern, international garb: skirts; simple, occasionally colorful blouses; a smattering of business suits; slacks and open-necked, short-sleeve shirts.

There appeared to be an endless stream of buses, all belching fumes into the air. But Lin knew the one they wanted. When it arrived in a few minutes, they boarded, paid the fare, and mounted the curving stair to the top deck. From there the dean had an even better view of the crowded city. They sat next to each other, and Lin took his hand. The last, small fragment of a long journey had begun.

Chapter Seventeen

And at Crabshaw...

Boomer was sitting at his desk, his lips drawn down. It had been a trying day in a trying week, a trying month, a trying semester and, so far, a trying year. Being dean, he had discovered, was like being the dartboard instead of the dart. Moreover, the faculty, disorganized and fractious, bore a suspicious resemblance to the defeated French army of 1940. Praise was seldom, complaints were often. The latter flowed downhill in a never ending stream, and he, unhappily, was situated at the bottom of the hill.

His thoughts turned to the events of the week. A faculty member had seen him the day before about his malfunctioning telephone, and when leaving the office, had inadvertently stepped on his foot. While somewhat painful, that had been an exciting moment in an otherwise dull day. Early in the week, sitting alone in a seminar room after a meeting, he had heard two students outside deride the quality of his daily broadcasts. Just because he had announced that all classes would begin as scheduled, they had had the unmitigated cheek to ridicule him. What if some classes did not? It was depressing.

He flipped through some correspondence, now several days old. Telephone message slips, all checked by Mrs. Ackerman in the 'call back' box, littered the side of his desk. Drudgery! If only a student would cheat on a paper or exam!

Hounding the hapless wretch would provide an interesting diversion. A committee would be appointed. Hearings would be held. Tut-tuts would be murmured in the faculty lounge, and he could seize the high moral ground. How nice to be remembered as the dean who stamped out this kind of student malfeasance.

Mrs. Ackerman opened the door and marched in, a sheaf of papers in her hand. She and her new boss were not overly fond of each other. It was not like the days with Dean Ansari. Boomer looked up, annoyed. On prior occasions he had told her, once with harsh embellishment, not to enter without knocking, but the effort was like trying to train a goldfish to come when called. Her worst violation had happened during an indelicate moment when he had thrust his hand inside his trousers to deal with a recalcitrant itch. His attempted explanation had only deepened her suspicion of him and all men.

"What have you there?" he asked in weary resignation.

"Some correspondence for you – nothing important. Mainly I wanted to remind you that you have an appointment."

"I know." Boomer looked at her as if she were a simpleton. He had, however, forgotten.

"Just wanted to make sure you remembered," she said primly.

With a meeting in the offing, there was certainly no point in working. Boomer picked up a pen and twirled it between his fingers. He did not have time, however, to return to his interrupted reverie.

There was a knock at the door, which then opened. A member of the faculty – his real name Norman but his nickname His Jollity – peered around it.

"Hi! Hope I'm not too late. I was delayed for a couple of minutes talking with Harry."

"No problem. There's always enough here to keep me busy."

"Mind if I shut the door?"

"Not at all. Come in and take a seat."

Boomer had risen as His Jollity entered. He now sank back in his overstuffed chair and put his feet up on the desk. His Jollity took a proffered chair in front of the desk but moved it slightly so that he could see around Boomer's feet. For several moments, they sat in silence.

"Well," the dean ventured, "what brings you here?"

"Well," echoed His Jollity, clearing his throat. He recalled the time, now nearly three years in the past, when he had sat in this same office conversing with Dean Ansari. Then, as now, his message had been difficult to convey.

"Well," he tried again, "I thought you ought to know." His voice was modulated, soft, calculated to be heard but not overheard. "Something funny's going on."

"Oh?" Boomer was staring at the ceiling. "Like what?"

"Like I don't know what," His Jollity answered. "But I've begun to get suspicious."

Boomer groaned inwardly. *Has this gossip nothing better to do than come to my office and waste my time with paranoid suspicions – all because he overslept and ate the wrong bowl of porridge?* His temper flared.

"Surely you didn't come here just to tell me that you've got some suspicion that somehow, somewhere, something might be wrong. No doubt. Why not check Armenia?" He swung his feet off the desk.

His Jollity looked stricken, suddenly aware that his

tentative approach had offended so busy a person. "No, no," he blurted, shouldering himself to a more aggressive posture. "No, I just… well… I just wanted to start by making it clear that I'm not… I'm not absolutely sure."

"Sure of what?" Boomer asked waspishly, unmollified, his unsatisfied urge to bully Mrs. Ackerman spilling over to this unrelated situation. The hapless butt of barbs in the past, Boomer had acquired newfound assertiveness in his recently acquired position of authority.

"Sure about… well," His Jollity grimaced at the words, "sure about whether criminal activity is going on… in the law school, that is."

Criminal activity? Boomer sat up straight, abandoning his aggressive demeanor. This was better than a student disciplinary hearing.

"What makes you think something criminal is going on?"

"I almost feel silly about this," His Jollity replied, again with hesitation. "But for the last month or so, after the class in Contracts – so, let's see, a little after eleven o'clock on Monday, Wednesday and Thursday – I've noticed a couple of the students meeting with others near the rear door. They gather on the landing where the door is on the stairs leading down to the boiler room and basement lockers. I know that shouldn't make anyone look twice, but the first time, when I was going outside, I noticed because there were about three or four people there and a couple of them didn't look like our students."

"How so?" Boomer asked.

"Hard to say. Older, or poorer, or tougher, or something. I noticed, but the thought was off somewhere in a corner of my mind, kind of unconscious. I was going to get a book, I think, from my car, and when I came back there was no one there. So I didn't think much about it. But then, a few days later, I was going out the same way to run an errand – same time of day – and the same people were there. And I wondered why.

"Maybe I'm a busybody. I hope not. I was curious, so the next day – Thursday – I went down just before class let out and pretended to be looking at one of the bulletin boards in the hallway just above the stairs. And sure enough, at the same time these two people, or maybe three that time, came in the back door and kinda hung around for a couple of minutes, and class let out with everybody busy and walking by, and they went over to the side – same spot – and met with these two students for maybe a minute, and then they all walked away from each other, and the two or three I was puzzled about went back out the door."

Boomer was stroking his upper lip. "I wonder what that was all about," he mused. "Are you sure those others weren't students? Maybe they were just exchanging outlines or something."

"You see, that's it. I can't be sure. I can only tell you what I saw. There's more, though, although not much. I was intrigued, so the next week I went to my car, and sat in it, and saw two guys – the ones I don't think are students – come to the building. One got out of a fancy car, and then four or five minutes later they left . Afterward I hung around the end of the corridor, and a funny thing happened. I saw The Duchess – oh, sorry, I mean Jane – walk up to one of the students just before the start of the next classes. The student handed her something, and she handed him something back. She had a bunch of papers in her hand, and it may have been one of them. I couldn't see very well, what with all the students milling about, but it seemed to me that they were acting in a secretive way.

"The last time, just last week, I had to go out, so I thought I'd check again. Something strange happened that time, too. Maybe because of me, maybe not. I wondered. I walked into the hall and stopped by the bulletin board again. They were all there on the landing and just stood around, and – I don't think it was my imagination – one of the students nodded in my direction. They didn't get together. And after a while they all left.

"I thought about it, and I decided I'd better come and tell you. That's when I made the appointment."

Boomer had been staring intently at His Jollity. For a few moments he closed his eyes.

"So what do you think is going on? I heard once about a ring that sold term papers to law students so they wouldn't have to write them themselves. Do you think that's it?"

"How about drugs?" His Jollity answered softly.

"Drugs? Oh come on… what was Jane doing there? She wouldn't get involved in something like that. And why inside the law school?"

"I have no idea, but I'll keep watching."

"Good idea."

* * * * *

"Are you free for lunch?"

Duxbury looked up from his desk and removed his reading glasses. Boomer was standing in the doorway, seeming to fill it like an oversized picture in too small a frame.

"Sure. Do you want to ask Jane and Rick?"

"That'll take too much time. Someone's always got to wait ten minutes, and I need to get back by one."

Duxbury rose, putting down a pencil on the yellow, legal-sized pad before him, and selected an umbrella from beneath a hat rack by the door.

"What're you up to," Boomer asked, "unless I'm being nosy?"

The two men by now were ambling along a corridor toward the front entrance. Doors to classrooms lined much of its length, illuminated by glaring fluorescent lights. Students, walking by, said hello and received nodded greetings in return. Boomer idly kicked the core of an apple to one side toward a bookcase half full of faculty publications.

"I was computing how much we'll need to raise tuition to be decently paid."

"What're you talking about? You know the university sets tuition and our salaries."

"Yes, my dear fellow," Duxbury continued, unabashed, "but that's why we supported you to become acting dean. You're a lawyer. You must use your hard-won skills and be persuasive."

Boomer, puzzled, cast his companion a questioning glance. They had exited the building and were walking briskly toward a restaurant across the street from the school's shaded front lawn.

"We took vows of poverty," Boomer protested with a snort of laughter.

"Wrong. We took vows for a less stressful life than practicing law, but it's becoming stressful to live with so little in this greedy society. I've been personally working on the problem, and I have an idea for the school."

Boomer raised an eyebrow. Whatever his faults, Duxbury did not lack an inventive mind. They had reached the restaurant, gone inside and slumped into a booth near the middle of the room.

Duxbury picked up a menu and, while scanning it, continued talking.

"My idea," he pressed on, "would be to quadruple tuition."

Boomer gasped. "Quadruple? And then file for bankruptcy!" His voice, characteristically, rose in volume and pitch, and several patrons at nearby tables turned to ascertain the source of the noise. "Who would come here? You're crazy."

"Not at all. I see, as usual, that you are not thinking creatively, despite the change in your job description. We'll open our enrollment to the, how shall I say, not very gifted sons and daughters of lawyers – including our graduates – who want to attend law school and can't be admitted elsewhere. We shall fleece the fleecers, justly skimming off a bit of the high fees the parents charge their corporate clients. Of course," he mused soothingly, "we may have to change from a three to a four or five year institution for slow learners, if the accrediting bodies will permit it… What do you think?" Duxbury's eyes twinkled in amusement. "I was just running some calculations when you arrived."

"I think you're a cheerful knave. I also think you're joking."

"Perhaps, perhaps. It's an idea worth playing with, so think about it. Now, tell me… I haven't seen you for a couple of days… how goes the battle in the dean's office?"

Lunch had arrived. Boomer bit into a large, greasy sandwich, then wiped his chin. A fleck of mayonnaise fell onto his tie but was lost in the medley of bright colors. His masticating jaws moved compulsively along the edge of the french roll.

"Same old crap," he said finally, his mouth half-full of food. "It's a boring job, and the worst is that I have to be there all day. No chance for a nap."

"Spare me your minor troubles! I know you like it. Why not shut the door?" Duxbury had ordered soup, and he sipped fastidiously at the edge of his spoon.

"Can't," his companion sighed. "Mrs. Ackerman keeps barging in on me. God, she's annoying. Always reminding me of things to do. Like yesterday."

Duxbury surveyed him attentively. "Yesterday?"

"Yeah. Just when I was gonna go out, she tells me of an appointment. Which, as it turned out, was kinda interesting." Boomer dropped his voice, but not enough to stop the adjoining diners from listening. "I probably shouldn't tell you this, but Norman came by and told me this crazy story. Sometimes, I swear, the guy belongs in a different kind of institution."

"What was he complaining about this time?"

"Not complaining, really. He has some crazy idea that a gang is selling term papers to our students. He's been watching them after the mid-morning Contracts class from the back hall."

Duxbury tilted his head. "How does he know? Just because people pass papers around… if that's what was happening… doesn't mean… Students could be passing course outlines to each other. What's he talking about?"

"Well… " Boomer looked embarrassed. "Actually, that was my idea. He saw Jane hand one of the students something, maybe a paper."

"Oh come, come, my dear fellow. Jane? Why in God's name would she be involved in such a scheme? The next thing I hear, you're going to say he's busted up a prostitution ring involving faculty and law students, or a plot to assassinate the governor, or a drug cartel."

"Actually," Boomer said ruefully, "he said it was probably drugs."

Duxbury put down his spoon. "Drugs? Our students could use some – the kind that keep dullards awake. Maybe someone's hawking anti-lobotomy medication without FDA approval." Reaching for the napkin in his lap, he turned his head to one side and coughed into it. Returning it to its place, he carefully smoothed it out. "What makes Norman think it's drugs?"

Again with a caveat that he should not be telling the story and an accompanying request for confidentiality, Boomer related the facts he had been told. Duxbury listened intently, occasionally sipping his soup but with his eyes fixed upon his companion's face. After a few minutes, Boomer finished talking and picked up the pitiable remains of his sandwich. Flagging the waiter, he ordered a cup of coffee.

Duxbury again took the napkin from his lap, and he dabbed it at his lips. "It does seem a little strange," he mused. "I wonder what those men were doing coming into the school."

"Hard to say. It's probably none of our business. Norman did say he's going to keep a lookout. I think he likes playing amateur detective. I suggested he get the license plate number of the fancy car he saw… just for the record."

"Not a bad idea. And for goodness sake, keep your voice down."

"Oh, right."

"Has he told anyone else?"

"Probably, knowing him," Boomer responded, forgetting his own propensities, "but I'm not sure. What do you think? Should I ask Jane to stop by and, maybe, just casually ask her what she was doing handing a paper – if that's what it was – to a student?"

Duxbury shook his head. "She probably won't even remember… and anyway, you need more than that to make an inquiry. It would be insulting… prying, sort of… like asking her why she was walking to the ladies room."

Boomer exhaled. The waiter had placed the check next to Duxbury. He eyed it, hoping that, contrary to their custom, his friend would pay the bill.

"You know," Duxbury said, "even if you don't talk to Jane, it would probably be a good idea to talk with Norman again. He should be careful, particularly if those guys are on to him." He picked up the check and examined it. "Let's see, I only had soup. You had the sandwich and coffee. I figure that brings my share to about a third."

His faint hopes dashed, with an inward sigh Boomer reached for his wallet.

* * * * *

His Jollity was in his office, seated at his desk in a rumpled cotton sweater. Despite the season, it was chilly outside, and a sharp wind tugged at his window, rattling the frame. He had turned on a table lamp only minutes before hearing a knock at the door. Not many students were in the building on a late Saturday afternoon, and those hardy few were invariably in the library. His colleagues were at home, or away, or in any event not in their offices. Only the solitary light from his window indicated that his office was occupied..

It was with surprise and some irritation, therefore, that he looked up from the article he was reading. He wanted to finish it without interruption and leave. A large spaghetti dinner and a glass or two of red wine beckoned.

"Come in." His voice was gruff and calculated not to be welcoming.

It was dark by the door and in the dimly lit corridor. The figure that came in seemed to be swathed in some kind of costume. Its movements were ungainly as it waddled into the room, and as the light from the table lamp caught its features, it appeared to be wearing a Donald Duck mask.

"What is this, a joke? Halloween is over."

The figure did not respond. It stopped about five feet from where His Jollity was seated.

"Who are you?" The gruffness was gone, replaced by a tinge of anxiety. His Jollity started to rise. Again, the apparition remained silent, but it slowly and carefully raised a black-clad arm. In its hand was a dull, metallic object.

* * * * *

Joe Walsh groped for his telephone, and the receiver clattered to the floor. How long had it been ringing? In his dream it had been a doorbell that he was determined to ignore. Half awake, he flicked on the light by his bed and, with wild sweeps of his hand, found and retrieved the receiver.

"What… I mean, hello… hello!"

"Hello. Is that you? Is Joe Walsh there?"

Oh no, Chief Pendleton. He glanced at the clock in the clock radio. Three in the morning. With annoyance he realized that the chief had forgotten the difference in time between them – if he had ever known it existed.

"Yeah. This is Joe speaking."

"Sounds like I musta woke you from a nap. Hard on the job, huh?" The chief laughed. "I got some news."

With conscious effort, Joe tried to dispel the wisps of sleep still clouding his brain. "It's one in the morning here. What is it?" he asked groggily.

"Really? Oh, sorry. There's been another murder at that law school."

"What!"

"Yeah, Another. Same kinda job, only this time one of the profs."

"How'd it happen?" Joe was awake.

"Shot three times. Torso. We think late Saturday afternoon. Nothin' touched, far as we can tell, so no robbery. A watchman saw the light on, found the body that night when he was checkin' the building. He's clean and scared shitless."

"Any leads?"

"Not really… not yet, anyway. We're talkin' to people, but no one was around when it happened. The lab's runnin' ballistics tests right now… just preliminary."

"That's something." Joe cleared his throat and swung his bare feet to the floor. "Nothing else? No prints? Was there a fight?"

'Nope. No sign of it… oh, one thing, kinda weird… some kid was comin' from the library. He was in the stairwell at the back – they keep the stairwells open so long as anyone's in the building – and he says, just as it was getting to be closing time, somebody in a costume, with some kinda mask, he remembers, that made him look like a duck, comes by him and real quick goes in one of the corridors."

"Tall? Short? Did it say anything?"

"He can't remember. We asked. Probably average height."

Did it say anything? *It?* His mind paged backward, the glimmer of a conversation surfacing into recollection. *What had that woman said, the dean's secretary? She said… she said, just before he disappeared, the dean told her… I wrote it down… it killed him.*

"Anyways," the chief was saying, "I called 'cause it looks like now our guy's committed two murders, and we gotta catch him. So how you doin'? Any sign of him?"

Joe hesitated, confused, a man trying to untangle himself from the toils of the chief's too ready conclusion.

"Whoa," he said slowly. "Not so fast. He's in Hong Kong with his girlfriend. They cleared customs four days ago from a ship, I found out, and said they were going to the YMCA on Nathan Road. But they didn't, and so far no one knows where they went."

"He came here, is what happened," the chief growled.

"Hey," Walsh countered crabbily, "not likely. Why would he go all the way back to America to murder someone? And take the risk? I wonder… maybe he's not our guy. In fact, the more I think of it, whoever was in that duck costume did it, and that wasn't Massoud Ansari."

"What makes you so sure? It's a good disguise."

"Yeah," Walsh mused, "for someone else. Maybe Ansari knows too much and is running away. Or he was an accomplice, which doesn't make sense for a murder right in his own office. He's too bright a guy. Or someone's after him, too. I'll tell you this… if he's here in Hong Kong, he didn't commit a murder there, and if he went there, he wouldn't likely come back here. So if I find him, we'll have the answer."

"That was just what I was thinkin'. So keep after him."

"And chief, listen… it's just a suggestion… but I'd check any stores that sell costumes. During the last year. Not everybody would buy that kind of thing, and some sales clerk might remember and give us a lead."

"That was my idea all along," the chief answered huffily.

Joe Walsh closed the conversation: "Thanks for calling, Chief. I'll be on top of it. I think he's here. It won't be easy finding him, but the local cops are working on it."

He tried returning to sleep, but he could not. After a time he rose, slipped on a light robe he had purchased two days before, and paced in thought until the dawn.

Chapter Eighteen

Dining Out

"Is this all there is?"

"Yes." Lin inflected her response, indicating her surprise. "What you expect?"

"I don't know. Maybe mud huts. Maybe those big water buffalo – they're always black – out in rice paddies. I've seen them in pictures. Or a new building. I don't know."

"You want to see animals, Gus, we go to farm. We give you 'Old MacDonald' experience." Lin and her classmates had sung the song, 'Old MacDonald Had a Farm,' in her English class in school, learning the names of all the animals. "We in town now."

She cast him a deprecating glance.

"Do you remember?" he asked. "Is this what mainland China looks like?"

"I not certain. That was long time ago. This place maybe nicer."

"Whew. Nicer? I mean, it's not that it's bad. It's clean. It's got electricity... all those wires all over the place... and I guess water, and everybody's, well, not fancy but, you know, dressed in good clothes, no patches or rags or stuff like that... like India – and they're obviously well fed. But it's so... so drab. I was thinking there'd be little alleys or people dressed up in costumes or teahouses. I guess... I guess I'm not sure what I was thinking."

"What you mean, costumes?" Lin asked archly.

"You know, those silk robes. The ones with dragons embroidered all over them."

"Those our clothes for fancy time, Gus. You the one wearing costume here, but these days not so much."

They were in the town of Fanling, a place in the New Territories not far from Guangdong Province in mainland China. The dean had wanted to see the 'real' China, and so, on the second day after their arrival, he and Lin had journeyed there for the day. She had been dubious, but he had insisted. Fanling was a junction in the western part of the former Crown Colony for bus routes that looped the Territories; it was also one of the last stops before reaching the border on the rail line from Kowloon to Guangzhou (formerly Canton).

A drab place set in a valley, Fanling was not large. Its streets, broad enough to accommodate vehicular traffic, were laid out in an even grid of squares and rectangles. The railroad station, at one side, was a focal point of activity. Most buildings in the town were no more than two stories in height and constructed of cinder block or cement. If they were ever brightly colored, the paint had long since faded.

Lin and the dean were standing on the side of a street near the railroad station, and the dean was staring at the row of ordinary, gray and dun colored buildings on the opposite side. It was late morning. The local inhabitants were going about their daily activities, moving past them in purposeful bustle and now and then entering or emerging from the retail establishments set in the walls of the buildings. Their functional clothing – slacks, open-necked shirts and simple dresses in muted tans and blues – mirrored their functional, workaday environment. Wearing a plain, faded blue dress and sandals, Lin blended in with them, indistinguishable except for her beauty.

Only the dean stood out, making a fashion statement of a sort. As in India, his feet were encased in large, floppy sandals. He had chosen to wear shorts, and so his hairy legs and knoby knees were exposed to view. Above his shorts he had donned a garish lavender T-shirt with 'Denver Broncos' inscribed across the front in flowing script. Lin had said nothing, although she had winced internally when he put it on. To complete his appearance – a final capstone – he was wearing a floppy, white tennis hat. With his luxuriant, flowing mustache and sunglasses, he looked somewhat like a strangely altered, gangly beetle dropped onto the street for a tour of inspection.

"I guess I've seen it," he declared with a note of resignation.

"So what you want do? We go back now?"

"Yeah, but we might as well eat first." He surveyed the street without enthusiasm. They had passed a local eatery at the corner, a small restaurant with bare tables and rickety wooden chairs. No doubt it was clean, at least by local standards, but the thought of a meal there was not appetizing.

"Lin, I don't think I want to eat lunch at one of these places on the street. I'd like a restaurant I can be… well, that's a little nicer and, maybe, better. That gets inspected."

There was not a wide selection. "How about railroad station?" she suggested. "Restaurant there maybe more what you like."

Turning, they trudged in that direction. The station was a bland, imposing edifice, neither elegant nor out of keeping with its environment. It contained platforms for travelers going in either direction, and above them was a large, noisy space containing a waiting room and restaurant. Perhaps, in another place at another time, the dean would have rejected the restaurant out of hand. But he knew it was the best they could do.

He and Lin jostled through a knot of people with bags and parcels and selected an available table near the center of the room. On it was a soiled tablecloth, some nondescript jars with condiments and a couple of greasy menus. The dean picked up one of them.

Had it not been for the Arabic numerals before each selection, he might not have guessed which side was the top and which the bottom. Everything was in Chinese characters. He stared at it blankly, then put it down. Helplessly, he looked at Lin.

"You've got to give me a hand."

"What you want?"

"I've no idea. Something you think I'd like."

Something he would like? Too many times she had watched him agonize over a selection, then push unwanted morsels to the side of his plate. Straightforward food, he often said, was the best – meaning, she had gathered, an unexciting offering of peas, potatoes and leg of lamb followed by jello or apple pie. In this restaurant no such inspiring delicacies were even a remote possibility.

With studied care, she scanned the menu for a simple offering with no spice. But the restaurant catered nearly exclusively to the native population, and the choice was difficult. She made her selection with qualms as a harried waiter, who was wiping his hands on a stained apron, bustled to their table.

It was obvious that he had neither the time nor the interest to reflect carefully with her on the choices she had made.

With harassed indifference, the waiter took her order after a brief exchange in Chinese – Cantonese dialect, Lin had explained, not the Mandarin Chinese she had learned as a child. After the pause for this formality, the waiter hurried away, stopped briefly at another table, and vanished behind a door at one end of the room.

They waited. The waiter emerged, along with others of like persuasion, and deposited bowls and plates here and there. But not in front of them. After several minutes, they attempted to catch his eye, but to no avail. It seemed he was always looking elsewhere, or, just as they thought he was moving in their direction, they would see his fleeting back as it disappeared again behind the door.

Lin put her hand on the dean's. "As long as we wait, I go to bathroom. I be back soon." And she too disappeared.

No sooner had she left, however, then the waiter emerged carrying a tray and sidled his way past a helter-skelter of occupied chairs to where the dean was seated. With rude informality, he deposited two bowls of victuals on the table, a small bowl of rice, cups for tea together with a carafe, and a bill covered with Chinese characters. As abruptly as he had arrived, he departed.

The dean looked at the bowls. Their contents seemed to writhe with earthworms, mushrooms, curds and bean shoots. Carefully, he picked up each one and sniffed. There did not seem to be a noticeable difference. The rice appeared innocent enough, but bland. Finally, after some deliberation, he chose the least menacing of the two bowls and shoved the other to the place before Lin's chair.

She did not return. How was he to proceed? With wild surmise, he had noted that there was no silverware, only chopsticks. How does one eat with sticks? He had eaten before in Chinese restaurants and in Lin's sister's apartment, but in an excess of fussiness, he had always requested a knife and fork. He glanced at the adjoining tables to discern the technique. Hunched over their bowls, their sticks employed with dexterity, people were shoveling food into their mouths or gracefully selecting choice items to savor.

He grasped the sticks. He was hungry. From long habit, having been well trained by his mother, he sat up straight at the table. Square-cornered eating! He had failed to note that the diners around him left little space between their mouths and their plates or bowls. Dipping his chopsticks into the food before him, he raised a chunk of meat to test the cuisine. He might, after all, enjoy authentic Chinese food! The morsel immediately fell from between the sticks that he maneuvered inaccurately and clumsily. How was one to hold them? With furtive consternation, he glanced around again, then grasped the sticks in two parallel lines with the ends butting into his palm.

This is tricky business, he thought. Once more he dipped the sticks into the food, pushing them under what he took to be another piece of meat. Slowly he raised the oily fragment into the air – half a foot, a foot, a half-foot more – balanced precariously on the sticks, then commenced the sideways motion to his mouth. The meat dropped onto his shorts, leaving a dark stain next to the fly. He had neglected to put on his napkin.

Surreptitiously, he reached for the meat with his hand. It was tasty. Again he tried, again forgetting to put on his napkin, this time with a piece of slimy pepper. The results were no better, and he added a second stain. He replaced the sticks on the table. *How do Chinese children ever learn to eat?* he wondered. Still hungry, he looked longingly at the food, close yet so far. And Lin, who could instruct him, had not returned.

However, the waiter, busy on another errand, passed close by the table.

"Excuse me." The dean attempted to catch his attention. Nothing happened. The man did not speak English. "Excuse me!"

Still there was no response. The dean plucked at the waiter's dirty sleeve.

"Have you, by any chance, a hamburger?" He received a blank, barely civil stare. "Something good to eat," the dean added helpfully and loudly over the raucous din. The waiter shook his head, jabbered something in Chinese, and moved away. Several people at adjoining tables looked at the dean, and one laughed.

Incongruously, in that setting, one of the onlookers was another Caucasian. He had not been sitting in the circle of tables directly surrounding the dean's, but he had heard the dean's question and the waiter's comment; he obviously understood the Cantonese dialect of Chinese, because he smiled thinly and then rose, crumpling his napkin onto the table before him. As incongruous as his presence, the man was wearing an immaculate white suit with a narrow, dark tie. He was tall and slender, with black hair and a manicured mustache, and he carried a matching broad-brimmed white hat in his hand.

He approached the dean's table.

"Monsieur would like something to eat?" he inquired urbanely.

For a moment the dean hesitated, adjusting to the man's thick French accent.

"Yes, yes, I would."

"Un hamburgair?"

"Yes, that would be wonderful," the dean responded, "if they have one."

"Alors, you hippee American monstrosity," the man purred, "may I suggest that you place your order in Denvair." He gestured at the dean's garish shirt.

Uncomprehending, the dean followed the thrust of the pointed finger. The Frenchman turned and commenced walking deliberately to the exit. A red glow suffused the dean's features as he grasped the import of the insulting comment..

"I am not a hippy monstrosity," he shouted after the white-dressed figure, "you... you rude French..." He rose, then perceived the stains on the front of his shorts, as if he had wet his pants. Quickly, he sat down and fumbled for his napkin.

Round, puzzled faces viewed him as if he were some demented street person. Had he made a scene? *What if someone called the police?* he thought fearfully. Then his anger resurfaced. *How dare that...* but the man had gone, and Lin had returned.

"What is wrong?" she asked with concern.

"The Frenchman. That man who just left. He called me a hideous... no... no, a hippy monstrosity."

Lin almost smiled. She saw the meat and piece of pepper on the floor and the curious, embarrassed expressions of the audience. In a crisp voice, she said something in Chinese, and the faces turned away.

"Let us eat," she commanded, sitting down.

Agitated and abashed, he said: "I don't know how."

"I shall teach you. Then we must go."

"How can we go? I have stains across the front of my shorts." This time Lin smiled – in fact, nearly laughed. "What you care what people think? Anyway, they think you just another crazy foreign devil who not know better. Come, Gus." She took his hand. "Now we have nice lunch. I show you how."

Reluctantly, the dean picked up his chopsticks. His expression was woebegone. He was concerned that he had attracted entirely too much attention to himself. And it was true. A short Chinese man seated at a table near the door had observed the scene. He paid his bill and walked outside where he loitered until they exited the restaurant. Then, inconspicuous and at a distance, he followed them.

Chapter Nineteen

A Voice Lost on the Wind

After lunch, they returned to the apartment. Lin had been correct. No one seemed to care. Or rather, if they did, it was he they noticed and not the stains on his shorts. But most people paid no attention. It was not as if Westerners were a rarity in Hong Kong, and even casually – some might say hideously – attired tourists were hardly a novelty.

During the afternoon, he had fretted about his encounter in the restaurant. Alternatively, he bristled, cringed with embarrassment and rocked with amusement at the absurdity of the situation. The last emotion began to predominate. It was material for a story worth retelling.

And Lin had admonished him: "If that is worst thing that ever happen to you, Gus, you very lucky man." He agreed.

For the next three days, they stayed in the apartment. Lin visited old friends, and he had two paperback books and a magazine to read. He soon grasped that his introduction to Chinese food had not been his last. It became his steady – and only – diet, although his hosts mercifully provided him with a knife and fork.

Finally, on the fourth day, he expressed his dissatisfaction. They were seated at a modest round table covered by a white cloth in the dining area of the apartment. It was midday, and the other occupants had gone out.

"It's not that I don't like Chinese food," he said. "You know

I don't mind." He was scowling, looking down at his plate. "It's just that… it seems like the same thing every day. Well, maybe not the same, but close enough." He looked up at her, his face softening. "I don't think you know what I'm talking about, but I'd give anything for a pizza or some apple pie."

"What is pizza?"

"Oh, nothing really… a kind of Italian food… actually, if I remember right, a kind of New York food first concocted by Italian immigrants."

"You mean like a Big Mac hamburgair," she smiled, imitating his imitation of the Frenchman, "or a peanut butter and jelly sandwich."

Her comment made him laugh.

"Lin," he responded, "I forget you've been to other parts of the world, and you can buy anything here… It's just that I'd like some variety."

"I get you variety, Gus. Big word you using. I promise." They were gazing at each other with unconcealed fondness. "Something not right, though," she continued. "I tell. You not happy, Gus, you say to me."

"No, that's not it." He looked out the window. "Well, maybe. I mean… " He turned on his chair and swung his arm in an arc. "I'm getting a little tired of sitting here every day."

His gesture was in reference to the adjoining living room of the medium-sized apartment in which they were staying. The furnishings – a red, overstuffed chair and couch, a black lacquered coffee table with matching end tables, and a standing lamp with a yellow, fringed shade – were sparse, antique and gaudy by western standards.

"But Gus," Lin protested, "you not say you want to go out. Why you not say?"

"Well, now I am. I want to explore the city, see sights."

"You promise to wear normal clothes? No hippy stuff?"

"Yes." He had learned. "Nice enough, if you want, to take you to dinner." He reflected. "Sorry, you'll have to take me. I forgot... you're the one with the money."

Lin's expression, as she glanced at him, was shy and enigmatic. "You behaving yourself, I happy taking you. Let's go this afternoon. I glad you want to see Hong Kong."

Rising, Lin removed the dishes from the table. She then scratched a note – in Chinese characters, he observed – and left it in the kitchen for her sister. As they were about to leave, she selected a handbag from a rack by the door, first fumbling through its interior to make sure she had keys and a sufficient amount of money in a small change purse. She had, he thought, been very frugal with her money, spending no more than necessary and always including him in her purchases. He surmised that her behavior was a trait of Chinese women – parsimonious to self, and generous, within careful limits, to her man. Somewhere he had heard that Chinese women were not to be trifled with. In this assessment, he concurred.

* * * * *

They boarded a train to Kowloon and again passed through bare hills dotted with highrise apartment complexes. Once they reached the eastern land terminus of the former colony, they walked along Nathan Road and its adjoining streets, exploring the various shops. The contrast with Fanling was startling. Everything, it seemed, was for sale: watches, cameras, clothing of all types, jewelry and souvenirs. And everywhere there was sparkling color in the signs, the displayed wares, and the throngs of busy, or merely curious, people.

Interesting though it was, they nevertheless tired rapidly of the experience. Lin had told the dean that it was possible to take a tram to the top of Victoria Peak on the island of Hong Kong, and after an hour or so, he suggested that they go there. She was delighted to comply.

It was a short walk – perhaps ten minutes in duration – from the basement of the Holiday Inn (an indoor, multi-level warren of hallways and stores where they had been examining the finely-crafted suits made at Esquire Taylor) to the Star Ferry terminal. With other passengers, they gathered at a gate, and as it swung aside, they hurried in the jostling crowd to secure seats. They need not have been concerned. The ferries plied the channel between Kowloon and Hong Kong each way approximately every ten minutes. They were the sole means of ordinary transportation between the two bustling halves of this vibrant, commercial enclave, and as a result they were in near-constant operation.

Once clear of the pilings by the dock, the dean surveyed the narrow expanse of water they were to cross. As on the day of their arrival, he was astonished at the amount of activity: the tugs and barges and pleasure craft in ample abundance. Particularly, he was fascinated by a junk off their starboard bow, with its orange, latticed, lateen-rigged sail, its high stern poop deck and its low center freeboard. Somehow, in his mind, junks were no longer supposed to exist. They should be as extinct as a Portuguese caravel, yet here was one that clearly had defied its natural demise.

Looming behind this activity, and rapidly approaching, lay Hong Kong. Massive modern buildings crowded its shoreline. Behind them rose Victoria Peak, its steep flanks descending directly to the edge of the strip of land, transected by city blocks, that hugged the waterfront. The dean could make out a few apartment buildings clinging with an uneasy foothold to the sides of the mountain. At the summit he espied another building that he took to be their destination.

Neither he nor Lin had paid attention to their fellow passengers. Had they been more attentive, they might have observed that one had followed close behind them on their walk to the Star Ferry terminal. This person had chosen a seat directly behind them – close enough, in fact, to overhear their conversation. He was dressed in an ordinary shirt and slacks, nothing distinctive. Nor was it noteworthy, in a cosmopolitan metropolis such a Hong Kong, that he was of Indian extraction. Of moderate height and build, his dark, well-chiseled features, sunken eyes and flaring mustache contrasted vividly with the soft, rounded features of the native Chinese. He sat, immobile, listening intently with a fixated stare while Lin and Gus chatted animatedly. Only once, when the dean compared Hong Kong to Mumbai, did he betray a flicker of interest.

The pilings groaned and creaked as the ferry berthed at the terminal on the Hong Kong side. Lines were quickly secured, and the passengers debarked. Lin knew the way. She and the dean emerged into a hubbub of arriving and departing taxis. Joining a stream of people, they walked across Connaught Road and through the lobby of the richly appointed Mandarin Hotel. From there they threaded several blocks before arriving at their destination: a platform on Garden Road at the base of a tramline that ascended the peak. Had they noticed, which they did not, they would have observed that their silent companion had kept pace with them, never allowing them out of his sight.

He stood, now, on the platform with them, and it was here that the dean first became aware of his presence. In his way he was a compelling figure, and the dean was struck by his piercing eyes. Was he mistaken, or had the man been staring at them? When discovered, he had averted his glance too abruptly, and for a passing moment the dean experienced a sense of unease. He wondered if once again his appearance attracted attention, but his clothing was innocuous: worn chino slacks and a pale yellow shirt. He had left his tennis hat behind. Certain that nothing about him was noteworthy, and in the exhilaration of his newfound freedom and his joy at being with Lin, his unease quickly passed.

The tram was a cog railway whose parallel, steep tracks ran up and down the peak, often through narrow gorges that had been cut in the mountain's side to maintain an even grade. When the train arrived, all of the passengers boarded it. There were only three cars, each with open windows along the sides, and Lin and Gus chose the center one. So did their shadow, who sat alone at one end. The ascent was swift, as the tram moved with surprising speed except in the steepest parts where it slowed and, with whirring clicks and clacks, labored upward.

At their destination, the summit, the tram stopped at a station adjacent to a building – an observation post – that housed a restaurant and souvenir shops. An outdoor terrace with tables under a spacious awning abutted the main structure. Surrounded by a lawn, it seemed an inviting place to pause and enjoy a cool drink. Upon sighting it, the travelers repaired there, choosing a table with ornamental iron chairs near bushes at the edge. The Indian, it seemed, also needed refreshment, and he chose a table at the opposite side of the terrace.

Happy together, joyful in their joint exploration of a new place, Lin and Gus each ordered a soda. Lin had carefully inquired about prices before the order was placed.

"This fun, Gus," she said.

"Isn't it!" He emitted a sigh and stretched out his legs, interlacing his fingers behind his head.

The drinks were served, and for several minutes they sat in silence, sipping them. Lin placed her nearly empty glass on the table. She looked at Gus with a mixture of admiration and contentment.

"You know, Gus," she said, "one thing puzzle me."

"What's that?" he murmured, also placing his glass on the table.

"You not mind?"

"Mind? How can I mind before I know the question?"

"Why you have name Honque? I nevcr hear that name in American movie or maybe magazine." A questioning furrow appeared between her eyes. "That very unusual name, I am thinking, and I wonder sometime where it come from."

She sat, her trim figure erect in her chair, and surveyed him with an expression of utmost concentration. For a fleeting moment, he nearly laughed at the strangeness of his predicament and wanted to tell the truth, but a cautionary hesitation intervened. Not yet. Not yet. Pressing his fingers and thumbs together under his chin, he returned her serious gaze.

"Why is it important to know?" he asked.

"I just curious. That's all." She reached her hand out across the table to take his. "Not serious, Gus, you not tell me."

"No, no. That's no problem. It *is* an unusual name," he stalled, "and it's been in the family a long time. As long as anyone can remember. Perhaps, in some form or other, it goes back to the Middle Ages. There's one tradition," he brightened at the thought, "that the name was originally Honkeszewski. From the Silesian part of Poland, I believe, near the Carpathian Mountains. Some lout of an official at Ellis Island – that's the island in New York harbor where all the immigrants from Europe came first – may have shortened the name because he couldn't pronounce it."

Lin's puzzled expression deepened. "Honkesze… ? How you say that name?"

"Honkeszewski. Of noble lineage, I believe. My great, great, great," he paused for breath, "great, great grandfather is said to have fought against the Turks at Vienna."

"Oh."

"But," he continued, "that's only one of the traditions in the family. Probably the accurate one. There's another. Some say that one of my forefathers was an Indian who was married to a captive white woman. I may be 1/32 American Indian. When this man had a son, his parents didn't know what to call him. One day, his father stepped out of the wigwam, very perplexed, and looked up. A flock of geese was flying south, calling to each other. It was a special sign. They named the boy Honque."

"That Indian name?" Lin's expression was quizzical. "I not very sure of word, but I think that is English word for goose noise."

"And right you are," he replied gravely. "The mother insisted on using the English word for his name, although spelling it as if it were French, but by an uncanny coincidence, the word is the same in both the Mohegan and English languages."

"Yes, Gus Honque," Lin said with a slight smile playing at the edge of her mouth, "very uncanny coincidence... We finish drink now. I see sign for path around Peak. We take walk and see sights."

Most of the soda had been consumed. The dean picked up his glass and finished the remainder with one gulp, then pushed back his chair and stood up. Lin also rose, and together they traversed the terrace and strolled to the start of a well-defined trail, several feet in width, that circled the mountain near its summit. The trail meandered in and around the folds of the peak, past rocky ledges and through dense bushes and trees. At several points, in breathtaking, panoramic views, it afforded unobstructed observation of the city, the harbor, the hills beyond and, in the gray distance, the former Portuguese colony of Macau on the opposite side of the Pearl River estuary.

Once they left the terrace, the Indian seated across from them also rose to depart. Possibly he had not been thirsty after all, for most of the liquid was still in the glass on his table. Losing sight of Lin and Gus as they rounded a curve of the trail, he hastened after them, then slowed quickly to a careless amble when he saw their retreating backs.

The two sightseers hiked around another bend in the mountain's side. Happening upon a clear place for observation, they stopped to enjoy the view. Their follower, who had been walking at some distance behind them, quickened his pace and also rounded the bend. His quarries, standing side by side, were only a few yards before him. He stopped, pretending to examine the bark of a tree, and surreptitiously attempted to step backward behind an outcrop of rock. At this moment, however, the dean turned. In a frozen moment he took in the man's appearance and intent stare. Their eyes met for a fleeting second.

"Lin," he said in a low voice, "I wonder if we're being followed."

"Why you say that?" She had been dreamily enjoying their time together, but his inquiry brought her senses to alert.

"I'm not sure. There was a man at the Tram Peak terminus on Garden Road who I thought was watching us. But I didn't pay much attention. I'm pretty sure he got on the tram, and now I just saw him behind us."

Lin, a worried frown on her features, looked back at the path. It was empty.

"He's not there now," the dean continued, still in an undertone. "When I saw him he was… well, kind of backing up, like he didn't want to be noticed. I guess that's what made me suspicious."

"What he look like?"

"An Indian. A little taller than Raji Rau. Nothing remarkable except… except his eyes. He has very deep-set eyes. Almost scary. They kind of look right through you."

"Deep eyes?" Lin clutched his arm. "An Indian… Oh, Gus, I worry. What he want?"

"Probably nothing. He has a right to sightsee, too, and he was probably embarrassed when he came on us suddenly. I'll just walk back and see if he's still there."

"No, no, Gus. You not do that." She fastened on his arm more tightly. "You not leave me… and we not go back. Maybe he's there."

"Well… " He was perplexed.

"Where this path go?" she queried.

"The map said around the peak. It shouldn't take long."

"Gus, we keep walking. Same direction, maybe more quick. When we stop again, I look back and see."

They started, an undercurrent of apprehension animating their steps. This time Lin took the dean's hand. There was no sound behind them. For several minutes they walked in silence, straining to hear. As before, the trail wound in and around the folds of the mountain, through trees and past boulders. Occasionally a vista opened before them, sometimes partially obscured by foliage. At one point, however, just before the trail curved eastward, they came upon a clearing that afforded a magnificent panoramic view of the entire estuary. Here they stopped.

"Oh Gus. This beautiful."

They stood side by side, still holding hands, Lin glancing from time to time to her right, back along the trail they had just traveled.

The sun was warm and sparkled on the water. It was a scene of infinite calm. The trees nodded in the heat, their leaves a dusty green. Below them, like toiling ants, they could see the harbor traffic, boats plying here and there, their white wakes barely visible from their vantage point on the peak.

Did he hear a crunch, or a stone being kicked? Lin heard it too. She stiffened and turned. No one was there. Still holding the dean's hand, she looked again at the view, then glanced to her right once more.

He was standing at some distance – at a place where the trail emerged from an indentation near overhanging, low bushes. This time he did not retreat. They were at the farthest point from the observation post and restaurant.

"I… oh my God, Gus… I think I know that man." Lin was speaking in a frantic whisper. Once again she clutched the dean's arm, this time in terror. "His eyes… that is man, I nearly sure, who sent me to Mumbai… to, to Raji Rau. Oh, Gus, what we do?"

He also turned and looked at the man, gauging the distance between them. A confederate of Raji Rau? The thought chilled him.

"We keep walking, that's what we do. Not that way, not toward him. We've got to find some other people or get back."

"Let's run," she gasped.

"Run where? No, no. We walk, but fast. Don't act frightened. There are two of us, remember."

"That no good, Gus, if he have gun or knife."

With purposeful, rapid strides, they began their hike again. No one else was in sight. The path seemed made of sticky resin, catching their feet and forcing them to move in some terrible, slow-motion tableau. And this time their shadow moved behind them; they could hear an occasional footfall, a stone scuffed to one side, a snapping twig.

Several minutes passed, a seeming eternity. Neither had dared to look back, but at a turn in the trail, as they were hurrying through a tall grove of trees and around a curve, Lin swiveled her head to see if they had gained ground. They had not. Their pursuer, in fact, had drawn closer, halving the distance between them.

"Gus, Gus, he right behind us!"

"Don't do anything."

"No, Gus, we must find help. Run, Gus! We must run!"

"Please," he grunted, "don't! We'll be… " But she had broken free of his hand and had started to race away. In consternation, he saw her fleeing form, then in the corner of his eye saw that the Indian was also running. Was he mistaken? There was something bright in the man's hand, something that flashed, reflecting the sun. Lin had been right! That glinting object was a knife.

It had been years since he had been in a race. In shambling, awkward strides he moved to catch Lin, who was now several yards ahead on the trail. Slender and nimble, she moved quickly, but she lacked training and endurance. Moreover, she was wearing sandals – as was he – which impeded movement on the path's uneven surface.

They had broken clear of the grove of trees and were in an open area. Here, as elsewhere, the trail had been cut into the mountain's side. Dense, scrub brush covered the hillside above them. Below, the mountain calved away in a long, steep, grassy bank. There was no sign of other people who might offer protection or at least the deterrence of identification. The running footsteps behind them drew closer – close enough that he could hear both the footfalls and the man's labored breathing.

"Keep running," the dean gasped.

And then he stopped. But only for a moment. Instead of waiting, a passive victim, he lunged backward at their assailant. By this time the men were very close, and the dean's unexpected movement caught his adversary off guard. They collided in a flailing heap, both thrown to the ground in the shock of collision.

The Indian rolled away with a loud exhalation of breath and attempted to regain his feet. His quarry was escaping; Lin had vanished, but her receding calls for help were clearly audible. His body aching from their jarring impact, the dean also attempted to rise. On one knee, his eyes locked fleetingly with the dark eyes of the Indian, and in their deep-set sockets he saw nothing – a blank, souless emptiness.

Wildly, without design, as much to break free as to defend himself, the dean staggered to his feet and tried to push his attacker away. But the Indian, with a snarl, slashed out at him with his knife. The movement was clumsy. The man was also groggy from his fall, and the blow missed. He started to cock his arm again, and in a frenzy of fear the dean grappled with him, trying to stave off the attack. He managed to grasp his antagonist's upper arm, partially immobilizing it, but the hand and forearm moved downward nonetheless.

The dean never felt the pain, although he was vaguely conscious of injury. In a paroxysm of effort and terror, he groped quickly along the man's arm until he reached the wrist. Gripping it in desperation, he thrust his head forward and bit the thumb and back of the Indian's knife-wielding hand. His mouth filled with blood as the man screamed. The knife clattered on stones beside the path. Grappling, the two men lurched backward and forward, blood spattering their clothing in the struggle.

Because of his smaller size, and without a weapon, the Indian was now at a disadvantage. They fell to the ground, rolling in the dirt, the dean successfully wrestling them away from the knife that his adversary struggled to reach with his uninjured hand. Despite the wiry Indian's strength, their frenzied fight was brief. They tumbled and flailed to the edge of the trail. There, half rising, his arms locked around his opponent, the dean with a loud grunt flung the Indian over the side of the path. He watched in groggy stupefaction as the man rolled crazily down the grassy embankment.

For a few moments, he simply stood, spitting and gagging and breathing in tortured gasps. His features were still contorted with fear. The Indian's descent had ceased, but his body showed no movement. Perhaps he was unconscious, the dean thought, or chose not to renew the struggle. Stooping, he picked up the knife and, slowly and painfully, limped with drunken steps up the path.

Where was Lin? He looked around in dismay and, still spitting the taste from his mouth, started to wipe his lower face with the back of his free hand. He noticed a cut, dripping blood, along the top of his forearm. In a convulsive movement of disgust, he flung the knife into the bushes on the upward side of the path. Stopping, he groped for his handkerchief and then clumsily bound the cloth around his wound. In the process, he noticed spots on his torn shirt and his cuffed, dust-covered trousers.

Where was Lin? What should he do? Even in his distracted state, he was aware that he did not want to draw attention to himself, did not want a report to the authorities, and did not want a probing investigation. Thinking in a confused, jumbled way, he walked slowly, experiencing his painful bruises and stretched ligaments. With his sleeve, he wiped the blood away from his mouth. *What a horrible way,* he reflected, *to end such an idyllic day.*

The dean's halting progress continued for only a few minutes when, in front, he heard running footsteps. Fearful, he crouched in a defensive posture. In a moment, however, Lin stood before him, accompanied by two uniformed male employees from the observation post, who were breathing heavily from their exertion.

"Gus, Gus, you all right?" Her hands fluttered to her mouth as she surveyed his disheveled appearance. "Gus… oh

God… what happen to your arm?" She had started to move toward him, then backed away.

"I'm all right." He smiled faintly. "How are you?"

"I bring help. I go get help quick as possible." She paused. "Where that man?"

"What man?"

She jerked her head to one side, looking at him in baffled surprise.

One of her Chinese companions broke in: "Madam says you were attacked. Where is this person? We must find him." The man said the words convincingly but without enthusiasm. His English accent was impeccable.

"There… there isn't anyone. I fell."

"But Gus, we… "

"Yes." He nodded his head emphatically. "Yes… you went ahead. I must have stumbled, and… and probably I got knocked out… or something. It seems," he added, peering down at his injured arm, "that I cut myself on a sharp stick."

"But… " Lin started to speak, then stopped when she saw his beseeching expression. Her companions, standing to one side, looked perplexed and dubious.

For several seconds, she hesitated, obviously confused. Reluctant, under the circumstances, to clasp him to her, she had taken his hand and was stroking it in her own. With concern and consternation, she bit nervously at her lower lip, and her eyes filled with tears.

"Okay. Okay, Gus. We get you help now. We take care of this cut you… you get on that stick."

The two men were whispering. One of them moved to one side of the dean, and Lin moved to the other side. Slowly, with halting steps, they started to walk back the route of her flight to the observation post. Lin noticed, but the dean did not, that the stockier of the two remained behind and began to walk, warily and cautiously, up the trail whence the dean had come.

At the observation post, their escort led them to a small, private office and fetched a first aid kit. The dean, recovering slowly from his traumatic experience, insisted that he go to the bathroom, and there he cleaned his face and arm, applied water to the spots on his shirt, and attempted to brush the dust from his clothing. When he returned, Lin applied an antiseptic salve to his wound and then attempted to close it by wrapping a bandage tightly around his arm.

During this procedure, the stocky man returned.

"I walked for some distance back on the trail," he said. "I was… ah… looking for the stick to prevent a further accident. No doubt it is there somewhere, but I saw nothing. And this even though I searched on either side of the path."

He looked impassively at Lin, then at the dean. Did he doubt her version of events? Or his? Or, possibly, did he suspect something else – a violent quarrel, perhaps? From his expression, it was impossible to say. After inquiring whether the dean had been attended to properly, and receiving an affirmative response, he excused himself and left the room.

Upon his departure, Lin and the dean exchanged a glance, but they said nothing. After feeling the bandage on his arm, and ascertaining that it was secure, the dean rose stiffly from his chair. Lin did the same. Somberly, they walked outside to the tram platform to begin their descent of the mountain.

* * * * *

Joe Walsh had had a tiring day. He had left the YMCA and secured a pleasant room at the Harbour Hotel in the Wanchai district of Hong Kong. Rising early, he had, with the permission of the local police, visited other hotels on the island to inquire whether an Augustus Honque or Massoud Ansari, or maybe a Lin Fei, might be registered. Or perhaps, he inquired, the clerk may have noticed an unusually beautiful Chinese woman with a tall, older Caucasian man, balding and possibly with a drooping mustache.

The response was invariably polite and invariably negative. No, the clerk would respond with a shrug, such a couple had not been seen. Thank you for bringing this matter to our attention. Of course, naturally, the police will be notified immediately if any people answering this description register at the hotel.

It had been frustrating. Several days of fruitless search had become wearisome and unproductive. His mission had taken him to scores of hotels in Kowloon and Hong Kong – the New World, Empress, Grand, Royal Garden, Hong Kong Hilton, Park Lane, even an Excelsior – and in the process he had seen much of the city. It had given a focus to his days, but he had not forgotten that his stay was also supposed to be a much-deserved vacation.

So, by mid-afternoon of this particular day, he decided to stop and devote time exclusively to himself. For days he had seen Victoria Peak brooding over the harbor, and he had long since determined that he would travel to its summit and enjoy the view. This was the day! He had stopped briefly to shop in the Chinese Arts and Crafts store on Canton Road in Kowloon. From there he strolled to the Star Ferry terminal and, like Lin and Gus before him, rode the ferry to Hong Kong island and proceeded to the tram terminus on Garden Road, visiting Saint John's Cathedral on his way.

The hour was growing late, but there was still ample time to enjoy this excursion and then return for a relaxing supper. He boarded a tram, and it began the steep ascent. Joe sat by a window, an enthusiastic tourist eager not to miss any sights. At approximately the half-way mark, the train pulled into a station. Another tram, descending the peak, approached from the opposite direction.

Idly, he looked out the window. *Maybe*, he thought, *a pretty woman will be seated opposite me. With perfect anonymity, we can exchange glances.* The side of the descending tram came alongside and, like picture frames of a movie winding to a halt, the passing windows slowed and then lurched to a stop.

Joe Walsh started. Then stared. Then jerked himself to his feet.

"Hey! Hey, Dean Ansari," he shouted out the window. "I mean, Gus. It's me… it's Joe."

"Look, Gus, it's Joe." Lin had also leapt to her feet. Her companion, however, sat frozen, a wan smile on his face as he glanced across to the other tram.

"Hey, Gus, what happened to you?" Lin looked the same, still beautiful, a glowing smile creasing her features. But not the dean. His face, bruised on the side, had begun to puff outward near his eye; his wrist and lower arm were swathed in a bandage.

The dean said nothing, but he nodded his head bleakly in mute recognition. The trams began to move in opposite directions.

"Hey… wait! Dean Ansari! I need to see you."

Their windows drew farther apart. Joe leaned out of his, craning his head to be heard.

"I really need to see you," he shouted. "I'm at the Harbour… Hey, Dean Ansari… Gus… you didn't do it. You didn't do it."

His voice was lost in the clattering of the cars and died, smothered, on the wind.

Chapter Twenty

A Revelation and a Proposal

The next morning, the dean visited a local doctor. The wound was deeper than he had thought and more susceptible to infection. Stitches were required and a fresh dressing. The doctor – a small, resolutely cheerful and energetic older woman – admonished him to apply an antiseptic ointment at periodic intervals and return in ten days. Lin accompanied him to act as translator, but her services were unnecessary. She did, however, hold his hand while the needle was inserted for the stitches, and she asked several anxious questions about his scrapes and bruised face.

The visit complete, they returned to the apartment. Their forays into the outer world had been unsuccessful, and each had good reason to retreat to a place of safety. Lin was terrified that she might again encounter Srinivasa, their Indian assailant; she could not help conjecturing upon the fate that might befall her if she did. Death was a possibility. A punishing injury or mutilation was another. Worse than these, she feared a kidnapping and forced repatriation to Mumbai and the not gentle ministrations of Raji Rau. Both she and the dean had noted that the man from the observation post had seen no sign of a body during his search for a sharp stick beside the trail. Yet when the dean staggered away from their fight, the Indian had been clearly visible. A close reading of the morning newspaper revealed nothing. The incident had gone unnoted and unreported. Srinivasa, it seemed, was still at large and armed with an additional inducement for revenge.

As for the dean, or Gus, he was equally frightened at the prospect of encountering Joe Walsh. By some uncanny wizardry – some intellectual feat that would place him forever in the annals of detective lore – Joe had tracked his quarry across half of Asia, and had, by the barest mischance, not cornered him at the summit of Victoria Peak. He would have been pinned like an insect to a board. All the more sinister was Joe's deceptively friendly greeting, designed no doubt to disarm him before making an arrest. The thought made him shudder.

During the remainder of their descent from the mountain, Lin had suggested that they return immediately to the observation post. Given his appearance, however, and their still urgent need for flight, it had not been difficult to dissuade her. The following morning, she had suggested calling several hotels to locate Joe. With some difficulty, not wanting to reveal the reason for his reluctance, he had talked her out of it, at one point going so far as to hint that perhaps Joe and Raji Rau were in reality confederates. It was a scurrilous suggestion, and he regretted the necessity for it, but it seemed to work.

Still, Lin would not stop talking animatedly about their chance encounter, about the luck that had thrown them back together. She had genuinely liked Joe, and while she chose to be cautious, she did not truly believe any ill that was spoken of him. The thought that he was somehow in league with Raji Rau struck her as preposterous; she knew too much to believe it, but she was willing to accede to the idea in order to calm Gus's fears, not her own.

"Just imagine," she returned again to the topic, "we meet after all this distance. Small world, Gus. Maybe God at work, try to tell us something."

"I can't imagine what," he grunted in reply.

"Joe look very good. He healthy, that something, and big smile. I like his smile. He enjoying Hong Kong, I bet."

"No doubt." His response was noncommittal.

"Maybe he here on business," she reflected, "but then why he travel up Victoria Peak? I think he here for fun time, want to see us."

"I suppose. But I've already told you. I don't think we should see him."

For a lingering moment, she studied him. But her enthusiasm could not be restrained.

"He really excited to see us. He trying to tell us something when trams started. Name of his hotel, maybe."

"Maybe," the dean countered. "Maybe not. It doesn't make any difference."

"Gus," she said, an idea occurring to her, "why he call you different name? He call you Gus, your right name." She hesitated. "He also call you Deenantz… or something like that. Why he say that?"

The dean, or Gus, started. He had forgotten, in the swirl and anxiety of the moment, that Joe had called him Dean Ansari.

"I… I'm not sure." His tone of voice was lame, unconvincing. A convenient lie eluded him, and Lin detected his confusion immediately.

"Why he say that?" She repeated the question.

"Because… " He looked at her, forcing his breath out in a quick exhalation. "Because… well, maybe because… because it's one of my names."

"You have another name you not tell me?"

"Well… maybe… well, yes… yes, I do."

"Why you not say?"

"I… I can't tell you. I mean, not yet. I can't tell you right now."

His eyes downcast, he did not look at her. Lin, however, was looking at him, registering his evident distress.

"Why?… Oh, Gus, you do something bad?" She paused. "I wonder and ask you, you remember? I ask you yesterday. I think, many time, Honque not a real name, and I not really believe that funny business about your grandfather being Polish count or Indian chief or that place Ellis Island."

"I haven't done anything bad." He looked up, riveting his eyes on hers. "I am not a bad person or a criminal or anything like that. It's just that… it's just that I can't tell you right now. I… I will. I promise."

"Sometime soon?"

"Yes."

"That's okay, Gus. We both… we both, maybe, have secrets."

"You too?"

"Perhaps." She smiled enigmatically. "Women always have secret, you know that. It keep men interested."

He dropped his eyes again.

"And Gus?"

"What?"

"You not mind, you always Gus to me. I call you that, whatever your name."

He reached over and squeezed her hand. His eyebrows were knitted together, and his jaw was working back and forth. Then he spoke: "And you… what is your name? Your sister calls you Fei Fei, not Lin… why does she do that?"

"Because Fei is first name in Chinese and Lin last name. You not know. Raji Rau not care. It's all right. We're Lin and Gus. No change, okay?"

Gus' smile wrapped around his lower face as he nodded his head in assent. "I tell you what," he said slowly. "It's time, I think, that I made a telephone call."

* * * * *

"Hel… hello. Hello, Bob?"

(Bob's response)

"It's me. It's Massoud."

(Bob's response)

"No, it really is me. Why, who did you think… ?"

(Bob's response)

"Very funny." (Forced laughter) "It's that late? It's the middle of the morning here."

(Bob's response)

"I, ah… I shouldn't say. Far… "

(Bob's response)

"Yeah. You too. You sound like you're right around the corner. It's absolutely fantastic."

(Bob's response)

"You haven't said anything? You know… to the police or anyone at the school or… "

(Bob's response)

"Good, good, that's a relief. You got my letter?"

(Bob's response)

"Okay. You're right. I went… you're not going to believe

this… to India. I've got some stories, let me tell you." (Leans back in chair, crosses legs) "Right now I'm in… I'm in Hong Kong."

(Bob's response)

"Yeah, it sure is. Very interesting… and beautiful, too."

(Bob's response)

"Well… listen, this call is long distance… We can chat about this some other time. I want to know how everything is… you know, has anything happened… any changes… has anything happened that looks better for me?"

(Bob's response)

"I… oh my God, that's horrible." (Sits up abruptly) "In… you say in his office? Some kind of costume?"

(Bob's response)

"Shit. I really liked the guy. How's, you know, his wife – how's she taking it?"

(Bob's response)

"That's right. You're absolutely right. I didn't think of it that way… But you know, why would I? I had enough on my mind just getting here."

(Bob's response)

"You already knew? How could you?… I didn't tell anyone."

(Bob's response)

"Then I guess you're gonna hear some more. I saw him again just yesterday. Funny thing is, he's a very nice guy."

(Bob's response)

"Really?… That's very interesting. That begins to explain a lot." (Speaks with animation) "Have they squeezed all the information out of him?"

(Bob's response)

"No… no, I never knew that was happening. You sure you've got it right? How come you know all this?"

(Bob's response)

"No kidding! That's really nice. Congrat… congratulations."

(Bob's response)

"Maybe I should. You think it would be safe."

(Bob's response)

"I'll, uh… I'll think about it."

(Bob's response)

"No. No, Bob, I don't think there's any danger."

(Bob's response)

"Bob, you can't catch germs from the door handle. You just can't."

(Bob's response)

"Sure, I suppose that's a theoretical possibility. But its just not going to happen."

(Bob's response)

"For Christ sake, it won't happen… " (Gesticulates with bandaged arm) "If you think it will, use a paper towel to hold the knob… or, but this is ridiculous… I guess the distances are right… just hold the door open with your foot while you lean back in and wash your hands. After you've touched the handle."

(Bob's response)

"It was just a suggestion."

(Bob's response)

"No, there was nothing personal about it."

(Bob's response)

"Okay. Sure. Maybe I'll see you. Or… or I'll call again soon and see how things are going. I've got some thinking to do."

(Bob's response)

"You too. Good to hear your voice… and, please, don't tell anyone I called."

(Bob's response)

"So long… "

(Bob's response)

"Yeah, thanks… " (Forced laughter again) "Take care… goodbye."

* * * * *

Lin looked at him expectantly.

"Would you believe it?" he said with excitement. "They've made Bob associate dean. I'm not sure I… " He stopped, frowning. "Dammit, I never asked who's the new dean."

Lin continued to stare at him.

"Gus," she said gently. "I have no idea what you talking about. Dean? Of what, some school? You all of sudden becoming some kind of mystery man."

"Ah, Lin." He sat down next to her on the couch. "I think it's time, sooner than I expected, that I told you a story."

Which he did, while her eyes widened. He told her about Crabshaw School of the Law, and that he had been dean, and about the murder in his office and his escape. He told her also about Joe Walsh, who Joe was, and how extraordinary it had been, how unexpected, that Joe had found him in India. He had been forced to flee again, but this time with the most beautiful woman in the world. Lin smiled slightly at the awkwardly spoken compliment. And then, when he thought he was safe in Hong Kong, who should he meet again but Joe. But… but that had not been a bad thing, because it had led to him calling home, and now, and now, everything had changed again.

"Changed in what way, Gus? You safe now?"

"Safe?" he mused. "I'm not entirely sure. I think so… But probably not completely. Joe's been in touch with his boss, and I gather Bob knows something about that. He doesn't think I did it."

"Who doesn't?"

"Joe. Joe doesn't. But the real murderer hasn't been found which… which I guess still means a problem for me."

"So what did this friend Bob say?" she asked firmly. "What he tell you?"

"Bob?… Bob said that… that a friend of mine had been shot, murdered, in his office. He was a member of the faculty, a very bright and jolly guy. In fact, that was his nickname. He was always ready to hear a joke… and laugh, even if it wasn't very funny. Everybody liked him. It was impossible not to. And now… just think, two murders. Two murders in the same year. I bet it made all the newspapers. This kind of thing… it never happens in a law school… no matter how unpopular a faculty member is."

He stopped for a moment and swallowed.

"But… but that's only part of it," he continued, swallowing again. "Right at the time it happened, or just afterward, a student saw someone in the back stairwell wearing a funny costume and carrying – and concealing – something, most likely a pistol. It was the same kind of costume… sort of like Donald Duck… that the person was wearing who shot the young man in my office. The student told the police, and Mrs. Ackerman… she was my secretary… remembered that I'd said *it* killed him. I'd forgotten I'd said that. It looks like the same person committed both murders. And the really important thing," he grew excited, "is that it couldn't have been me. Why would I return, and then come back here? Anyway, you and I were at sea on a ship at the time… and I've got lots of witnesses to prove it.

"Bob said Joe doesn't think I did it. He thinks it couldn't have been me. And he's right."

The dean stopped, panting. Lin, still perplexed, continued to stare at him, a baffled expression on her face.

"I not understand," she volunteered hesitantly. "Not about you. You very good man, Gus, I know that. But why would anyone kill this jolly professor? Or first man? What they do, so bad someone want to kill them?"

"I don't know. I really don't." He blinked once, twice, his face somber. "Except… except, I forgot, Bob did say the police had caught this punk, and the kid wanted to talk – turn state's evidence – in return for a lighter sentence."

"Punk? What is this punk?"

"Oh, sorry." He laughed, then explained. "Some young person who's no good, who's kind of tough, a real bad apple, but I guess not necessarily a criminal."

"Punk is bad apple – some kind of rotten fruit? That's what you mean. Okay, what this punk… this bad apple," she asked, savoring the words, "what he say?"

"Not much. Not yet… But," he said, recalling the telephone conversation, "Bob did say the kid talked about selling drugs at the law school. I gather that's what they picked him up for. Dealing drugs… can you imagine? Selling drugs, of all places, at the law school?"

Lin could not imagine. Indeed, she could not imagine most of what she was being told, and her curiosity was mixed amply with alarm.

"Why this Bob," she queried further, "why, I mean, how... how he know this?"

"He's now the associate dean."

She looked at him blankly.

"Because he's part of the law school administration; the acting dean would have to be told, and naturally, he'd share the problem with the associate dean. They'd talk it over. You know, what to do, whom to contact... that sort of thing. The police must have asked the kid about the murder... the cops... kind of a routine question, because it didn't happen too long before, and I'm guessing the kid got scared and talked... and in a roundabout way – from the kid to the chief of police, to the acting dean, to the associate dean – that's how Bob found out about the drugs. And something else... something else I forgot to tell you. The police chief said that Joe had seen me in Mumbai. So Bob already knew about that."

Lin's alarm deepened. "Bob know all this? Gus, how you know he not go to police? He tell where you are."

The dean smiled. "You forget. They already know where I am. Since yesterday."

"This Bob may be bad apple too. You so trusting, Gus. Good quality, but sometimes bad one, I tell you. Why you call this man?" she blurted. "Why you think he a friend?"

"I've known him a long time," he answered emphatically.

"How well you know him? You know him like brother? Even then I not sure."

"No... not like a brother. But a long time – time enough to make a judgment. I do trust him. And another thing... there's so much to tell, I forget... How do you think I got out of the building? Out of the law school? When I escaped, I didn't do it alone... Bob helped me."

"He help you? How he help you?" Lin was baffled. One revelation had tumbled upon another. Now one more was to be added. It was as if, like the hollow Russian nesting dolls that pull apart in the middle, each time revealing another, smaller version inside to be opened in its turn, every one of her questions invited another.

"I told you," he began. "Or maybe I didn't. When the young man in my office got shot, I was standing there with the pistol in my hand that the person in the costume had thrown to me." He caught Lin's stricken face. "I swear. I didn't do it, but it looked like I did. It wasn't me."

She responded quickly to his pleading: "Gus, I believe you. You know that."

"It wasn't me," he repeated earnestly. "But it looked like it was. I… I made a mistake. I think now, looking back, I only made it worse. I ran away. I went down the hall… and I looked back… and my footprints were on the floor. It had been raining, and I was only wearing socks because… because I'd taken off my wet shoes, and the footprints showed, and I was scared, and I went into the bathroom.

"And Bob was in there. He's always in there, checking for germs. He thinks they're on the handles of the toilets and the urinals and the door. I went in, and he… he was standing there. I think he was cleaning a handle on the sink. He could tell I was terribly upset, and he asked what was wrong. Probably I shouldn't have said anything, but there I was, really scared, in wet socks, and as quick as I could, I told him what had happened and that someone was going to follow me any minute.

"He didn't hesitate. I didn't know what to do, except keep running. Whatever else… he's a very bright guy. He helped me. He said, 'Get up on my back.' I did. I'm pretty heavy, or I was, but he made it to the door. He even opened it without a towel and looked out and no one was there. We went down the hall, piggyback… it must have been very hard for him… he kind of lurched and staggered… but we made it to some stairs and down them. I don't know how he did it… to the outside door.

"When he put me down, he said he wouldn't tell anyone. I believed him, and I don't think he has. We couldn't ever be buddies but, you know, we've known each other for so long, he's a loyal friend. He… he said he'd keep his eyes open for me, and I should contact him. I had no choice. I agreed… and thanked him, and went out into the rain, and never looked back. When we were on the way to Kolkata, I wrote him… stupid, of course, once he got that letter, he would know I was in India. He didn't need Joe Walsh. And, just now, as you know, I called… and now you know, well, maybe not everything… I can't recall it all right away… but everything important."

He stopped. Lin loved 'Gus'. She had been in love with him for a long time. For both of them, the seed had been planted in Mumbai, and her affection was reciprocated. Nevertheless, she was experiencing difficulty adjusting her new image of him to the old. He had been a vacationing American with a small inheritance. Now he was a law school dean on the lam, unjustly suspected of murder. Poor, bumbling, terribly bright Gus, or was it Massoud? No wonder he had been is such a panic to leave Mumbai, and no wonder, despite his scrapes and bruises, he had not been overjoyed to see Joe again.

"It seem to me," she said finally, "that you can go home."

"Yes, I suppose so."

"You go back, clear your name. No more shame. No more running from police."

"Yes." His voice was flat, the animation gone. "But it may still be difficult. Inquiries will be made. Maybe there's no job waiting for me, although… although I'm not sure tenure can be removed for a suspected crime, even murder. I didn't do it, and no jury could say I did beyond a reasonable doubt."

Lin nodded her head, the import of his words beginning to come clear.

"The circumstantial evidence was against me," he said, his lawyer's mind continuing to work. "Now, it seems, it's in my favor."

"Gus," she broke into his train of thought, "when you go, I not go with you. It's not so easy, go to America, unless you go just to see sights. I know this. There is long line of people who wait many years."

The dean put his hand on his chin – a reflex movement when he pondered a problem – and stroked it. With a bewildered expression on his face, he then put his arm around Lin and hugged her fiercely to him.

"That's impossible. I can't go without you. I won't. You mean… you are far more important to me than going home."

"What you do here, Gus?" She sat stiffly in his embrace. "What job you get? I wonder before now. You get some job like my father, make clothes, cough yourself to death? That not job for you. You are important man in home country."

"No, not very important. America is too big. And… and I have to get a job. We have plenty of time to think. I have no money. I can't just go to a travel agency and buy a ticket. With what? With a credit card I don't have… and a name that's not my own."

"Gus, I give you money. It's… it's not… " She stopped speaking and turned her head toward him. "You take rest of money and go home. You not run away all your life."

"Run away from what? Run away toward what? Don't you see, I can't do it. And Lin," he cried bitterly, "what about that man? That horrible man who tried to kill you – and me – yesterday. He's still out there, waiting. You can't stay here. He may know where you live. If I should return, you should come with me. You can't hide in this apartment for the rest of your life."

Lin shuddered, and her stiffness melted. For several minutes they sagged together, their mutual plight bearing in upon them, each in its own way. Silence lengthened in the room.

"Lin," the dean said finally, and softly, "of course there's a solution. There wouldn't be any problem with immigration if… if you want."

She looked at him, questioning.

"We could," he continued resolutely, "we could get married… and go together to America as husband and wife."

Chapter Twenty-One

Going Back

It was early October. The trees lining the gravel walks were garbed in dull green mixed with red and yellow, and their richly laden branches drooped in the heat of an Indian summer. Once the campus had been dotted with graceful elms, but disease had destroyed them, and the trees now were oaks, maples, chestnuts and sycamores. No errant breeze stirred their branches. Fallen leaves tagged about on the ground. The air was still, and the browning, parched lawns between the walks seemed to crackle in the heat. Only a billowing dark cloud on the western horizon promised relief.

The man and woman standing on one of the walks before the building were dressed appropriately for visiting tourists on such a day. She, of Chinese extraction, had on a light-colored pink dress with sandals. He, older than she and Caucasian, was wearing khaki shorts and a loose-fitting, yellow sports shirt. Only his soiled, floppy tennis hat seemed out of place. With his drooping mustache, had he pointed a finger, one might have mistaken him for Kitchener of Khartoum.

"This is it," he said as they approached the building at the center of the walks. He gestured toward a modest sign that, in capital letters, proclaimed 'CRABSHAW SCHOOL OF THE LAW.' The sign was low to the ground, the letters inscribed on a solid plank fastened to two stout stakes that had been driven into the earth by the side of a short flight of stairs leading to the main entrance. A couple of students sat on the steps, obviously on a break between their classes, and others were leaving the building.

Most were oblivious to the visitors, but one peered with barely concealed curiosity at the dean as he walked past.

"Isn't that Badger?" he whispered to his companion.

"Who? The weirdo in the shorts and dirty hat?"

'Yeah, Dean Ansari. Except for the mustache, I could swear that's him. He must be out on parole."

His friend turned for a second look. As he did, the dean and Lin mounted the stairs and entered the law school. Lin squeezed the dean's arm. She had overheard the whispered comment outside.

"You have still another name? How many names you have?"

He laughed. "Just a nickname the students gave me. It's nice to be remembered."

They were struck immediately by the cool dimness of the entrance hall compared to the glaring heat outdoors. They were struck also by a blaring noise, some sort of announcement that appeared to be emanating from a public address system.

"Now hear this: the library opened at eight o'clock this morning," the familiar announcer's voice was saying, "on schedule for fall semester hours. Way to go librarians for setting an example for us all. The administration only wishes it could express its appreciation in raises. Everyone is reminded that it will be time for lunch in forty-five minutes."

Puzzled, the dean frowned. Lin looked at him quizzically. He took her hand and gently tugged her in the direction of a corridor off to the right. They walked past several doors that led to classrooms. Large poster boards, which had been mounted on the walls at frequent intervals, were nearly obscured by a blizzard of announcements tacked to them.

There was a stairwell at the end of the corridor. A half flight down, it exited to a parking lot. Two flights up, it exited through a swinging, hollow-metal door – with a small, wired window in the center – onto a corridor leading to the dean's office. The visitors mounted the stairs, and the dean pushed the door open, allowing Lin to walk through first. They then proceeded together down the corridor and strode into the acting dean's outer office.

To his surprise and disappointment, Mrs. Ackerman was not there. She had taken a week's vacation to be with her mother. A temp – a slatternly looking young woman – was lounging in Mrs. Ackerman's secretarial chair reading a paperback novel. She looked up in lethargic surprise as the dean walked brusquely by her toward the open door to his former office. Lin, more deferential, was two or three paces behind him, visibly uncertain whether they should barge in unannounced.

The dean had no such concerns. But he paused on reaching the threshold. The office had changed. In place of the dark bookcases and his old, brown leather couch, the walls were now white, with a faint tint of lavender, and the couch had been redecorated in a mauve fabric. Before it was a glass table with gleaming brass legs. His old desk remained, although it had been refinished, and instead of the clutter of books, articles and memoranda that used to crowd its top, it was now bare except for a microphone in a stand that reposed near the edge before a large chair with a high, curving back.

The change surprised him, a tangible reminder that this fragment of territory might no longer be his. Of equal surprise was the scene before him. Boomer was grappling with an elderly member of the Board of Trustees, trying with his outstretched arm to retain possession of a piece of paper. The latter was struggling to grasp it, but because of his smaller stature and frail condition, he was unable to do so.

"I've got to make another change," the smaller man snarled.

The dean surmised that some document pertaining to the law school was at issue.

"That's not necessary. You've done enough." Boomer was panting from his exertion.

"No, I haven't. I've got to review it again, just to be sure."

"Sure of what?" Boomer heaved in response. "I tell you, it's enough." He lunged for the pen in the older man's hand, and they wrestled for it. "You've already gone over it five times."

"What has that got to do with it?" The small man attempted to jump upward toward the paper.

"We're paying you by the hour."

The member of the board stopped struggling and relinquished his hold on one end of the pen. He drew himself up stiffly. "As counsel to the board, I'm only doing my job. And as a law school dean, you ought to know a lawyer's stock-in-trade is time."

"I'll say," Boomer responded sarcastically.

The older man glared at him, then reached down and picked up his attaché case that was by the desk. "I estimate that I've been trying to get this document away from you for at least five minutes," he said huffily. "That will add twenty-five dollars to the bill."

He marched to the door, nodded curtly to the dean as he

stepped around him, and was gone. Only then did Boomer realize that he had a new visitor.

"Yes?" he said in a tentative, questioning tone. "May I help you?" He stooped to move the coffee table that had been kicked aside in the scuffle. His puce-colored tie was askew, and as he rose, he began to straighten it. There was something familiar about his visitor, and his glance was arrested.

"May I help you?" he inquired again. His large ears had turned red from exertion, and he was still breathing heavily.

"Don't you recognize me?"

Boomer started. "Massoud?"

"Of course, who'd you think it was?" The dean removed his floppy hat and, with outstretched hand, walked into the room.

"Well… well, how… good to see you." Boomer's tone was not entirely convincing. He stretched out his own beefy hand in return and managed a reasonable facsimile of a smile. "We were… ah… wondering when you would return." He paused. "Who's this you've brought with you?"

"I've gotten married. In fact, I guess you'd say we're still newlyweds. This is my wife, Lin."

She had placed herself slightly behind Dean Ansari, but now she moved to his side and, shyly, held out her hand.

This time Boomer did not feign enthusiasm. He took it warmly. "You've done well, Massoud. How'd an old codger like you ever land such a beautiful woman?" His tactless query was followed by a raucous laugh that filled the room. "Come in. Come in and sit down. I'm not sure whose office this is now that you're back… Maybe we'll share it." He laughed again.

The dean and Lin, who had been standing near the

threshold, entered the office. With a wave of his large hand, Boomer gestured toward the couch, inviting them to sit down.

Lin did so, but the dean walked toward a bookcase in the corner of the room.

"What's all this?" he asked. "These aren't books." He had put on glasses and was peering at one of the shelves.

"Those are… those are tapes of my broadcasts." Boomer made this pronouncement with a mixture of pride and uncharacteristic shyness, as if he were a third grade pupil who was showing a drawing of a rhinoceros to his teacher.

"Broadcasts? You mean what we heard a few minutes ago?"

"Yes, that was me," Boomer perked up. "It must be obvious, being here in your old… I mean, the dean's… office and all, that now I'm the dean… actually, acting dean… I naturally had to keep the school moving forward. I've had a public address system installed so that announcements can be made to the student body."

"Why the tapes?"

"That's so, if I'm not here, Mrs. Ackerman can still play a message about anything important that I've announced before."

"I see." The dean nodded. "Interesting idea," he added after a moment.

Boomer, who had been expecting praise, looked slightly deflated. "It's good for morale," he said defensively.

"No doubt. No doubt." Dean Ansari took a seat next to Lin. "Now tell me what's been going on. That is, if you have a few minutes."

"Right now we're pretty jammed, Massoud, it being only five weeks into the fall semester, but for you I've got the time. Maybe I should call Bob and see if he's in. I'm sure he'd like to join us, if he's here. We'd both like to hear about your adventures."

"Why Bob?" the dean asked ingenuously.

"Bob's the associate dean. He was appointed not long after you left. Surprised the faculty, but he's doing a great job."

Boomer, who had been standing by the coffee table, padded on his over-sized feet to the rear of the desk. He picked up a telephone on a credenza. Bob was obviously in, because Boomer spoke animatedly for a couple of minutes, conveying the reason for the call.

"He'll join us in a second," Boomer said as he replaced the receiver. "I guess he just got in. There was some problem about the plumbing in his bathroom at home, and he had to be there."

The dean raised an eyebrow but said nothing. There was an awkward interlude of silence, and Boomer started to talk with Lin about China. Their brief conversation was interrupted by Bob's arrival. He looked the same, although dressed more formally than usual in view of his new position. He and the dean greeted each other warmly, and once again there were introductions. Boomer fetched a chair from the corner, and the four of them sat around the coffee table.

"Well," said Boomer, clearing his throat. "Lots has happened – that's for sure. It was a real shock when you left, and to be honest, I think it's fair to say most of us thought you'd done it. Or done something, because all we had was Mrs. Ackerman's word for it and a missing person's report. And no dean. Oh, and blood on the rug." He pointed his shoe at a slightly discolored spot near the front of the desk.

"It's really great to have you back," Bob added enthusiastically. "I mean," he continued, noticing Boomer's downcast expression, "it's not that the place hasn't been well managed. Enrollments are up. I'm sure you're glad to hear that. And it must be a real relief to know you're no longer under suspicion."

"It sure is," the dean responded. "It sure is."

"So tell us what you've been up to. We know you were in Hong Kong. Is that where you both met?"

'No, I met her... " the dean began. "You know, it's a long story. First tell me about the school. That's really good news about enrollments being up."

"We've worked hard at it," Boomer replied. "It meant we had to hire new faculty. And then – oh, of course, you don't know this – we also had to replace The Duchess and Duxbury."

"Replace? But they're tenured."

"They're gone, is what you mean. About a month ago. They didn't show up. Missed appointments, didn't turn in grades. Finally we asked the police to check where they live. Nothing really missing at either place, except clothes... sort of like you. No doubt about it, though. They've left."

"Why?" The dean was visibly perplexed. "Why'd they do that? Where'd they go?"

Boomer was silent. Duxbury had been his friend. Bob answered for him. "At this point, we really don't know. It's made everyone very nervous. We hope they haven't been murdered. If that happened and the news got out, it would really be bad for the school... but so far, we've kept a lid on it."

"Oh my," the dean interjected. "How strange. How very strange."

"Yes," said Boomer quietly. "It sure is. Maybe we'll find

out something soon. Your detective Walsh is back… the one who followed you, so we heard. He must be pretty good."

"He's very good," the dean answered. "At least I think he is. I also think the suspected murderer he was following was a clumsy oaf."

Boomer laughed, dispelling his melancholy mood. "All's well that ends well – assuming, that is, that we're at the end… I suppose you want your office and job back."

"I'm not sure. Can there be a dean if there's also an acting dean?"

"I don't see how." A gloomy frown momentarily puckered Boomer's features. "You never resigned, and 'acting dean', as I understand it, means acting in the absence of the appointed dean. I think the job is yours."

Dean Ansari made a face. "Let's talk about that later. For the time being… I won't take too much more of your time, but let me tell you about my adventures."

Chapter Twenty-Two

It All Comes Clear – Sort Of

A week later, back in his now redecorated office, Dean Ansari was staring pensively out the window. It was drizzling, and a mist hung over the lawn and caressed the branches of the trees. On the window ledge there sounded a slow, rhythmic drip from a clogged gutter above. It was, as the Irish say, a soft day.

The old, treasured tennis hat was gone. So were the floppy sandals, the shorts and the brightly colored T-shirts. The dean was once again in uniform, attired in a medium gray summer suit, his neck appropriately strangled by a dark blue, conservative necktie. Only the droopy mustache remained, a visible, solitary reminder of his adventures in a faraway land .

It seemed like a dream – and from the perspective of his confining office, a wonderful, happy dream. Screened from consciousness were the discomforts, the heat and the tedium punctuated by agonizing moments of fright. He could, in rosy recollection, visualize the first moment he had met Lin, their romantic dinners by the window at the Excelsior, and their languid passage from India. It seemed odd to think that they were now ensconced in his apartment, a married couple, with Lin searching for a job. She had also firmly announced, shortly after their arrival, that his bachelor quarters were unsatisfactory. Her searching, therefore, also included a determined hunt for a larger space, perhaps a townhouse or condominium.

These reveries were interrupted, not rudely but certainly without welcome. Mrs. Ackerman had knocked on the jamb of the open door, but it was a knock to announce her arrival, not to request permission to enter. She had been ecstatic to see Dean Ansari again, her stout affirmation of his innocence finally vindicated. But that euphoria had been several days ago. Boomer had moved out, the microphone shelved in a file cabinet. Dean Ansari had moved in, and they were back in the tedium and routine of daily work.

As usual, she was wearing a floral – and florid – printed dress, and in her hand she carried the daily stack of announcements, letters and memoranda. Some of the letters were incoming; some were outgoing; all, to the dean, represented a mind-numbing chore that he had escaped for a delirious interlude.

"Here's your mail," she said unnecessarily.

"Yes," he answered absent-mindedly. "Just put it on the desk."

"I think you should sign your letters," Mrs. Ackerman persisted, observing his distraction, "so we can get them in the afternoon mail."

He had turned, and now he held out his hand. "Anything else?"

"That detective, the one who was here right after the murder… such a nice man, really . He should be here in a few minutes. He called this morning. He's bringing his boss."

"Um." The dean had been looking forward to seeing Joe, a tangible link to his memories. Lin wanted to see him too, and he made a mental note to invite him to the apartment for dinner. He leafed through the three letters in his hand.

"Ah, Mrs. Ackerman," he said, almost deferentially, "this needs correcting."

"Where?" Mrs. Ackerman peered over his arm.

"Here," he pointed. "The word is 'alleviate', not 'levitate'."

"That's the way you dictated it," Mrs. Ackerman replied in a wounded tone. "I have it in my notes." She turned to fetch them and demonstrate, not for the first time, how one error could justify another.

"That… that won't be necessary. Just… "

But Mrs. Ackerman had departed. He heard her speaking to someone in the outer office, and shortly thereafter she returned, beaming, and stood just inside his office door. Introductions were her forte.

"Dean Ansari," she announced, gesturing to two chunky, square-set men who were standing behind her, "I have the honor of introducing… "

One of the men brushed past her.

"Gus! I mean… " he faltered, smiling, "Dean Ansari. It's great to see you again!" He took the dean's outstretched hand in both of his and pumped it warmly. "Damn. You sure look different, 'cept for that mustache." He stepped back and surveyed the dean, who was smiling broadly. "Let me introduce you to my boss."

Mrs. Ackerman's announcement had been ruined.

"This is Chief Pendleton," Joe said. "The chief's been actively involved in your case… " He stopped, interrupting himself. "That file's closed, of course. That's why we're here. He's been looking… "

The chief stepped forward. "Dean Ansari, it's a pleasure to meet you." He said these words gravely, as the two men shook hands. However, the formality of the occasion was offset by the chief's rumpled suit and loud tie that, askew, failed to close his shirt collar around his beefy neck.

The dean waived them airily to seats in the room and asked if either would like coffee. They declined. Mrs. Ackerman continued to stand by the door.

"Mrs. Ackerman… ah, we won't be needing you. You, ah, can get that letter fixed… and I'll sign the others when you do."

She looked at him reproachfully, then left, noisily closing the door to his office.

Joe, who was seated at one end of the couch, gazed directly at the dean. "You're off the hook," he said. "And no one could be happier than me."

"Off the hook? Was there any question?"

"No, not really. Suspicion?… Well, yes, to be honest, you were a person of interest… pretty high on a short list. Now you're in the clear."

The dean smiled and shook his head. "How so?"

"We got this kid in custody," the chief interposed in his gravelly voice. The dean turned to look at him. "He finally decides, you know, to tell us somethin'. We got it wrote down and signed. Guess he got scared and decided to deal."

Joe picked up the thread of the story. "It turns out, from what he told us, that the guy who got shot was a courier – the one who got killed here in your office. He was trying to build a law practice, didn't want people to know he was a homosexual, and they blackmailed him."

"Who blackmailed him?" the dean asked. "I'm lost."

"Your profs. The ones who took off. They found out about this kid when he was a student. The thin one – the one the

259

students called Duxbury – was selling cocaine… would you believe it, out of his umbrella. It was hollow inside. We found it a couple of days ago in his front hall at his home, just where the kid said it would be."

"Selling cocaine? In the law school?" The dean's voice rose slightly. "Why kill the young man in my office?"

"He'd come back from Colombia. As best we can figure it out, he was going to tell them it was his last trip and… I dunno… spill the beans to us or blackmail them in return."

"I can hardly… a courier? John? Are you sure you've got this right?"

"Hey, dean," the chief said condescendingly. "You do your job, right? We do ours."

"What'd they do with his body? And… and why kill him in my office?"

"They musta found out," the chief took charge, "that he was comin' to see you. The kid said they were afraid he'd talk. So they hid in that narrow stairwell – the one hardly anyone uses – near your office. We think the man was the leader but it was the woman who did the dirty work. First time, anyway. When you and that dopey broad you got for a secretary leave your office, which was blind luck, they snatched the body. Best we can tell, they wrapped it in your raincoat that you'd left behind so the blood wouldn't leave a trail. The victim was a mule; he had little balloons of cocaine in his stomach. Lots of them. That's how he got the stuff here… then he'd shit it out."

Joe winced at the chief's inelegance. "That cocaine was worth a lot," he said, "and they wanted it… In fact, it seems they were willing to do anything to get it. Your other faculty member got killed by them, 'cause he was getting wise to what they were doing."

"I can't believe… " The dean was flabbergasted. Stunned and bewildered, trying hard to absorb this revelation, he stared at his guests. "Where… where'd they go?"

"We don't know," the chief said, "and we're not sending Joe to find out. Maybe we should. Maybe they went to Bombay… or is that now Mumbai?… Hey, Joe, how'd you like to go back and start all over? You wanna take another vacation?"

Joe shook his head slowly, forcing his lips into a tight smile. "No… no, I don't think so. Once is enough, but that reminds me. I forgot to tell you. We have some reason to believe that there's a connection in Mumbai to this drug cartel that sells the cocaine… and I've a good hunch it's Raji Rau. These guys are international. If my guess is right, he's their Indian connection."

"Raji Rau!" The dean exhaled. "For a while, I'd stopped thinking about him. It makes sense, you know. He's a bad man. A very bad man."

There was a momentary interlude of silence.

"Are we safe?" the Dean asked.

"Who?" Joe responded, perplexed. "You and Lin?"

"Yeah. He was after us – or Lin, anyway – in Hong Kong."

"I wouldn't worry. You've got different names, although I guess those faculty members… the ones who disappeared… could tell them the real ones. But they're not going to try anything here, and they don't need more publicity. I hope it doesn't hurt your feelings, but you're small change."

Again, there was an interlude of silence.

The chief fidgeted his square bulk restlessly in his chair. After glancing surreptitiously at his wristwatch, he heaved himself to a standing position.

"Busy day," he said. "Dean, it was a pleasure, a great

pleasure, to make your acquaintance. But there's a real world out there, ya know. Me and Joe, we gotta work in it. So c'mon, Joey boy, let's get up and at 'em."

Both Joe and the dean rose. "I hope you'll join us soon for dinner," the dean said. "Lin very much wants to see you."

"Love to. Gimme a call."

"Chief Pendleton, it was nice to meet you." The dean and the chief shook hands. "I really appreciate you taking the time to come over and tell me what happened."

"Our pleasure, dean. Distinctly our pleasure."

"Do you know your way out?"

"We came in the main entrance," Joe said. "Maybe you could tell us a different way to leave."

"Why?"

"There's a bunch of people on the steps carrying signs. Real scruffy types."

"Those would be our students," the dean laughed. "What kind of signs?"

"I dunno. Crazy. Something about saving the gnatbasher seven, or liberating the gnatbasher seven, or something like that."

"You got it right," the dean laughed again. "A gnatbasher, I found out, is a squirrel that catches gnats by squashing them with its foot. I gather the government is trying to build a six-lane highway through some woods, and these squirrels live there. A few of our students are trying to bring the highway program to a halt."

"Your world," the chief said, shaking his head. "Your world. C'mon Joe, I think we can brave some students."

Joe opened the door. The two men said goodbye to Mrs. Ackerman in the outer office and departed.

* * * * *

A week later, the dean spoke with Mrs. Ackerman. It was the end of the day, and he had asked her to sit on his couch. Alerted by that gesture of civility, she waited expectantly, with a tinge of apprehension, to hear what he had to say.

The dean sat down wearily in a chair by the coffee table. His features were composed, betraying no emotion, and he looked at Mrs. Ackerman for several moments with his soft, brown eyes.

"I've decided to resign," he said finally, "or maybe," he faltered, "take a leave of absence."

"Re… resign? Is something wrong?" In the first moment of bad news, Mrs. Ackerman comprehended the words, but her emotions lagged behind, unable to keep pace with understanding. "Is it something I've done?"

"No. Nothing's wrong. It's not you, not at all. It's just that I'm not… I'm not happy. It's not the same anymore. I've talked about it with Lin. The school has lost three teachers, and she agrees… I can go back to teaching. It's a good time to do it."

"But everything's going so well. You should enjoy it. The job's much easier now."

"I know," he said. "But maybe that's the problem. The challenge is gone." He still had to tell her what, to her, would be equally distressing news. Bracing himself, he half blurted: "I've talked about it with Boomer. He… he can have the job back."

Mrs. Ackerman stared at him.

Continuing, the dean said, "I know, I've heard he complained a lot. But it's obvious he liked the work."

263

"That's because… " She stopped. "Oh dear, this means we'll have announcements again."

"Well, yes, probably. I mean, if he's dean, well, that's his choice." She seemed so crestfallen that he hurried to add: "But don't worry. Before I step down, I'll revise your job description. I will. I'll make sure you won't have to play martial music before the late Friday afternoon broadcasts. Or… or the ones on Monday morning."

"Have you really made up your mind?"

"Yes."

"You'll come back," she said with determination. She inhaled deeply. "You should just test out this idea. Live with it awhile. And only take a leave of absence."

"I'm not sure."

"You'll come back," she said again. "You did before."

"Well… maybe. Maybe not. I can't predict the future. For now… for now I just want some peace and quiet."

* * * * *

Five days later, at ten o'clock on Monday morning, the law school's loudspeaker boomed: "Now hear this! Now hear this… " There was no martial music.

Epilogue

"Is that it?"

"What do you mean? Isn't that enough?"

"Well, do they live happily ever after? That sort of thing. Does Gus – I like the name Gus – does he ever become dean again?"

"You can see the future as well as I. It's all laid out, if you want to look."

"I know… but… I don't like peeking. It ruins the fun."

"You don't have to peek to appreciate one thing. Even they appreciate it, as much as they appreciate anything. Happily ever after? Do human beings ever live happily ever after? Their capacity to get restless and mess things up is nearly limitless."

"That's what makes them so interesting."

"Um. I'm not sure I'd use that word. I'd say pathetic. Or comic. Or, even better, tragic. Or maybe all three. Watching them is like watching a gigantic farce, but all swept to doom."

"Hey, that's our job. Don't knock it."

"Your colloquialisms are appalling. You've been listening to them for too long. Anyway, we are Fate, my dear fellow, not Doom."

"It's all the same."

"Only ultimately, from their point of view."

"What about the two who ran away – the two professors? What do you think may happen to them?"

"If you insist on not finding out for yourself, then I'm not going to say. Not now. Perhaps, like Dean Ansari – Gus, to you – they've fled to India. Or Africa. Of one thing I'm reasonably certain, their penchant for trouble-making is not at an end."